THE MYSTERY OF GATEWOOD AIRPORT

A Vanessa Mystery

By

Madalyn S. Kinsey

First published by Dog Ear Publishing
4011 Vincennes Rd
Indianapolis, IN 46268
www.dogearpublishing.net

ISBN: 978-1-4575-4163-6

This book is printed on acid-free paper.

This book is a work of fiction. Places, events, and situations in this book are purely fictional and any resemblance to actual persons, living or dead, is coincidental.

Printed in the United States of America

TABLE OF CONTENTS

Appreciation is expressed to Stanley D.
"Butchie" Gatewood for his technical assistance with the flying passages in this book.

Appreciation is also expressed to Kenneth
L. Turchi for his editing and proofreading
assistance, and to Nils Nordell for his editing assistance.

CHAPTER ONE

Return to the Heartland

*A*h, summer! It was great to be a fourteen-year-old girl on a warm and sunny Indiana morning like this in early August 1967. I was fully entrenched in making the most of what remained of the precious days of summer vacation. For Labor Day would inevitably roll around, together with the start of a new school year and the end of summer's carefree ways.

Being home for the summer wasn't entirely without its challenges, though. The good news was that I was too young for the typical summer jobs reserved for teenagers trying to make a little spending money. On the down side, I was too young to have a driver's license and the independence it afforded. Still overall, life wasn't too bad.

I lived in a house my parents had built about ten years earlier in the Indianapolis suburbs. Besides my parents, I lived with my older sister Karen, who was going to be a college sophomore next year, and two brothers — Brian, who was sixteen, and Bruce, who was seven. I was the typical middle child, doing my best to keep a low profile and out of the daily dramas the others perpetrated. My sister, in particular, seemed to exist in a daily crisis of one sort or another. Perhaps that was part of being a teenager, or maybe that was just her. Whatever the reason, my goal most days was to stay out of the way.

As I slowly awakened that morning, I heard the faint strains of the lyrics of "San Francisco (Be Sure to Wear Some Flowers in Your Hair)" coming from my mother's radio sitting on top of the pink refrigerator in the kitchen. The song beseeched hippies to come to San Francisco to wear flowers in their hair and enjoy a summertime love-in. I just knew it must be great to live in a place like that, where people were involved in amazing stuff all the time. Nothing exciting ever happened to people who lived in Indianapolis. Not ever. Well, at least not to me.

I noticed that my sister's twin bed was empty and rumpled. She probably had already left for her summer job as a cashier at Hook's Drug Store. Could it be that late? I had no idea what time it was, except that the bright summer sun was already peeking in around the edges of the green pleated curtains that spanned the high windows that stretched across the front of my bedroom. After staring at the ceiling for several minutes and scratching the whiskers of my Siamese cat, I finally got up and shuffled into the hall bathroom. Yawning, I looked at myself in the large mirror hanging above the side-by-side sinks in the long pink vanity.

I was tall for my age, with a light complexion and long, strawberry-blonde hair that I wore in the popular style of the day — — long and straight and parted down the middle. I wore amber-colored eye glasses that my mother promised could be replaced with contacts once I turned sixteen. Why that was the magic number, I didn't know, but it was one more good reason to look forward to the passage of two more years. I didn't know if I was pretty, but I hoped I was. Every day I looked in the mirror and studied my face, hoping to see the emergence of high cheekbones and other attributes I thought would make me more beautiful, as though a magic beauty wand had been waved over me as I slept. Instead, each day I saw just the same old me looking back, for better or for worse.

I had just taken a hairbrush out of a drawer to brush my tousled hair, when my mother knocked on the bathroom door.

"Vanessa! Are you in there?" she asked, rapping lightly. "Emma's on the phone for you."

Emma on the phone? This was good news, indeed. Emma was my cousin who lived with her family on what had been my mother's family farm in Fishers, Indiana. It was about a forty-five minute drive from our house. I hadn't known her or her siblings well until I visited them earlier this summer while my parents were out of town. That visit changed everything. Before that, Emma and I had nothing much to say to each other, or any reason to be friends, for that matter. We came from such different worlds. Hers — — the farm and a rural life, and mine — — the suburbs.

Something happened, though, during that visit that brought us together forever. I knew I could count on her no matter what, even when no one else would listen to or believe me, and she knew the same about me. We swore after that visit we'd be the closest of friends forever, and always keep in touch by writing letters and calling. Although we'd traded a couple of letters since that visit, I hadn't spoken to her in several weeks. It'd be great to hear her voice again.

I quickly jerked the door open and ran to the kitchen and picked up the receiver of our turquoise wall phone lying on a table.

"Emma! Hi. It's me. How *are* you?" I shouted eagerly into the phone.

"Fine, I guess," she replied meekly.

"What do you mean?" I asked. I was surprised there wasn't more energy in her voice. She sounded sad or upset. "You don't sound so good. Is everything okay?"

"I — . . .I guess so," she stammered. Then, after a brief pause, she continued. "Well, not really. Do you think you could come stay for a couple of days? I could sure use a friend right now."

"Sure. I'd love to come visit. But what's wrong?" I coaxed. "You sound kinda down. Is everything okay? What's going on?"

"I'll tell you about it when you get here. I'd rather not talk about it on the phone," she hedged. "Do you think you could come today?"

"I'll check with my mother," I replied.

Today? She must really need to talk about something urgently, I thought.

After we finished our brief conversation, I ran down to the laundry room and found my mother unloading the dryer. Mom said she had a very busy schedule, but was willing to drive me out to Emma's in a couple of hours. I was delighted. She told me to get dressed right away and to pack an overnight bag.

I ran back to my bedroom and quickly dressed in a pair of light blue shorts and matching cotton knit shirt. Then I ran back into the bathroom and looked at my face again. My mother didn't allow me to wear much makeup, but she allowed me to wear a little eyeliner and mascara, which I quickly applied. I finished my look by coating my lips with Yardley Slicker pale pink lip gloss. I pursed my lips together, feeling the slippery effect of the gloss, and stared into the mirror. Not too bad, I thought. I brushed my hair and placed a tortoise-colored headband on my head and was ready to go.

When I left the bathroom, my mother was in my bedroom packing a small suitcase for me.

"Why did Emma want you to come out today?" she inquired as she folded my white eyelet cotton shirt. "Did she say if there was anything in particular on her mind?"

Mom was tall with shoulder-length, blonde hair that she wore lose and bouncy. She was a pretty lady, in my opinion. Today she had on a tan shirtwaist dress with a gathered skirt.

"She didn't say," I answered, plopping down on the edge of my bed. "She didn't sound like herself. She sounded worried. I wonder what's going on. Do you know, Mom?"

"I haven't a clue. She probably just misses you. You girls haven't been together in several weeks. It'll do you both some good to get together again. You two can do more ghost hunting like you did last time. That'll be fun, won't it?"

She gave me a motherly smile, and I knew what she was thinking. She thought Emma and I were silly little girls obsessed with ghosts. Well maybe we were when Emma felt haunted by the ghost of a Civil War soldier buried in a cemetery on the farm, but that was earlier in the summer. We'd grown up a lot since then and were more mature. Now we thought about more serious things.

"Ha! Ghost hunting. I think we're done with that," I scoffed.

"Okay, if you say so," Mom conceded, smiling slyly. "Well, I've got you started packing. You'd better finish filling this suitcase, or you won't like what you end up having with you."

With that, she left the room. I placed a few more summer outfits in the suitcase until it was full. A person of taste needs a lot of different things to wear when traveling, you know. When I was done, I had to practically sit on it to zip it up. By then, it was almost time to go.

I walked into the living room where my little brother was watching a summer rerun of the TV situation comedy, *The Andy Griffith Show*, and sat down to watch as I waited for Mom. I couldn't focus on the show, though. My mind was consumed with thoughts about a boy I met the last time I visited Emma. His name was Jim Sparks. He was a friend of Emma's older brother, Luke. I guess you could say Jim and I had gotten fairly close during that visit. He gave me my first kiss, and said he cared about me in a special way. I really cared for him, too. I had to confess that I had a major crush on him.

But since that visit, I'd seen him only once. That was when we met for a Coke at G.C. Murphy's lunch counter at the Glendale shopping center about four weeks ago. Mom was with me, and I was self-conscious and didn't feel free to be myself. It was a nice visit, just the same. But countless days had passed, and I hadn't seen or heard from him. Not a note or a phone call. Nothing. Every time the phone rang, my heart stopped, hoping it was him. I was beside myself wondering why he didn't contact me. I knew there was a good chance I'd see him during my visit, because he hung out a lot with Emma's brother at her house. Thinking of Jim made me even more impatient to get on the road.

Mom came into the living room and jolted me out of my daydream about Jim with last minute instructions. She sent my little brother next door to play with a friend, and then said it was time to go. We got into our beige 1966 Chevrolet Impala and were on our way. We drove across Kessler Boulevard, and then north on Allisonville Road. It didn't take long for the scenery to change from suburban houses on large, grassy lots, like ours, to nothing but tree-lined fields and a few old farm houses spotting the landscape. "Monday, Monday" by The Mamas & The Papas played on the car radio as we rode along. Mom always let me listen to the local rock station when I was in the car with her as long as I didn't play it too loud. I usually tuned in rock station WNAP-FM, as I did today.

"These farmers should be very happy," Mom observed cheerfully as we sped along. "The corn looks tall and healthy this year. Should be a good harvest." As a former farm girl, Mom often looked at the world through the eyes and soul of a farmer. She looked as pleased, as if the abundant fields we passed were her own.

We finally approached a small airport and a large farm, both of which belonged to my Uncle Forrest who lived with his wife, Aunt Loretta, and their five children. The airport was located almost directly across the street from where Emma lived with her parents, Aunt Louise and Uncle Evert.

We turned onto a long gravel lane leading up to Emma's house. A large white barn sat at the end of the driveway. Emma's one-story house was situated off to the left, perpendicular to a detached two-car garage. Both structures were wooden and very old. Their windows and doors were trimmed in dark green paint. They sat in the middle of an expansive grassy lawn with several old trees providing soothing shade.

My mother was born and raised here with her older sister, Aunt Louise, her brother, Uncle Forrest, and three other sisters. Grandma and Grandpa were no longer living, and the farm now belonged to Aunt Louise and Uncle Evert. My uncle was a plumber and didn't farm the property. Some of the fields were leased to other people to cultivate, but most were left to go natural. The farm animals that my grandfather once had were also long gone.

A push mower stood abandoned in the yard as if someone had temporarily stopped to go inside for a lemonade, or perhaps had called it quits for the day. All of the windows were pushed open to allow in an occasional breeze, as the house wasn't air conditioned. I studied the scene as the gravel lane turned and made a complete circle around a maple tree in front of the house. It was so quiet it appeared no one was home, although I knew that couldn't be.

"Well, we're here," Mom said, turning off the engine.

Aunt Louise bounded out of the house to greet us as we stepped out of the car. She was tall and wore light tan pants that revealed her slim figure, paired with a white, short-sleeved cotton shirt. She wore her dark blonde hair very short in a natural, sporty style that was different from the permed, stiff styles most women her age wore. The hairstyle suited her artsy, free-spirited personality.

"Welcome, welcome!" she said warmly. "Welcome back, Vanessa. Let's see if we can get some excitement going for you again while you're here."

"Thanks, Aunt Louise," I said as I walked around the car and gave her a hug. "I could sure use some." Wasn't that the truth! Aunt Louise was a very intuitive person.

"Thank you, Louise, for having Vanessa as a house guest again," my mother said. "She's been longing to return for quite some time. I think she finds life back home a bit dull after all the fun she had out here earlier this summer."

"We're delighted to have her," Aunt Louise said. "Let's get you inside and settled in," she said, gesturing toward me.

I grabbed my suitcase and we walked down the short walk leading from the gravel driveway to the end of the house, and then opened a screen door and went inside. The familiar staircase leading down to the cellar was on the right, and straight ahead were the two steps leading up to the kitchen and the rest of the house. I went up the steps, through the narrow kitchen, and into the dining room. It felt good to be back in the house again. A wide arch separated the dining room from the living room, which was in the front of the house overlooking Allisonville Road. There was an official front door in the living room, but people rarely used it. On the right-hand wall of the living room was another large arch in which old gold brocade curtains created a makeshift wall and a door to Emma's bedroom on the other side.

The home's furnishings were somewhat sparse. There was a large oval table with several wooden dining chairs encircling it in the dining room. The living room was furnished with only a green couch, a gray metal desk that Uncle Evert used in his plumbing business, and a mahogany wooden chair from China with carved arms that looked like serpents encircling them. I called that the dragon chair. An upright piano stood against the wall just to the left of the gold curtains. The Beatles album, *Sgt. Pepper's Lonely Hearts Club Band*, was currently spinning on the turntable of a record playing sitting on the floor. I knew that only because the album cover by the same name was lying next to it.

"Shall I put my suitcase in Emma's bedroom?" I asked, turning toward Aunt Louise who walked in behind me. I knew the answer, but thought it wise to be polite and check first.

"Yes, that'd be great. Where *is* Emma, anyway?" Aunt Louise asked, looking around. "Emma, are you here?" she shouted. "She's been very impatient waiting for you to arrive."

Suddenly, Emma emerged from between the two long gold curtains leading to her bedroom. "You're here at last!" she said excitedly.

Emma was thirteen and slim like her mother, with curly, white blonde hair that fell just to her shoulders. She was tall, but not as tall as I, and had a pretty face with bright blue eyes. "What took you so long?" she demanded, looking worried. "Come on. Bring your stuff in here."

She turned and disappeared behind the curtains. I followed her into the bedroom, and placed my suitcase on the floor near the white canopy bed that stood in the corner of the generously sized room. I sat down on the bed and gazed around. Sheer white curtains hung over two large windows facing the backyard. An old dresser with a large, frameless mirror stood against the wall next to the arch. A large walk-in closet with a sin-gle hinged door occupied the wall opposite the bed.

Emma sat down on the bed next to me. Her brow was furrowed, and she didn't seem at all like her usual happy self. Clearly, she had something on her mind.

"Emma, what's going on?" I implored. "You're acting weird. What *is* it?"

"Thanks for coming," she began. "Things haven't been going so well."

"What do you mean?" I asked.

"I don't know if I should talk about it here — — in the house, I mean," she whispered, looking anxiously toward the gold curtains. "Mom, or someone else, might overhear us."

"I think your mom went back outside and is hanging with my mother," I informed her. "She won't hear you. Go ahead." I wanted her to talk.

"No. No. We'll have to go someplace else," Emma insisted. "I want to make sure no one hears us."

"Maybe out to the barn?" I suggested.

"No. Dad might be out there working. Or Luke could be out there doing who-knows- what," she said. She paused, then exclaimed, "I know! We can go over to the treehouse. No one will be *there*."

"The tree house?" I asked. "Where's that?"

"I'll show you," she said. Looking intently at me, she added, "I need your help, Vanessa. We *have* to talk."

"Then *tell* me!" I pleaded. It was too much to be teased like this, whether she meant to or not. "What *is* it? You're scaring me. Can't you please just whisper it to me right now?"

"I'll tell you when we're up in the tree house," she answered, stand-ing. "Come on. Follow me."

We got up and walked through the living room to the kitchen, down the steps, and out the screen door. I was beyond curious and couldn't bear to be kept waiting to hear what was on her mind. She was clearly in dis-tress about something important. I could see that in her eyes. Still I had to do as she asked, so I followed her instructions and tried to be patient.

CHAPTER TWO

The Ghost Plane

Outside, my mother and Aunt Louise were still chatting near our car.

"Come say good-bye, babe," Mom called to me as I exited the house. "I'm going to have to leave now if I'm going to get your sister ready to leave for college next week. I know you know how to behave when you're a house guest, so I don't have to remind you, right?" She opened the car door and got in.

"Bye, Mom," I said, approaching the car. "I'll call you when I'm ready to come home." It was my goal to be the one to decide when I was going home.

"Let's just say I'll come pick you up in four days," Mom countered through the open car window. "That should be enough time for you two girls to say everything there is to say to each other for now, don't you think?"

"Oh, Mom," I whined. Four days seemed much too short a time.

After making a few further farewells to Aunt Louise, Emma, and me, my mom started the car and drove down the driveway and out of sight. Aunt Louise went back into the house, leaving Emma and me standing alone in the driveway.

We had just turned to start walking toward the back yard when I suddenly heard, "Hey, city slicker!" in a loud voice from behind. Turning, I saw my cousins Luke and Daniel walking across the yard from the field on the other side of the driveway, holding fishing poles. "Well, well, look

9

who's here. It's the city slicker!" Luke shouted playfully. "I guess we should have known you'd return someday, like it or not."

Luke was Emma's sixteen-year-old brother. He had the same white blonde hair like Emma, only his was perpetually tousled all over his head as if it hadn't been combed in weeks. He had a muscular and slightly stocky build, and an air of tremendous pent-up energy that might explode at any moment. He also had a somewhat annoying tendency to refer to me as "city slicker," which I hated, but had to tolerate in good humor.

Daniel was one of Aunt Loretta's and Uncle Forrest's six children. They lived almost directly across the street on the property adjacent to Gatewood airport that Uncle Forrest owned. Daniel was thirteen and almost as tall as Luke, but very thin, with curly dark brown hair, a quick smile, and a perpetually cheerful air. It was fortunate he had such an easy-going temperament, because that's what was needed to hang with Luke. Daniel was wearing the over-sized, hand-me-down suede fringed jacket that he always wore, no matter how hot it was outside. It made me smile to see him in it again.

"I understand your family has dumped you on us again," Luke lamented. "Well, I guess that's our burden, like it or not."

"Oh, cut that out," Emma reprimanded. "You're so mean! Simply uncivilized. Let's go Vanessa. You don't have to stand here and take that."

"It's okay, Emma," I said, chuckling. "Hi, Luke. You too, Daniel. What're you guys doing?" I was glad to see them, even with the teasing.

"We were just fishing in the creek, but the water's pretty low right now and there aren't many fish in there," Luke said as he walked to the door of a workroom in the garage where yard equipment, tools, and other odds-and-ends were kept. He and Daniel propped their poles up against the wall in the back and then re-emerged as Emma and I watched from the walkway. "Didn't catch a single one. It's a good thing we don't have to rely on what we catch for our meals around here."

"Yeah, you're no Daniel Boone when it comes to fishing," Daniel taunted.

"What did you say?" Luke asked, slowly turning toward Daniel. "I don't think I heard you correctly."

"Ha! You heard me," Daniel laughed, taking off running in the direction of the barn, as if he knew what to expect. Luke ran after him and overtook him about halfway to the barn. They fell to the ground, arms and legs flailing in a confused jumble. "Let me up, let me go!" Daniel yelled, kicking his feet as Luke sat on his chest and appeared to punch Daniel playfully with his fists.

"If you don't behave, then you get the five-minute treatment. I've told you that a thousand times!" Luke admonished as he continued to sit on Daniel and pinned Daniel's hands over his head.

"Oh, get off of me, you big ox!" Daniel shouted. "Let me go. You've given me the treatment, now get off!"

Luke stood up and brushed himself off. "I just hate it when I have to teach you a lesson like that," he said sarcastically.

"Yeah, you and me both," Daniel complained, sitting up slowly, straightening his tousled hair, then rising to his feet. "I didn't deserve the five-minute treatment that time. No fair."

"Is Daniel okay?" I asked.

"Oh yes," Emma said, nodding. "They do that all the time. I guess they think it's fun. I really don't know why Daniel runs around with Luke. I guess he must enjoy the punishment."

"He doesn't ever do that to you, does he?" I asked, hoping *I'd* never be on the receiving end of the so-called five-minute treatment.

"No, and he'd better never, ever try," Emma declared emphatically. "Let's go. I don't want them to know where we're going."

"Okay, let's go," I seconded eagerly.

Emma and I resumed walking toward the back yard. I hadn't seen the tree house before and my curiosity about it was growing by the minute. It had to have been built since my last visit. I was also running out of patience waiting to learn why Emma summoned me so urgently.

We hadn't gone very far when Daniel ran up to us. "Hey, where are you guys going?" he asked. "Buzz and Lars just finished putting in the floor of the tree house, and you can actually get up in it and walk around. We should all go over and hang out. What do you think?"

Buzz was one of Daniel's older brothers, and Lars was Emma and Luke's older brother. Buzz and Lars frequently worked on interesting projects together, I'd noticed before. The tree house must have been their most recent undertaking. Emma flashed a look indicating she wasn't in favor of Daniel's suggestion.

"Nah, I'm not interested," Luke answered before Emma could come up with a reply. "Been up there before. You guys go ahead without me."

"That's okay. I'll just bum around with you here, then," Daniel said. "Let's go back down to the creek and look for arrowheads. Whad'ya say? When the water's low like today, we should find a bunch of them real easy."

"Sounds like a plan. See you guys later," Luke said as he and Daniel walked toward the creek that ran through the fields beyond the barn.

"Thank goodness we got rid of them," Emma exclaimed as got underway. "I want to talk to you alone."

"Can't you tell me what it is now?" I asked as we walked along.

"Nah. Just hang on," she insisted. "I don't want anyone interrupting us. You'll understand when I tell you."

Emma and I crossed the back yard and followed the narrow trail through the weeds at the edge of the yard down to Allisonville Road. We walked along Allisonville Road a few yards, then crossed and walked past Aunt Loretta and Uncle Forrest's house poised at the crest of their large, gently sloping yard on the other side.

"The tree house is in a maple tree along the access road over there," she said as we continued on, pointing to a row of large trees lining a dirt road in the distance. I squinted, but couldn't see it yet.

"Which tree is it in?" I asked as we walked. "I don't see anything."

"You'll see," Emma reassured me, as she turned and strolled up the dusty dirt road that ran along the edge of the airport. A row of about ten or fifteen forty-foot maple and oak trees lined both sides of the road. A chain-link fence just a few feet beyond the dirt road marked the northern boundary of the airport on the other side. The mature trees were full with their summer foliage blowing in the afternoon breeze, making it difficult to see anything in them until you were up close.

"This is the access road," she explained as we continued walking up the dirt road. She stopped at the base of the largest tree and pointed up. "Look up there," she said. She had the expectant look of someone revealing the secret of a hidden tomb.

I stood close beside her and looked up. Sure enough, there it was. The little house was nestled into the crook of the enormous old tree on a giant limb about three stories above the ground. It was magnificent.

"Wow. There it is," I said, gazing up at it. "How do you get up there?"

"You just climb up this ladder. Like this."

A ladder was constructed by nailing flat pieces of wood into the trunk of the tree about every foot or so. The first step was about four feet off the ground. She jumped up and her right foot landed squarely on the first step. Then she stepped up to the next step and the next.

"See, you just take it one step at a time." She continued upward until I heard her foot steps on the wooden floor high above. "Come on up," she beckoned, looking over the railing at me.

I stared at the first step and realized I was going to have to really jump to reach it. I jumped, and happily my foot connected with the step. I climbed up the next step and the next until I finally reached the tree house floor. A small opening cut into the deck floor was just large enough to climb through, and I pulled myself up to the deck and stood up. I was in! I had made it.

"Wow, this is nice up here. What a view!" I exclaimed, looking down over the airport grounds at the six or seven small private planes tethered to the ground in neat rows below. "I love it!"

The tree house consisted of a single room about the size of a small bedroom, with a roof made out of large sheets of corrugated tin laid on wooden rafters. It was surrounded on two sides by a four-foot-wide deck that had a single two-by-four piece of wood as a railing. The walls of the house were made from large sheets of wood. It had a carved door that looked as if it had been salvaged from an old farmhouse, and still had traces of badly weathered light green paint. It was open and pushed back flat against the wall, and there was a small padlock hanging on its old brass door knob.

After checking out the deck, I stepped inside and looked around. A large window was cut out of each wall, except the wall with the door. None of the windows had glass in them. Except for the paint on the door, the house was unpainted, both inside and out. The only furniture in the house was a small wooden chair and a small, square farm table with carved legs, both of which were positioned under a window. From the looks of things, the roof wasn't very weather-tight, but at least it was a roof, and it was high enough that I could stand up comfortably and walk around.

"Did Buzz and Lars really build this?" I asked as I admired the house and walked inside and out, checking out everything. "They're very talented, aren't they?"

"Yep, they sure did," Emma replied from out on the deck. "Buzz scavenged wood from old houses and barns being torn down, and he and Lars started building it a few weeks ago. They finally found enough wood to finish it up like this last week."

I stood at the window facing the airport and studied a small, single-engine airplane slowly taxiing toward the gas pumps that stood in the middle of a large refueling circle in front of the single-story airport office building. You could really see what was going on all over the airport from up there. It was a private airport for people with their own planes to fly as a hobby or for company business. No commercial airlines landed there. A large airplane hangar stood in the distance, and beyond that were three smaller hangars lined up in a row. There was also a large hangar not far below clad in turquoise aluminum. The airport had only one runway that appeared to head in the general direction of the tree house. As I stood at the window, a plane took off, coming toward us until it flew high enough to pass over us and turn to the west. It was exciting, and a bit startling, to see the plane fly so close.

"That's a Colt," Emma said, studying at the plane as it flew by. "Yeah, I'm pretty sure that's what that one is."

"A Colt?" I repeated, squinting at the plane.

"Yeah. That's a kind of plane," she explained. "You get to know the different kinds of planes when you live near an airport like this."

I was enthralled by the new experience of being in the tree house, but I hadn't forgotten the reason we'd come there.

"I'm dying to find out what's on your mind. Why did you bring me up here?" I asked, changing the subject. "Can you please tell me *now*?"

"I need your help, Vanessa. Desperately," she confided, turning toward me looking perplexed.

"Okay, okay. Just tell me what it is," I urged. "I promise to do what I can."

She paused, took a deep breath, and then began. "Okay. Here goes. The other day I overheard my parents talking when they thought they were alone in the house. I had gone down to the creek with Daniel to fish, but came back to get some safety pins to use as hooks. I was looking for the pins in my dresser when they started talking. I'm pretty sure they didn't know I was there."

"What did you say?" I asked, eager to hear. "It must have been something pretty serious."

"It was. They said that the bank sold the mortgage on the farm to someone — — I forget who. The people who have the mortgage sent Dad a letter saying my parents didn't do something technical when the mortgage said they should, and now they're going to foreclose and kick us off the farm unless my parents pay off the entire mortgage in two weeks. My parents don't have the money to do that, so that means we'll lose the farm!" As she spoke, her face reflected her torment.

"Are you sure?" I asked. "Isn't there something they can do? Can't they talk to the people who own the mortgage and ask them to be patient? Can they fix whatever they said was goofed up?"

"They said they don't even know who to talk to, and they don't have the money right now to pay off the mortgage," Emma explained. "Whoever sent them the letter is playing hardball, I heard Dad say. My mother cried. The farm's been in the family a long time. Dad said we might have to move back to New Jersey to be near some family. I can't bear the idea of losing everything and leaving!"

"Can't they ask Uncle Forrest for help? Or my parents? Surely they'd help if your parents asked," I suggested.

"No. They won't ask anyone for help. My parents are too proud to ask. They said they won't do that, no matter what," Emma continued. She looked as forlorn as I'd ever seen her. "Can you imagine if they take the farm from us and we have to leave? I'll miss the creek and the fields and the barn. I'll have to change schools. I'll have to leave all my friends. I won't get to see you anymore, either. I don't know anyone in New Jersey. I don't want to move to New Jersey!" She started sobbing.

"Don't cry," I consoled her. "Everything's going to be okay."

I smiled feebly and tried to look encouraging, but I was frightened, too. I had a real attachment to Emma and her family. If they lost the farm, where would they go? Would they really have to move so far away? Was I going to lose them all so soon, just when I'd gotten to know them? Something had to be done. But what could two girls like us do? I had to think this through carefully.

"I could ask my parents for the money," I proposed. "That's different from your parents doing the asking. I'm sure my parents would help if I explained the situation to them."

"No! Don't you dare mention this to your parents," Emma shot back. "This is super-secret. You have to keep this our secret, no matter what. On your honor. Promise you won't say a word. Pinkie swear." She held up her right hand and crossed her heart with her index finger.

"Okay. If you say so," I reassured her.

She seemed pretty worked up about it. I wanted to tell my mother, but it was important that I keep my promise that I wouldn't. I sat quietly for a moment. Then an idea occurred to me.

"Maybe you and I could do something to raise the money," I offered. "You know, babysitting, odd jobs, running errands for people. Stuff like that."

"My parents need thousands of dollars," Emma replied dismissively. "How could we raise that kind of money by baby–sitting and running errands in just two weeks? There isn't enough time."

She was right. There was no way we could baby–sit or do enough odd jobs to earn that kind of money in just two weeks. I had to think harder and come up with a better solution.

We sat in silence on the edge of the deck with our legs dangling over the side. I struggled to absorb all that she had just told me. I was surprisingly relaxed sitting so high from the ground. It was pleasant to perch there and gaze mindlessly into the distance and watch the people and planes at the airport below. After a few minutes, Emma spoke again, breaking our silence.

"I got something else to tell you. Did you ever hear about the ghost plane?" she asked.

"Ghost plane? What?" I sputtered, looking at her with wide eyes. "No, I haven't. Tell me about it."

This was a new one on me. Maybe if we talked about a ghost plane, she'd be distracted from her parents' financial troubles.

"They found a Cessna, with its engines still running, sitting at the end of the runway one night a couple of weeks ago. It had no pilot and no passengers," she began. She spoke slowly and deliberately, like people often do when telling a ghost story.

"What happened to the pilot? Did he get out and just disappear?" I asked.

"No one seems to know. The night security guard saw it land and drove his car out to see why it just sat at the end of the runway and didn't taxi in. He said he never saw anyone get out of the plane, and the doors were closed."

"Did someone in the plane radio the airport before they landed?" I inquired.

"Nope. There's never anyone in the airport office at night, so there was no way to communicate with the plane before it landed."

"Well, the plane didn't just land itself," I reasoned. "Someone had to land it. Aren't planes registered or something, like cars? Couldn't they trace it back to the owner somehow?"

"I heard it was registered to someone in California, but the owner said he didn't fly it here. Maybe someone stole it and flew it here. But no one saw it on radar or received any radio messages from it between here and California. There was no record of it landing anywhere between California and here to refuel. It just appeared on the runway here one night — — propellers spinning — — with no one inside," she recounted.

"That doesn't make sense. Was there luggage or anything inside?" I asked. "Maybe they left a clue."

"Uh-uh. There was no luggage. Nothing," she continued. "Except *one* thing."

"Well, don't keep me in suspense! What was it?" I asked impatiently.

"A crate full of turtles."

"Turtles?" I repeated. "Why would someone — — or a ghost — — fly a crate of turtles here? You can get all the turtles you want down by the creek."

"It's true. They found a bunch of turtles," she said, shrugging. "Daniel said they were special turtles, though. I think he said they were Eastern box turtles, and that they're endangered. Uncle Forrest took them to Mr. Jefferson, the guy who runs the pet store in Noblesville, and he agreed that's what they were."

"I see," I said, thinking out loud. "So, let me get this straight. Someone stole a Cessna and flew it here from California with a bunch of special turtles in it. Landed the plane, disappeared, and left everything on the runway, including the turtles, and didn't even bother to turn off the plane's engines? Why would someone do that? That makes no sense. It's nutty."

"I don't know. As for me, I don't think the plane was stolen," Emma said, looking far off.

"What then?" I asked. "How do you explain it?"

"I think the plane was enchanted, and flew itself here all by itself without a pilot," Emma declared with a decisive nod of her head. "I've heard of planes being inhabited by evil spirits, and maybe that one was, too. That's the only explanation. That plane was haunted!"

"Nah. There has to be a logical explanation," I disagreed, shaking my head. "Haunted planes don't have turtles in them, do they? The turtles were real, right? What happened to the plane?"

"Last I heard the police wanted Uncle Forrest to keep it here so they could look it over before the owner has it flown back to California," Emma said. "I guess it's still in one of the hangars." She pointed over to the three small hangars lined up in the distance. "I sure wouldn't want to be the person who has to fly it back to California, would you? You wouldn't know *what* that plane might do."

"You really think the plane flew itself here?" I asked, looking squarely at her. "Come on!"

"I sure do," she said. "A lot of other people think so, too. That plane has its own spirit. There's no other explanation."

"Hmm. Sure is strange, no matter how you try to explain it," I agreed.

"Yep, it was a ghost plane, pure and simple," she repeated decisively.

I stared into the distance. A ghost plane? Now I've heard of everything. Perhaps it was possible. I didn't know. I looked across the airport, deep in thought. After a second or two, I slowly realized that there was a man in a beige jacket standing near the edge of the large turquoise hangar looking up at us. He stood motionless, just staring in our direction. I looked around and concluded he was definitely fixed on us, as there was nothing else around us to look at.

"Why is that guy down there looking at us?" I asked Emma casually. "Is there any reason we shouldn't be up here?"

"Who? You mean that guy down there?" she asked, pointing at him. "Beats me. Why?"

"I don't know. Just wondering," I replied.

It made me uneasy to think someone was watching us. Even with all of the leaves, he must have been able to see us pretty clearly. I returned his stare until he finally broke off and walked to a white panel truck parked near the two large doors of the hangar and climbed inside. I watched as he drove out to Allisonville Road and out of sight. Maybe he was just admiring the tree house. Or perhaps he was looking at something else.

CHAPTER THREE

Love Hurts

The shadows the sun cast became long as the afternoon wore on, and Emma and I became hungry. We decided to climb down and go back to see if dinner was ready.

"Hey, watch this!" Emma said as she ducked under the deck railing and crawled out on the large limb supporting the tree house. A thick rope hanging almost to the ground was tied near the end of the limb.

"What are you *doing*?!" I shouted as I stood up and ran to the edge of the deck. "You'll fall and break your neck!"

"Nah. This is fun!" she answered playfully as she took the rope in her hands, shimmied down it, and jumped the final five or six feet to the ground. "We call that the tree house elevator," she shouted up to me from the ground with a look of triumph. "Now you try it."

"No, I don't think so," I declined without hesitating. "I don't want to break my neck."

"You won't. Just crawl out like I did, and hang onto the rope and shimmy down slowly," she urged. "Go on. Try it. You can do it. I have faith in you."

I looked over at the rope as it swung at the end of the limb about six feet away on the other side of the railing. This was something I was definitely *not* going to do. But what could I say to maneuver out of this situation in such a way that I wouldn't be the city slicker she and the others expected me to be? I stood steadfast on the edge of the deck and stared at the rope.

"Are you coming?" Emma shouted up impatiently as she paced below.

"Okay, okay. Don't rush me," I answered, stalling.

Just then, I heard a "Yoo hoo!" and saw Luke walking up the access road with another person I couldn't quite see. "Yoo hoo! Anyone up in these trees?" Luke called as he approached. "Tarzan? Jane? Anyone home?" I exhaled with relief that he had arrived just in time to distract Emma from forcing me to execute the rope trick.

"What do you want?" Emma demanded impatiently as Luke walked up to her.

"Hi, Cheetah. Where's Tarzan?" Luke teased.

"Cut it out," Emma chided. "Who are you looking for?"

"Well, you're in a bad monkey mood today, aren't you?" Luke said, smiling. "We're looking for Daniel. Is he around? We thought we'd do some target shooting with our bows and arrows."

"No. We haven't seen him," Emma answered. "We've been up in the tree house by ourselves. Besides, I thought he was with you."

I was stunned when I looked down and saw that the boy standing next to Luke was Jim Sparks! I took a deep breath and felt my heart start to race. There he was, at last. He looked as great as ever. He was sixteen years old and about six feet tall, with hazel eyes and straight, dark hair that fell across his forehead and over his ears. He had a handsomely rugged face that was tan from being outdoors most of the time, and broad shoulders. My old feelings for him welled up inside me, and my heart skipped a beat when I saw him standing there. I had ached for so long to see him again. Now that the moment had finally arrived, I choked inside and felt like disappearing into a wisp of smoke.

"Is that you, Vanessa?" Jim asked, squinting up at me.

"Yep. The city slicker has returned!" Luke answered for me. "Just like the seven-year locust, she keeps coming back. No matter what precautions you take."

"Oh, cut that out!" Emma scolded, nudging Luke on the arm. "You think you're so funny, but you're not. Don't pick on Vanessa."

"Hi, Jim. Yes, it's me," I said, smiling. I was tongue-tied, not certain how friendly I should be. After all, I hadn't heard from him in more than four weeks.

"Vanessa, just use the ladder and come on down," Emma urged. "You can learn to use the rope later."

"What? Don't tell me you're trying to teach the city slicker how to come down the rope," Luke scoffed with a playful snort. "I'd pay money to see *that*!"

I didn't mind Luke's teasing. Not even in front of Jim. I was just relieved that the rope-climbing lesson was suspended for now. I lowered myself through the hole in the deck floor and slowly and carefully managed the rungs and made my way down. Once on the ground, I turned around and stood face-to-face with Jim. It sure was good to see him! His smile had the same warmth that I remembered so fondly. What could have happened to make him give me the cold shoulder the last few weeks? I wondered — — should I act a bit aloof — — play hard to get? Maybe he'd find me attractive if I did. Still when I looked into his handsome eyes, I melted, and there was no way I could act cold toward him. It felt so natural to be near him, as though no time at all had passed since we had last been together.

"Come on, Jim" Luke said. "Daniel got a new bow and some fancy arrows at Ed Schock's last week. I bet he's up at his house. Let's go get him." Luke charged off toward Daniel's house without waiting for a response from Jim.

"Well, nice to see you again, Vanessa," Jim said. "I'd better go. You know how Luke is. We'll talk soon. Okay? See ya." He turned and followed Luke across the yard.

"Sure, that'd be great," I managed to utter as he walked away.

I felt a sinking feeling, and was disappointed our conversation had been so brief. He said we'd talk soon, though. What did that mean? Did he have something to tell me? Was he as eager as I was to be together again? My emotions were all over the place, and I had no idea what to think.

"Well, let's go back to the house and watch TV and see what's for dinner," Emma suggested after a moment of silence. "Come on." She knew from my last visit that I had a crush on Jim, and could probably tell from the look on my face that I was disappointed we hadn't had a more in-depth conversation.

Emma and I walked down the access road and then along the shoulder of Allisonville Road until we crossed it and walked up the gravel driveway to Emma's house. Aunt Louise stood at the stove stirring something in a pan when we entered.

"It's about time for dinner," Aunt Louise announced as we passed through the kitchen to the dining room and sat down. "We're having spaghetti and meatballs. Are you hungry?"

"I'm starving," Emma confirmed. "How about you, Vanessa?"

"I don't know," I answered with a shrug. "Guess so."

"Let's snack on some Chips Ahoys while we wait for dinner," Emma proposed, standing to retrieve them from the pantry. "Want some?"

"No, thank you," I replied. I was preoccupied with thoughts of Jim, and suddenly had no appetite.

"Aren't you feeling well?" Aunt Louise asked, standing in the dining room doorway. She had the radio in the kitchen tuned to a rock station. "Help!" by the Beatles was playing.

"No. No, I'm fine. Just fine," I stuttered. "I'm just not very hungry today. I don't know why."

"I know why," Emma said, looking sly.

I gave her a stern look conveying the message to be quiet. Surely she wouldn't discuss Jim in front of my aunt. I hoped not, anyway.

"She's got boy troubles," Emma continued, giggling.

I was shocked she'd give me away like that. It was new to me to feel this way, and I was a little embarrassed for Aunt Louise to know. I frowned at Emma to show my disapproval. I hoped my body language cut short any further comments she might make.

"You mean Jim Sparks?" Aunt Louise answered, to my surprise. How did she know Emma was referring to *him*? Did *everyone* know about my crush? "He's a very nice boy. Very nice," she continued. "But he's got a girlfriend, doesn't he, Emma? Isn't it Monica Calhoun? Am I right? Isn't that what Luke told us?"

Hearing those words cut through me like a knife. *He's got a girlfriend.* How could that be? I thought *I* was his girlfriend. At least I thought that's what I was earlier this summer. With so little contact from him recently, I had no rational expectation that I meant anything to him. But in my heart, I wanted to think — — to hope — — that I still did. This completely destroyed any delusions I could hang onto.

"I guess so. I'm not sure. You see them together everywhere, that's for sure," Emma observed. "They always look pretty cozy, too. Know what I mean? I'm not sure if they're boyfriend and girlfriend though." I could tell she was backtracking, but it was too late.

"Sorry to just lay it out there so bluntly, Vanessa," Aunt Louise said. "But it's better to know, don't you think?"

"Oh, no!" I blurted before I could stop myself. "I didn't know he had a girlfriend. He never told me. I feel so foolish!" I covered my face with my hands. I wanted to act cool and collected in front of Emma and Aunt Louise, but my feelings were pouring out, and I couldn't stop myself.

"Oh, there, there," Aunt Louise consoled me, walking over and placing her arm around my shoulder. "No harm's been done. Honest emotions are never anything to apologize for. You're a lovely young lady, Vanessa. There'll be plenty of young men in your life before you're done. He's just one of many. You'll see."

Yes, but I wanted *Jim*, not any other boy. I didn't dare say that, though.

"I think he's a big flirt to lead you on this way," Emma protested indignantly. "I used to like him, but now I don't. I'm putting him on my blacklist."

"No, don't say that, Emma," I said, looking over at her. "He's a good guy. Really he is. It's not his fault. He didn't lead me on. He never promised me anything. I just didn't want it to end so soon, that's all."

"Emma, why don't you two go outside and get some fresh air while I finish heating up dinner," Aunt Louise suggested. "That'll make Vanessa feel better. Fresh air always helps clear the mind. You girls go on, now. Dinner will be ready in about half an hour."

Emma and I took Aunt Louise's advice and walked outside. The sun was just starting to set as we walked aimlessly across the yard toward the barn. As I gazed at the gracefully angled roof of the barn, thoughts of Jim dominated my thoughts. Everywhere I looked I was reminded of him and of the fun we'd had together only two months ago. How things had changed. At least now I knew why I hadn't heard from him since we met for a Coke at Glendale. Who could blame him? I was younger and lived in another city. It was only natural he'd get involved with a local girl his own age.

"Sorry I said that to my mother," Emma apologized softly as we walked along. "I was just trying to tease you. I never figured it'd go the way it did."

"Oh, it's okay," I said, wiping a tear from my cheek. "Glad to know what the score is. I can take it."

I was lost in my feelings when Daniel suddenly ran up behind us, panting hard as though he'd run flat out all the way from his house.

"Have you seen him?" he asked. His eyes were large with panic.

"Who?" Emma asked. "Who are you talking about?"

"Bobo's missing," he said excitedly. "I locked him into his climbing house out by our barn this morning, but he wasn't there when I went out to feed him this evening. I think someone must have taken him. He's pretty smart, but I don't see how he could have gotten out all by himself."

"Who's Bobo?" I asked, puzzled.

"My black spider monkey," Daniel explained. "Have you seen him over here? I sure hope so."

"You have a spider monkey? Since when?" I asked. I'd never known anyone who owned a monkey.

"My dad got him from an animal dealer in Muncie. He was born in captivity, so it's legal to own him. Spider monkeys are an endangered species, but if they're born in captivity and you purchase them from a reputable dealer, it's okay to own them," he explained. "There're some bad guys out there who sell them illegally, though. There's a black market for spider monkeys, you know. You've got to be careful. That's why I'm so worried he's missing!"

"He's a cute little thing," Emma said, chuckling as she thought of him. "His little hands will pick up and throw just about anything that's not nailed down."

"I know," he replied breathlessly, his eyes still searching the yard as he stood next to us. "He really likes to hurl things. When we first got him, we tried keeping him in the house, but my mom got fed up with all the stuff he broke, so now we keep him mostly in his climbing house out back," Daniel said. He turned and peered slowly and carefully around the barn yard.

"That's awful. Do you think someone took him?" I asked. "That would be a really rotten thing to do."

"I don't know. I really don't. Are you guys doing anything right now? Can you help me search for him?" Daniel pleaded. He looked sad and agitated.

I was hungry suddenly, and dinner was probably ready by now. But we gladly delayed our meal and joined him in the search for his missing pet. We went out to the barn and up into the hay loft. We walked through the fields, through the old graveyard behind the barn, and down along the little creek that cut through the property. There was no sign of Bobo anywhere. It was growing dark, and we knew we had to give up our search for now. It took a lot of convincing to get Daniel to discontinue the search, though.

"Someone took him, I just know it," he said, inconsolable. "He was so cute. Now it's nighttime and he's out there somewhere, all alone and scared."

"We'll help you look for him after dinner if you want," Emma volunteered.

"Nah. That's okay. It's too dark now. You're right. We'll have to wait 'til morning. I just hope he wasn't snatched — — that he got out on his own. If he did, he'll come back when he's hungry. I just can't bear the thought that someone kidnapped him to sell on that wicked black market," he lamented.

Daniel gave us a half-hearted wave and walked off toward his house with his head hung low. I watched him check the bushes and undergrowth as he made his way across the back yard to the path down to Allisonville Road. I felt sorry for him. Did someone kidnap Bobo? I knew Daniel's heart must be broken. I had a Siamese cat at home that I loved very much, and I'd be devastated if I lost him. But you never know. Maybe we'd find Bobo tomorrow.

CHAPTER FOUR

The Wishing Tree

After dinner it was time to watch prime time television on the one and only TV in the house. It had a black and white picture, and sat on a tripod with wheels in the archway between the dining and living rooms. Emma still seemed preoccupied. I assumed she was thinking about her parents' financial problems. As for me, I was still trying to shake off my disappointment about Jim. It would be therapeutic to watch a good show and think about something else. She and I took our positions on the floor in front of the tiny TV screen, while Uncle Evert and Luke pursued what appeared to be the nightly ritual of wrestling the picture into focus.

"There. Well, darn it! It got all fuzzy again," Uncle Evert said in an exasperated tone as he manipulated the antennae attached to the back of the set from side to side. "I thought I had the picture that time for sure."

Uncle Evert was average height, with a stocky build and had a thick head of silver-gray hair. He wore glasses only when reading or working on something up close like the TV. It was remarkable how much Luke resembled him in build and mannerisms.

"Come on, Dad. Let me have a go at it," Luke demanded impatiently. "I bet I can get it." He hovered over his father watching everything he did.

"No, I've got it. There it is. Voilà!" Uncle Evert stepped back and examined the picture. Satisfied with the results, he picked up the *Indianapolis Star* newspaper from the dining room table and walked to the green couch. It appeared he had no intention of watching TV himself.

"Want to watch *Star Trek*?" I asked Emma and Luke. It was one of my favorite shows.

"Nah. I don't want to watch that science fiction stuff," Luke said, settling into one of the dining room chairs. "*Daniel Boone* is on tonight, isn't it? Let's watch that instead."

"*Star Trek* isn't on until after *Daniel Boone*, so we can watch both. Okay?" I cajoled. I had the TV schedule practically memorized, as I took my TV-watching very seriously.

"Okay with me," Emma replied. "I like *Star Trek*. That Mr. Chekov is cute!"

"He's a Commie, isn't he? How can he be cute if he's a Commie Ruskie?" Luke argued. "You know those guys have nuclear warheads aimed at us at this very moment, don't you? We're one push button away from annihilation. People like that are not exactly what I call cute."

"He's from Russia, but that doesn't necessarily make him a Communist!" Emma returned. "The show takes place in the future, like the twenty-third century or something. There aren't any communists in the twenty-third century. By then the people of the earth have become united into one federation. You know that very well. You're just trying to start an argument, as usual." She tossed her hair scornfully.

"Ha! Me? Argue? I'm as agreeable as a lamb," Luke insisted with a smirk as he stood and stretched. "Doesn't matter anyway. I think I'll go outside and wait for Randy. He said he might come over tonight. As far as I'm concerned, you can watch anything you want until he gets here."

"Who's Randy?" I asked.

"Just one of his friends," Emma replied. "Kind of a nerd."

"Better watch what you say about your future husband, Sis," Luke said with a grin.

"Yuck!" Emma replied, rolling her eyes. "No way."

"Luke, are you bullying the girls again?" Lars asked, entering the room from the back hallway. He was Emma and Luke's older brother, in his early twenties. He was tall and slim with dark, almost black, straight hair that he wore parted on the side. He carried a *Time* magazine under his arm. "I'm trying to read about Soviet Premier Kosygin and President Johnson meeting in New Jersey at the Glassboro Summit, and all I can hear is Luke in here creating static noise, as usual."

"What? You're reading about a Ruskie? I'm surrounded! It's a Commie conspiracy!" Luke exclaimed as he marched through the kitchen and loped outside.

"I just don't see how I can be related to such a barbarian," Lars observed dryly. Then, glancing over at me, he said, "Well, hello, Cousin. Is that you? I almost didn't see you sitting over there."

"Hi, Lars," I replied, smiling. "Did you miss me?"

"Of course I did!" Lars exclaimed. "Where have you been? We like having you around. You're a good influence on my little sister. She can run wild at times, and needs a sensible friend like you to help tame her."

Emma rolled her eyes again. I could see that living with her two brothers required thick skin to withstand all of the teasing they dished out. On the plus side, though, Lars had been part of building the tree house. He strolled into the kitchen and opened the refrigerator. Then walked back through the dining room holding a Mountain Dew bottle and shuffled into to the middle bedroom and closed the door.

Emma and I decided to watch *Daniel Boone* anyway, after rejecting the choices available on the other two networks, one of which was *Batman* followed by *F Troop*. Ironically, Luke didn't return until after *Daniel Boone* was over and the opening sequence of *Star Trek* had started. He stomped up the stairs to the kitchen with his usual heavy gait. Trailing behind him was a boy I'd never met before; I assumed it was Randy. The boy was Luke's age, average in height, with dark blonde hair and a slight belly visible under the oversized, green t-shirt he wore hanging out over his baggy jeans. His face had a dark pinkish tone to it, set off by black-rimmed glasses sitting slightly crooked on his face. The two boys took a seat at the dining room table.

"What's the name of this episode? 'Mudd's Women'?" Luke asked, reading the TV screen when the commercials finally ended and the episode began. "Well, that has promise, anyway. As long as the women don't have pointy heads and eyes in the middle of their foreheads, that is!"

"Hi, Randy," Emma said to the boy.

"Oh, yeah, I forgot. Guess I'd better introduce you. This is Randy," Luke said. "That's Vanessa," Luke said, pointing at me. "She's my cousin. Visiting for a few days. She's kinda different. A real city slicker, if you know what I mean. You'll want to steer clear of her."

"Hey," Randy replied in barely audible voice. He seemed awkward and shy.

I nodded in return, and then resumed watching TV.

"Oh, I've seen this episode before. It's a good one," I shouted, excitedly. "Mudd's an intergalactic cargo ship captain who transports women to remote outposts to become wives. The women are stunningly beautiful because they take this special drug. I think they call it the Venus drug, or something."

"Shhh! Don't give the whole story away," Luke warned. "Hey! Maybe those women'll wear sexy little outfits. They usually dress the women on this show like sex kittens."

Ignoring him, I continued. "One of the three women who are brought by Mudd to be wives on barren planet Rigel XII runs away, not wanting to become the wife of a miner and a sex object. She wants more out of life than that."

"What's her problem?" Luke muttered. "She's lucky that miner will take her to be his wife. Captain Kirk ought to show her who's the boss."

"I don't know," Randy observed. "That Rigel XII looks pretty dusty and barren. I don't think I'd want to live there, either, no matter who I was. Can't Mudd and Captain Kirk can find a better planet for that woman to live on than that?"

Good for Randy! He wasn't shy, after all. I sat up straight and managed to get a good peek at him. He wasn't really too bad looking, but he was certainly sloppy and unfit. Not the athletic type like Jim.

"Who cares if it's dusty and barren?" Luke complained. "She needs to know her place. Just like all women should."

"I hope you don't mean what you're saying," I replied. "Women don't exist for the sole purpose of becoming wives and serving men. What century do you live in, anyway?"

"Says who? Why, sure they do! And, the costume that troublemaker is wearing isn't very sexy at all. It looks like the evening gown Ginger wears on *Gilligan's Island*. She needs to up her sexy game. Don't you think so, Randy?" Luke asked, looking at Randy and giving him a quick wink.

Randy smiled and shrugged. "Communications Officer Uhura is her own woman. She doesn't need a man. I think she rocks."

"Randy, you're really starting to get on my nerves. You know that?" Luke growled, giving his friend a dirty look.

"You sexist pig!" Emma shouted. "Go outside and leave us in peace. You're ruining the show."

"Ha! Call me all the names you want, but I'm a man, and I'm just saying what all men think," Luke declared, puffing out his chest. "It's time you ladies learn how men think."

"I don't want to know how men think. I want to watch the show," Emma chastised.

"Oh, for crying out loud. Let's get out of here, Randy. This is a stupid show, anyway. We can find better stuff to do," Luke said.

"Good," Emma replied. "Go outside and do something manly, like fall in the creek."

"Bye. I guess," Randy said, giving me a self-conscious smile as he shuffled out behind Luke and down the steps.

The house was peaceful once again. When the show ended, one of the women, Eve, discovered that she didn't need the Venus drug to be beautiful, and she chose to stay with the chief miner on barren Rigel XII.

"What was the point of that ending?" Emma asked as the credits rolled. "I don't get it."

"I don't know — — maybe they're saying you're only as beautiful as you think you are?" I concluded after giving it some thought. "The Venus drug turned out to be a phony. When she took it she became beautiful only because she *thought* it made her beautiful. I think the message is that every woman is beautiful in her own unique way."

"Yeah, but I thought she wanted off the planet. I still don't get it. But whatever. It's late and I think I'll go to bed. I'm going to think myself beautiful so I can wake up gorgeous."

"Ha! That's the spirit," I laughed.

It was late, so I followed suit. When I crawled into bed that night, it felt good to be back in my aunt and uncle's home again. I could hear the sounds of applause and laughter coming from the TV as Lars sat up late watching *The Tonight Show* starring Johnny Carson, and the muffled sounds of Aunt Louise and Uncle Evert speaking in low tones in the next bedroom. A little later I heard Luke return, and soon heard his bedroom door close. All of the sounds and smells of the house were familiar, and it felt safe and cozy to be there.

"Thanks for coming out here today," Emma said softly after a few minutes. "I know we can't save the farm, but having you here makes me feel better."

"Of course," I replied. "I just wish I could help."

"It helps to just have you here to talk to," Emma answered as she rolled on her side and pulled the sheet up over her shoulders.

I wished I could do more to help than just talk. I stared at the white canopy arching over the bed and thought hard to come up with an idea, but I couldn't think of a single thing. How I wished Emma would allow me to tell my parents! That was all I could think of to do. I just knew they'd know what to do. But I had to honor my promise not to tell them.

Emma fell asleep right away. I looked around the room and my eyes came to the half-open closet door. I thought about the dark, cavernous space inside. The last time I visited, Emma told me her older sister Margret saw glowing red eyes in there. She swore it was true. I smiled recalling her telling me that, probably to scare me, since we didn't get along that well when we first met. Now we were the best of friends and there was no mention of the glowing red eyes. Still, just to play it safe, I fixed my eyes on a macramé wall hanging of an owl on an opposite wall until I finally fell asleep.

The next morning came quickly. It was one of those sunny, warm summer mornings that seem to come endlessly one after the other this time of the year. I was awakened by the sound of Emma rifling through a drawer in the dresser next to the bed.

"Hey. What are you doing?" I asked, yawning. "Is everything okay?"

"I'm looking for that silver ring with the tiger's eye that Margret bought for me when she was down in Broad Ripple a couple of weeks ago," she explained as she continued noisily moving things around in the drawer.

"Why?" I asked.

"I want to sell it," she replied.

"Why?" I asked again.

"So I can give the money to my parents to help pay the mortgage," she answered as she continued digging through lingerie, scarves, and jewelry.

"How much could you get for it?" I asked.

"I don't know. I could take it over to the airport. Someone flying through might buy it. Those people usually have extra money for stuff," she said, continuing noisily moving things around in the drawer.

"Oh," I replied. I sat up in bed and watched her. "Do you really want to sell it? Will Margret mind since she gave it to you as a gift?"

"Here it is!" she shouted, triumphantly holding up a tiny silver ring. "I knew it was in here. Hurry and get dressed so we can go over to the airport."

She darted through the gold curtains as I climbed out of bed. After I was dressed, I joined her as she sat at the dining room table eating a bowl of Alpha-Bits cereal. She said nothing as I sat down beside her. She had lost the happy, determined demeanor she'd had when she'd left the bedroom only minutes before. After a few moments of silence, she suddenly burst out sobbing.

"Oh, no! What's the matter?" I asked, stunned. She continued crying and didn't answer.

"What's going on in here?" Aunt Louise demanded, entering the room. "Emma, why are you crying? What's the matter, dear?"

Emma continued sobbing. Aunt Louise bent down over her and asked again what was wrong. When she still didn't get an answer, Aunt Louise looked at me with questioning eyes. I shrugged, because even though I knew it was probably about the foreclosure, I didn't want to give away the fact that I knew about it.

"Emma. I insist you tell me. What on earth has gotten you into such a state this morning?" Aunt Louise implored. "What's in your hand there?"

Emma uncurled her fingers and revealed the little ring sitting in her palm.

"What are you doing with that?" Aunt Louise asked. "Are you crying about that ring? But why?"

"She's going to sell it," I volunteered.

"What?" Aunt Louise blurted. "I thought you liked that little ring. You said you did when Margret got it for you. Why would you want to sell it?"

"The farm! The farm!" Emma cried.

"What do you mean? What about the farm?" Aunt Louise asked, looking bewildered.

"I heard you and Daddy talking. We're going to lose the farm. . . and have to move far away," Emma replied between sobs. "I don't want to. I'll just die if we have to move away. I thought. . . I could sell the ring and, and. . . .get some money to give you. But I know it isn't enough, and I don't have anything else to sell!"

"Oh, that," Aunt Louise said, straightening up. A solemn look came over her face. "That's nothing for you to be concerned about, Emma. We'll figure out something. You'll see. Don't worry your young head about that."

"What if you don't?" Emma said, tears streaking down her face. "We'll have to move away. *Move away*! To New Jersey! Mom, I don't want to go. Please don't make me move to New Jersey! I don't know anyone in New Jersey!"

Emma seemed inconsolable, and continued weeping bitterly.

Aunt Louise gazed out the window, deep in thought, then turned and spoke. "You're not selling your special ring, Emma, and that's all there is to say about that. I have a better idea. I want you girls to come with me," she said decisively, exuding an inspired air. "I want to show you girls something."

"What?" Emma asked, blinking back her tears.

"You'll see. Come along now," Aunt Louise insisted, gesturing to get up.

Emma and I looked at each other with confused looks, but dutifully rose and followed her. Once outside, instead of heading in the direction of the barn as we typically did to go just about anywhere on the farm, Aunt Louise walked across the back yard to a narrow ridge of land that followed the creek as it wound around and cut through the woods behind the old cemetery. We eventually came to a finger of land carved high into the creek bank by fast-moving water flooding the area for decades. At the highest point stood an enormous old sycamore tree. Its smooth, white-and-gray bark glistened in the morning sun like a tall, white lady. It had to be as tall as a five-story building. Its branches spread out gracefully for several feet all around it.

"This is the wishing tree," Aunt Louise said, raising her arms upward at the tree as if she were greeting it.

"What do you mean?" Emma asked, looking confused. "Why is this the wishing tree? I've never heard it called that before. Is this what you wanted to show us?"

I'd never seen the tree before. Or perhaps I'd just never taken particular note of it before. It was a very beautiful tree, for sure, and had an impressively huge trunk. It had to have stood watch high over the creek for well over a hundred years.

"There's a story about this tree," Aunt Louise continued. "It was about eighty years ago, when this area was just being settled. A young woman named Hannah McClintock lived in a little house just south of here with her husband, Jacob, and their baby. They were struggling to farm a few acres and establish a life for themselves. One winter day, their baby took ill with scarlet fever. Jacob took their horse and buggy in a terrible snowstorm to get the doctor in Noblesville, while Hannah stayed home with the sick baby. Jacob was killed in an accident on his way back with the doctor, and their baby later died of the fever. Hannah lost both of the people she loved, and without her husband to farm the land, she also lost her homestead. She lost everything that mattered to her."

"That's a very sad story, Mom," Emma said. "If you're trying to cheer me up, it's not working."

"Well, hang on. I'm getting to the good part," Aunt Louise said. "Hannah was so grief-stricken, that a few months later she came right here to throw herself into the creek and end it all. But before she did, she looked up into the tree, and something spoke to her that stopped her."

"What do you mean something 'spoke to her'?" Emma asked, looking up at the tree suspiciously.

"Just what I said," Aunt Louise replied, looking triumphant.

"A voice? A real voice?" Emma asked. "That's kinda spooky."

I looked up at the tree, unconvinced. "What did the voice say?" I probed.

"The voice told her to have faith. That her life was worth living, and that something better would come," Aunt Louise related.

"So, she didn't drown herself, like she planned?" Emma asked. She looked intensely at her mother as she waited for her mother to answer. "I have a feeling I know the answer," Emma added.

"No. The voice inspired her, and the desire to die completely evaporated," Aunt Louise said. "She eventually remarried and had several more children, living to a ripe old age. But any time she felt at the end of her rope or in despair, she'd come here, to the wishing tree. As the story goes, she'd make her wish, and receive comfort and advice."

"Comfort and advice, eh?" I repeated. "Did she actually hear a voice? A *real* voice?"

"Who knows?" Aunt Louise speculated. "Sometimes voices are thoughts in our heads or in our hearts. They're not necessarily voices outside of us."

Aunt Louise looked up into the tree with a blissful look on her face. I wondered if she came to the tree often and talked over her concerns and troubles. Maybe she'd already been to the tree this morning to make a wish to save the farm.

"Why don't you wish for something while we're here?" Aunt Louise suggested. "You don't have to wish out loud, unless you want to. You can wish in your thoughts."

Emma and I stood below the tree and peered up into its high, graceful branches. I closed my eyes and, in my thoughts, wished that the farm would be saved. I wasn't certain how many wishes I was allowed, so I left it at that. I didn't wish for anything involving Bobo or Jim. After wishing, I opened my eyes and looked over at Emma. Her eyes were still closed. I think I could guess what she was wishing.

After a few minutes, the three of us turned and strolled back to the house. I looked back at the wishing tree as we walked away. Yes, I had to admit there was an undeniably cheerful, positive energy surrounding it. Maybe it, or another power, spoke to poor Hannah McClintock eighty years ago. I hoped it would work for us, too, even though I didn't hear a voice. That sounded loveably hokey to me. Still, Aunt Louise had been very wise to bring us to the tree. Emma seemed much more peaceful all morning after that. And I had to admit I felt a little better too.

CHAPTER FIVE

Cubs and Monkeys

As we strolled along with Aunt Louise back to the farmhouse from the wishing tree, Emma told me that Daniel had called earlier that morning and invited us over to his house.

"Did he find Bobo? I hope so," I asked. "Or does he want us to help him search for him?"

"I don't know. He didn't mention Bobo," Emma answered. "He just asked us to come over. We could go up in the tree house again, or we could go over to the airport and hang out. You've never been over to the airport, have you?"

"Not really," I answered. "That sounds okay to me."

I didn't have anything particular in mind that I wanted to do today, except hang out with Emma, so going to Daniel's house seemed good. I pondered whether I'd run into Jim if we went to the airport, though. I didn't want to run into him again if I could avoid it. It didn't seem very likely that he'd have a reason to be there, so that was a point in favor of going there. He told me earlier this summer that he had a part-time job at the pool at Northern Beach Swim Club, so he'd probably be at the pool today.

"Is it okay if we have lunch over at the airport restaurant, Mom?" Emma asked.

"Yes, but don't let Aunt Loretta give you the food for free. Be sure to pay for it," Aunt Louise instructed. "She's running a business and should be paid for her food just like anyone else. You be sure to tell her that. I won't allow you to go over there again if she gives you any argument about that."

Aunt Louise went into the house while we waited outside, and returned with two dollars for our lunch. We said good-bye, then walked down the path to Allisonville Road. We crossed the road and walked up the long driveway to the single-story house where Daniel lived with his parents, sister, and three brothers. When we got to a breeze-way door, Emma opened it without hesitating and walked inside. I gathered that unlocked doors and a lack of formality were the hallmarks of country living.

"Daniel! Daniel!" Emma called. "Where are you? We're here!"

"Down here in the basement," Daniel beckoned. "Come on down."

We crossed the family room to stairs that lead to a basement. We walked down and emerged in a large, well-lighted room with a large table set up in the middle where Daniel and Buzz were working on model airplanes in various stages of completion. Their six-year-old brother, Rex, ran around the room holding a small plane over his head while making jet engine noises.

"Hi, guys!" Daniel greeted us, holding a small plastic model of a fighter plane. "What do you think of my P-51? It was a fighter plane during World War II." He gazed at the small green- and-tan plane with pride.

"Very nice," I replied. The pungent odor of model–airplane glue hung heavily in the air, and took some adjusting to get used to.

"Hi, Cousins!" Buzz said cheerfully from the opposite side of the table. Buzz was Daniel's older brother and was about twenty years old. He was tall and had the same curly brown hair that Daniel had. His eyes almost twinkled when he spoke, and like Daniel, he too, had an easy smile. He appeared to be working on a fairly sophisticated, large model plane made out of balsa wood and some kind of fabric.

"What are you guys up to today?" Buzz asked, looking up from his work holding a small paint brush.

"We thought maybe we'd help Daniel search for Bobo, unless you've already found him," Emma said, looking at Daniel.

"No, I haven't found a trace of him," Daniel replied, carefully setting his model plane down on the table. "I've spent hours looking everywhere, too. I even searched all the neighbors' yards along 106th Street on both sides of Allisonville Road, and all along the creek. Someone *must* have taken him. That's all I can figure."

"I'm so sorry," I said. "I'll help you keep looking, if you think it'd help."

"Thanks anyway, but there's nowhere left to search," Daniel replied dejectedly.

Emma and I stood awkwardly in silence, not knowing how to respond.

"Why don't you guys go over to the airport and show Vanessa around? Vanessa's never been over there, have you?" Buzz asked.

"That's a great idea. I'd like to see it close up," I said.

"Maybe Vanessa will decide to get a pilot's license when she's a little older," Buzz suggested playfully.

"Oh, I doubt that!" I replied quickly. The idea of flying, even as just a passenger, was very frightening to me. Piloting a plane seemed very complicated and well beyond my capabilities, no matter how old I became.

"It's not so hard when you've been trained and know what you're doing," Buzz observed. "I got my pilot's license when I was just sixteen. Lots of people we know have their licenses. Even Aunt Louise is studying to get hers."

I had no idea Aunt Louise was doing that. Good for her. She was more adventurous than I figured.

A record player sitting on a kitchen stool off to the side was on, and a record album I'd never heard before was spinning on the turntable. There was a clever song that included the sounds of war planes swooping and shooting, and someone counting in German in the background.

"What song is that?" I asked. "It's funny."

"That's 'Snoopy vs. the Red Baron,'" Daniel explained. "It's about Snoopy from the *Peanuts* comic strip shooting down the Red Baron during World War I."

"Only Snoopy was good enough to shoot down the Red Baron," Rex suddenly blurted as he continued running around the room with his toy plane in pretend flight.

"These guys are airplane crazy," Emma observed. "Just like their dad. He built the airport, you know."

"Uncle Forrest did? Well, I guess I knew he was responsible for the airport, but I didn't know he actually constructed it," I replied.

"Yes, he did. It used to be part of our farm," Daniel chimed in. "Buzz helped, too. He operated the bulldozer, and he was only fourteen." You could tell Daniel was very proud of his father and older brother.

"You did?" I replied, watching Buzz busily working on his model. "How'd you know how to run that equipment? That sounds scary to me."

"Oh, it was nothing. When you're a kid growing up on a farm, you have to figure out how to do lots of things. Dad told me to get up on the Tournapull earthmover and run it, so I just did," Buzz answered.

"The propeller on this model needs to dry before I can do anything more, so this is a good time to take a break. Wanna go over there now?" Daniel asked.

"I tell you what," Buzz began. "If you guys are still over there a little later, I'll take you up for a ride in the Piper Cub. Would you like that?"

I knew their family owned a Piper Cub airplane. I'd never flown before, whether in a commercial or private plane, and was intrigued by the idea of taking a ride. Even so, I was cautious about the idea of flying, and wondered how I could wiggle out of going up without being viewed as cowardly. If I was lucky, something would come up and I wouldn't have to confront the situation.

"Dad wants me to move a couple of parked planes around, so I'll do that and then we can go up," Buzz continued. "It's a fairly calm day without much wind, so it should be a good day to fly."

Emma, Daniel, and I left Buzz in the basement, and walked down to Allisonville Road and then over to the airport next door. We crossed the parking lot to the single-story brick building Uncle Forrest built to house the airport office, lobby, and restaurant. Its outer walls consisted almost entirely of floor-to-ceiling windows so that people could see everything going on outside. We walked up to the small building and went inside.

Three men chatted at a counter at the opposite end of the large lobby. Except for them, no one else was around. Various airplane-related things for sale were hung on racks and hooks on the wall behind the counter. Several chrome and leather chairs were placed in conversational groupings in the middle of the lobby. Through the back window I saw two fuel pumps where planes taxied up to refuel. A large plane was slowly taxiing up to one of the pumps as we entered.

"So this is the airport," I said, looking around.

"Yep. This is it," Daniel said proudly. "What do you think? Want to see the restaurant?"

"Sure. Where is it?" I asked.

"It's through that doorway," he answered, pointing to a glass door off to the left.

Emma and I followed him through the doorway into the coffee shop. It was larger than I expected, with five or six tables in the middle of the room, and eight or ten turquoise booths lined up along the windows on the two outer walls. The room had a casual and contemporary feeling, with amber pendant lights hanging from the ceiling. An older man sitting at a booth having a cup of coffee was the only customer when we entered.

"Let's sit here," Emma said, eagerly walking to a booth along the windows facing the runway. "You can really see everything from here."

I slid into the seat next to Emma, and Daniel plopped down on the opposite side. I could easily see the refueling area and the entire runway without any obstruction. The large plane in the refueling circle was right outside the window by our booth.

"What kind of plane is that? It looks like an old-style commercial passenger plane," I said, studying the twin-engine, round-nosed plane only a few feet from my window. It had a red stripe that extended across its silver nose and down the side, a red "S" inside a circle on its tail, and six small passenger windows on the side. A door at the back stood open, and several metal steps extended down to the ground. It was at least three times the size of all of the other single-engine planes at the airport.

"That's a DC-3," Daniel answered. "That's the kind of plane flown by the airlines in the forties and fifties, until the Convair, the DC-9, and other planes came on the scene and replaced them. It's one of the largest planes the airport handles."

"Does that one still carry passengers?" I asked, peering at the glistening giant.

"No," Daniel explained. "That DC-3 is probably owned by some bigwig who stopped in to refuel. The airlines don't use them anymore, so people buy them second-hand for their own use."

"Do you know who owns that one?" I asked.

"Nope. I don't recognize it. Some of the car dealers own planes like that, but I don't know who owns that one," Daniel answered, staring out the window. "I don't recognize the red 'S' on the tail."

Just then two men entered the restaurant. One of them was heavy-set, balding, and smoking a cigarette, which he puffed on frequently. He wore a noticeably large gold ring on his right pinkie finger. The other man was only average in height, but stocky and muscular. He had brownish-gray hair and a receding hairline, and wore a lightweight beige jacket with a red circle design on the pocket.

"We've got to get to Houston as soon as possible," the heavy-set man said to the man in the beige jacket as they walked to a table. "I've got some serious commitments tied up in this cargo, and need to make the trade as soon as possible. I can't sit on this for too long."

"I know. I know, Pete. Just calm down, will you?" the man in the beige jacket replied. Looking over at us, he lowered his voice considerably. "It's under control. Trust me."

"Well, I just hope so," Pete answered, gesturing with his cigarette. "I've got a fair amount of change on the line, not to mention my credibility."

"That's Pete Scaggs, the home builder" Daniel whispered, leaning across the table. "That must be his DC-3 outside. He's a big-time operator."

The two men sat down, noisily moving their wooden chairs across the linoleum floor. Almost immediately, a girl about eighteen years old, with a long pony tail and wearing a blue waitress dress and white apron, emerged through a door behind the counter. She hurried over to them holding an order pad and pen.

"Can I help you?" she asked.

"Just some coffee, thanks," the man in the beige jacket replied.

"I'd like some pie with that, too, honey," Pete added. "You got any of Loretta's homemade apple pie back there today? I could sure go for a piece."

"I think so," the girl said softly. "You want that warmed up with ice cream?"

"That'd be perfect. I like things warmed up," Pete said, leaning back in his chair, studying her. "What's your name, sugar?"

"I'm Patsy," she answered, looking down shyly.

"Well, Patsy, it's a pleasure to meet you," Pete continued. "Loretta sure improved the décor around here when she hired you. How long you been working here? I don't think I've seen you in here before."

"Just a week," Patsy replied. "I'm out of school for the summer. I just work here a few hours a week." She looked uncomfortable.

"Well, do say," Pete continued, smiling slyly.

"Leave her alone, will ya Pete?" the man in the beige jacket remarked impatiently. "She's just a kid."

"Butt out, Ralph," Pete barked back sharply. "This is none of your business."

"We should be fueled up any minute. You may not have time to finish that pie," Ralph added.

"That ain't any of your business, either," Pete replied curtly.

Patsy turned quickly to walk back to the kitchen. As she crossed the room, she saw us and came over.

"Oh, sorry, Daniel. I didn't see you guys over here," she said. "Are you going to eat something, or are you just hanging out?"

"Hi, Patsy," Daniel replied. "We want to eat some lunch. What did my mom make today?"

"She made homemade chicken and noodles that looks pretty good," Patsy answered. "Served over mashed potatoes."

"I love chicken and noodles, so I'll have that," I said enthusiastically.

"I'll have a cheeseburger," Emma said politely. "With potato chips and a Coke please."

"Me, too," Daniel chimed in. "The same as Emma."

"I'll have a Coke, too," I added.

"Okay. Two cheeseburger platters, one chicken noodle dinner, and three Cokes. Coming right up," Patsy said, rushing off.

Pete lit up another cigarette. Its smoke curled up and drifted toward us, making me wish they'd taken a table on the other side of the room.

I looked out the window to get my mind off the smell of the cigarette, and became fascinated with the DC-3 just outside. It was a beautiful plane, with a very rounded nose and fat body characteristic of older passenger planes. I guessed the large red "S" on the tail stood for Scaggs. I scanned the small square windows running down its side, and wondered what it would have been like to be a passenger on it years ago, looking out one of those windows as the plane flew across the country. Twenty years ago I bet it would have been considered a very glamorous way to travel.

As I stared at the plane, I was startled by seeing a very small face looking back at me from one of the plane's passenger windows. It was a small, black furry face, like a monkey's. As quickly as it appeared, it disappeared. It happened so fast, I wasn't sure what I'd seen.

"Uh, Daniel," I said. "I think I just saw a monkey looking out of one of the windows of that plane out there. Could it have been Bobo?"

"No way!" Daniel exclaimed, turning abruptly to look. "Which window? I don't see anything. Which window?" he demanded impatiently.

"That one," I said, pointing to the fourth window from the front. "I'm pretty sure I saw a monkey's face — — it was black and furry — — looking out that window. But I don't see it now."

"I don't see anything," Daniel said, still staring intently out the window. "Are you sure you saw something? Maybe it was a kid, or a dog, or something."

"Yeah. I don't see anything either," Emma said, studying the plane. "Are you sure you saw a *monkey*?"

"I sure thought I did," I said, my eyes still fixed on the plane. "I guess I could be mistaken. Whatever I saw, though, I don't think it was a person or a dog."

"Why would Bobo be on Pete Scaggs's plane?" Daniel whispered, looking over at Pete and Ralph to observe if they were hearing us. "It doesn't make sense. You must be mistaken."

"Maybe Bobo crawled inside the plane on his own through the open door in the back," Emma suggested. "That could have happened, couldn't it? Why don't you ask Mr. Scaggs if you can search the plane for him?"

"It sounds as though they're in a big hurry to push off. I don't have the nerve to ask him," Daniel said softly. "Besides, it'd be crazy if Bobo were on that plane. Vanessa, you must be seeing things."

"Maybe it was just wishful thinking," I agreed. I knew I'd seen something, but I didn't want to upset Daniel any more than he was already.

By now, though, my imagination was ignited, and I was really intrigued. What had I seen? I knew I'd seen something. One by one I studied each window of the plane carefully for that furry little face. I really wanted to find Bobo for Daniel, even if it meant finding him in an unlikely place like Pete Scaggs's DC-3. But the face didn't reappear.

I guess I could have been mistaken about what I saw. I must have been. But no. I saw something. If I didn't see a monkey, what *did* I see?

CHAPTER SIX

Earning My Wings

Patsy had just delivered lunch to us when Buzz entered the restaurant. "Hey, you guys!" Buzz said, strolling over to us. "I thought I might find you in here. Are you guys ready to go flying, or are you just going to sit in here all day?"

"Vanessa thinks she saw Bobo in that DC-3 outside. Do you think that's possible?" Daniel asked immediately. He looked at Buzz as though he believed Buzz knew everything there was to know in the world.

"Nah. Probably not. But we could ask the owner if we could look around inside, just to be certain," Buzz replied. "He shouldn't mind. Is that Pete Scaggs's plane? I think I recognize its markings."

Just then Pete looked over and appeared to recognize Buzz. "Well, Buzz Kingwood!" Pete shouted. He stood up and walked over to Buzz with his right hand outstretched. "How're you doing these days, young man?"

"Mr. Scaggs. How nice to see you," Buzz said, shaking Pete's hand. "Is that your DC-3 out there? That sure is an impressive aircraft."

"Sure is. Got her from a retired car dealer up in Michigan City," Pete replied. "I thought I'd feel her out on a quick hop out to Vegas on a little pleasure trip. There's a lot of pleasure to be had in Vegas, if you know what I mean." Pete winked and laughed in a loud, raspy voice.

Buzz looked uncomfortable. "Yes, sir," he replied politely.

"Well, maybe one of these days you can come with me," Pete said, slapping Buzz on the back. "I mean it. I'll even step aside and let you fly her in the right seat on the way out if you like. Would you like that? Huh? Sure you would. Well, gotta go. Say hello to your dad for me, will ya?"

44

"Sure thing," Buzz replied. He hesitated for a moment, then added, "Uh, one more thing, Mr. Scaggs, if you wouldn't mind. My brother lost his monkey and thinks it might be on your plane. Do you mind if Daniel has a quick look around inside before you take off?"

Pete and Ralph exchanged odd looks. "Well, I don't know," Pete replied slowly. "I'd like to help, but there's no way a monkey got on that plane. You kids sure do have crazy ideas! I hope you find your pet. Gotta go now."

"I'm pretty sure I saw it," I insisted. I was surprised I spoke up so boldly, but I was certain I saw something worth investigating. Pete shot me an exasperated look.

"It'll only take a minute, sir, I promise," Buzz continued. "What could it hurt to take quick look?"

Pete and Ralph looked at each other again. "Tell you what. I'll look through the cabin before we shove off and report back to you. How's that?" Pete suggested. "I can do that while Ralph goes through the pre-flight checklist."

"Great," Buzz replied. "That'd be awfully good of you."

As Pete and Ralph passed the counter on their way out, Patsy emerged from the kitchen holding a coffee pot and a plate with a slice of pie on it.

"Sorry, sir, but it took some time for the pie to come out of the oven," Patsy explained.

"That's all right, sweetheart, but we gotta go," Pete said, throwing a ten dollar bill down on the counter. "That should cover it. Keep the rest for yourself."

Buzz sat down in our booth, and the four of us watched through the window as Pete and Ralph went inside the plane to look for Bobo.

"What if Pete is the kidnapper?" I wondered out loud. Buzz, Emma, and Daniel gave me shocked looks. "Well, he might be. I mean, think about it. Why wouldn't he let Daniel on the plane to look for Bobo? Makes me suspicious."

"Oh, you're always suspicious," Emma laughed. "Of *everyone*."

"Pete Scaggs a monkey-napper? A successful builder and businessman like him? That's pretty far-fetched, even for you Vanessa," Buzz said, laughing.

I shrugged. Who knows? A few minutes later, Pete emerged from the plane empty-handed, and walked back into the building.

"Sorry kids," he shouted from the door. "Like I said before. No monkey. Good luck finding it."

"Thanks for looking, Mr. Scaggs," Buzz yelled back.

"Sure thing, Buzz," he said, making a small, salute-like gesture.

"It was a long shot," Daniel replied, looking disappointed. "It's cool. I'm okay."

I watched Pete walk to the plane and climb in through the rear door. Just before he pulled up the back door to close it, he looked back at me through the restaurant window and frowned. I wondered again if I was seeing things. I gazed at my cousins to see if they'd also seen him do that, but they were talking and not looking out the window. Who or what else could Pete have been looking at, if not me? It gave me a shiver. *Why would he look at me that way?* What'd I do? I thought about mentioning it to the others, but decided it was wiser to keep it to myself. They probably already thought I was imagining things. One more false report from me today might be one too many. I decided to just shrug it off and say nothing.

After a few minutes, the two large piston engines of Pete's DC-3 finally fired up. It was thrilling to hear them. The plane made a thunderous rumble as it slowly taxied away and made its way to the opposite end of the runway. There, it made a U-turn and sat motionless with its propellers spinning for what seemed like a long time. I was impatient to see it go forward and soar into the sky.

"Why is he taking so long to go up?" I asked. "Is there a problem?"

"No. He's just doing his final run-up," Buzz explained.

"What's that?" I asked.

"It's when the pilot conducts a series of engine checks just before he takes off, to make sure the engines will give the thrust he expects," Buzz explained.

After a few more minutes, it began slowly rolling forward. It went faster and faster, gaining momentum, until it was finally airborne. Daniel stood up and leaned against the windows, totally enthralled as he watched. It continued gaining altitude until it finally disappeared into the horizon. It was magnificent to see, especially from our close vantage point.

"That Pete Scaggs. He's quite a character, isn't he?" Buzz said when the plane had finally flown out of sight. "He runs a successful home construction business. He's quite a pilot, too. That DC-3 of his is a really fine plane. Must be nice to fly off to Vegas just for the fun of it."

"I overheard him talking to the other guy, and he said he was going to Houston tonight," I replied. "I wonder why he told you he was going to Vegas. Houston's not on the way to Vegas, is it?"

"No, not unless you're confused," Buzz joked, "and want to go the long way."

"Then why would he tell you he's going to Las Vegas when he's really going to Houston?" I asked refusing to drop the subject. There was something about Pete that made me distrust him. I couldn't put my finger on what it was exactly.

"Who cares where he's going?" Emma replied impatiently. "Are you looking for another mystery to solve? You're always playing detective."

"Vegas or Houston. It doesn't matter. I'm much more interested in going up for a ride in the Cub. Anyone else up for taking a little flight this afternoon?" Buzz asked, raising his eye brows with a questioning look. "How about you, Vanessa? Do you feel like Amelia Earhart today?"

"She crashed and was never found, you know," Daniel warned, laughing.

"Hush, little brother!" Buzz scolded playfully. "Everyone will be quite safe flying with me."

"I'm, uh, kind of nervous to go up," I confessed. "I've never flown in a plane before, and the idea scares me." I had hoped to disguise my fear, but now that the reality of flying was imminent, I felt a compulsion to confess.

"Oh, you'll be fine," Emma volunteered. "Buzz is the best pilot in Hamilton County."

"Buzz, it's not you," I was careful to explain. "I know you're a good pilot. I just don't think I can do it." I looked at Emma apologetically, but she looked away with exasperation.

"I tell you what. Let's take it one step at a time. I've got to tie down a couple of planes before it gets too late," Buzz said "Walk over to the first T-hangar in about thirty minutes and you'll see me outside there with the Piper Cub. We'll figure out a plan then. Don't be late."

Was he really going to insist that I fly? It was a sunny, warm August day, with hardly any wind and only a few big, fluffy clouds. Surely, there was no better day for flying, but that gave me little comfort. Those little planes had only one engine. What if it failed? When you fly, there's no place to pull over like there is when a car engine conks out. Watching from the ground as other people went up was much better as far as I was concerned.

We quickly wolfed down what remained of our lunches. Then Daniel left us and went back to home to work on his model airplane. I guess he went up in the Cub all the time, so it was no big deal to him. Emma and I went out to the lobby to wait. We watched a steady flow of people come in to freshen up or purchase a cool beverage while their planes refueled, and then go back outside and take off. To those people, traveling by plane must be as routine as driving by car was to the rest of us, and I envied how casual they were about flying.

We watched the clock on the wall, and after exactly half an hour, strolled outside and walked across the tarmac to the first T-hangar, just as Buzz had directed. We found Buzz standing next to a bright yellow single-engine plane. It appeared to be an older, vintage plane. A portion of the engine protruded from each side of the bright yellow engine cover.

"Hi, there!" Buzz said enthusiastically as we approached. "How do you like our J-3 Piper Cub? She was built in 1946. One of the best training planes ever built. I learned to fly in this very plane." He looked up at the plane with the kind of infatuated gaze one often sees a man give his favorite sports car.

"Nice," I replied. What did I know about planes? It looked like a good, basic plane to me, but older. Did its age have any bearing on its safety? I wondered. It had a black lightning bolt painted down both sides, probably in an attempt to give it a jazzy feel, although it was rather boxy and wasn't racy looking in the slightest.

"Almost done with the preflight check. We want to make sure it's safe, don't we?" he asked rhetorically.

He walked around the plane, studying it carefully. He screwed open a cap on the side of the front of the plane and pulled out what looked like an oil dipstick, examined it, and then slid it back into position. I was glad he was being so careful. Flying looked like it could be dangerous business if you weren't.

"Are you ready to go up?" he asked when he was finally finished with his check.

"Um, Emma can go first," I replied. "I don't mind waiting."

"Oh, no, you don't!" Buzz laughed. "We're going to get you over your fear of flying today, so you're first up young lady."

"I don't have a leather flight helmet. Don't I need one?" I asked. I was only kidding, of course, and stalling.

"No. Only Snoopy wears one of those," Buzz replied, chuckling. "Okay, step up and get in the back."

Emma's watchful gaze forced me to go along, even though I was petrified. I took a deep breath and stepped up and sat down in the only seat in the back. There were two pedals on the floor in front of my seat and a big stick protruding out of the floor. I fastened my seat belt as Buzz climbed in and sat in front. He closed the door and locked it. The sound of the lock sent a shiver through me, and I wanted to open the door and jump out, but didn't.

"Those pedals on the floor move the rudders that make the plane go left or right, depending on how you move them," he explained. "The joystick there in front of you controls the movement of the plane up and down. Don't touch any of them. We could have a *big* problem if you do. I have my own controls up here, and I'll manage them. All you have to do is sit back and enjoy. Sound good?"

I nodded in agreement. I carefully placed my feet as far from the pedals as I could so I wouldn't accidentally step on one and make the plane spin out of control. I watched as Buzz turned various switches and pushed a lever, until I finally heard the engine start. Then, we began to move. My heart raced with excitement. I was about to take my very first plane ride!

Buzz guided the plane along a narrow paved taxiway from the hangar to the end of the runway, where he turned the plane around so the runway stretched out ahead of us. We sat motionless briefly while he checked the rudder pedals and the joystick, and raced the engine. *Oh, god! It's really going to happen!* Then, he slowly let the plane roll forward down the runway. I held tightly onto the sides of my seat and closed my eyes as we gained momentum and climbed into the air.

The side window was open and the wind blew back on me as we climbed. I opened my eyes and timidly looked over my shoulder and watched as the airport office and hangars became smaller and farther away. I snapped my eyes shut again and held onto my seat even more tightly. After a few moments, we stopped climbing and I relaxed a little and looked around. Ahead was a patchwork of golden and green fields. I looked down and searched for Aunt Louise and Uncle Evert's house and barn. I just barely spotted them through the green canopy of the tall trees as we flew over. It was fascinating to see them from this vantage point, I had to admit. So far so good, I told myself.

We flew north above Allisonville Road to the town of Noblesville. The courthouse in the middle of the downtown square was easy to spot, with its five-story Second Empire clock tower. When we got close to it, Buzz made a gentle loop around it. Once again, I had to admit it was fascinating to see the clock tower and the other buildings from the vantage point being in the plane allowed. The engine appeared to be performing well, and the flight was smooth so far. I took a deep breath and studied the horizon, and told myself to loosen up. But it wasn't easy to do.

He changed course after we few around Noblesville, and flew east toward the quarry on 96th Street. He went on until we were over Geist Reservoir. The deep blue sparkling water gleamed in the sun as far as the eye could see. I tried my best to appreciate the beauty of what I was seeing. Then he looped around and guided us west in the direction of the airport. Although the engine was noisy, I could hear Buzz when he occasionally turned and spoke to me from the front seat.

"What do you think?" he asked loudly, beaming as he looked over his shoulder. "Are you having fun?"

"Yes!" I shouted, nodding. I didn't tell him that, even so, I'd be very glad when we were safely back on the ground.

"Look down there," he said, pointing down as we flew above 116th Street near River Road. Below us was a boy on a bicycle. The street was deserted, and no cars were coming from either direction for quite some distance. "Wanna have some fun with that guy? I'll cut the engine so he can hear us, and when I do, yell down at him with me and wave. Ready?"

I looked down and studied the figure on the bike. He wore a t-shirt and long shorts, and was muscular and young, with brown hair. He appeared to have a tall build. Could it be Jim? I squinted and tried my best to confirm if it was. It sure looked like him from up there.

My next thought was whether it was it a good idea to cut the engine. Is that something reasonable and prudent pilots do? I knew Buzz was both, so it must be okay. I didn't have time to evaluate the situation further, though, because Buzz suddenly cut the engine. As instructed, I joined with him and yelled and waved out the open side window.

The boy must have been startled by the spectacle we made overhead, just as Buzz had hoped. He pulled off to the shoulder and stopped, looked up, and waved back. That's when I could see that it was indeed Jim. It seemed as though he may have recognized us, given how heartily he waved. But how? Maybe he recognized the unmistakably bright yellow Piper Cub and knew it belonged to Buzz. He probably had no idea it was me in the back, not that it mattered.

I wondered, where was Jim going? To his job at Northern Beach? Or, to visit Monica Calhoun, his girlfriend? Yes, that probably was it. He was going to visit Monica. She must live nearby. It seemed as though I couldn't escape running into him, not even in the sky.

Buzz restarted the engine, and I sighed with relief. I hoped he didn't have any other aeronautical practical jokes planned. We flew on until I saw the airport runway lying in the distance like a light gray ribbon. We'd be on the ground in minutes, and then I could unwind. Buzz lined up our plane with the runway and appeared to be preparing to land. He pushed the stick slightly forward and pulled the throttle back, and we started gliding down. We sank lower and lower. Finally, when we were only a few feet from the surface of the runway, he pulled the stick all the way back and the plane gently settled onto the pavement.

We continued moving down the runway until he turned off onto the taxiway that led back to the hangar. Once there, he stopped the plane, turned a switch over the window, and the propeller stopped. The ride was over, and I was alive and in one piece! I was elated the ride was over and I was safe.

"Well, what'd you think?" Buzz asked, turning around with a big smile. "Did you enjoy the ride?"

"Yes. It wasn't too bad," I replied as enthusiastically as I could. "Too bad we didn't have any water balloons to drop on that guy, though."

"Oh, you're a mischievous girl," Buzz laughed. "I'd only do something nasty like that to someone like Luke. Not to a nice guy like Jim. That *was* Jim Sparks on the bike, wasn't it? Do you know Jim?"

"Yes. I think that was him," I said.

Buzz left it at that, and got out first, and then helped me squeeze myself out of the back and step down out of the plane. Emma ran up as I stood by the plane getting my bearings.

"You were a trooper," Buzz declared. "Now you won't be afraid to fly ever again. Right?"

I nodded, but didn't totally agree. While the ride had had its pleasant moments, I figured it was just a lucky break that we didn't crash and burn. I was, and figured I always would be, a nervous flyer.

"Me next!" Emma said, enthusiastically. "I thought you'd never get back."

"Okay, okay," Buzz said. "Let me take a pit stop and I'll be right back." He walked hurriedly toward the office as we took cover under the wing, enjoying the shade it offered on a hot and sunny afternoon.

"How'd you like it?" Emma asked. "Did you get queasy or anything?"

"It was okay, and I didn't feel sick at all," I answered. "We saw Jim Sparks riding his bike," I added. Just as soon as I did, I chided myself for mentioning him. I wished I hadn't said anything, so I quickly tried to sound nonchalant. "We played a little prank on him and yelled hello when Buzz cut the engine." I gave a forced laugh that I hoped sounded real.

"Oh, that. Buzz does that all the time. Did Jim see you?" she asked, studying me.

"Probably not. He waved back, though," I said.

Buzz returned before we could say much more, which was fortunate. Emma and Buzz quickly boarded the vintage aircraft. She obviously had flown before, and knew how to get in and where to place her feet without Buzz instructing her. Moments later they taxied off to begin their joy ride.

CHAPTER SEVEN

Tree House Surveillance

After Emma returned from her flight, she and I said good-bye to Buzz and walked back to her house. When we entered, Lars was sitting on the green couch reading a small book with an orange cover.

"Listen to this, you guys," Lars said, looking down at the book. "This is a poem written by Rod McKuen called 'A Cat Named Sloopy.' It's from his new best-seller, *Listen to the Warm.*"

"Sloopy?" Emma interrupted. "That's a funny name. Are you sure it's not Snoopy?"

"No, it's Sloopy," Lars confirmed, emphasizing the pronunciation as he repeated the name. "It's a sad poem about a cat Rod McKuen had once."

"If it's sad, don't read it to me," Emma insisted. "I'm still too upset about losing my little Tinker."

"Was Tinker your cat?" I asked.

"Yes," Emma replied wistfully. "She was black and white. I found her when she was a kitten abandoned by her mother. I let her go outside and one day she never came back. I guess something got her."

"That's kind of what happened to Sloopy," Lars said. "Except Sloopy disappeared from her window ledge in New York City, not Fishers, Indiana."

Aunt Louise suddenly entered the room holding folded laundry. "Why are you two girls back in here on such a lovely day?" she asked. "Go outside and enjoy this beautiful summer day."

"We were just over at the airport," Emma answered. "Buzz took us up in the Cub."

"That's great!" Aunt Louise replied. "Flying provides a different perspective on life. You can't stay stuck in your petty concerns when you're up there looking down on the majestic world below, amazed by the greatness of all you see."

"Is it true that you're getting your pilot's license?" I asked.

"Oh, who knows," she answered. "I'm taking lessons, and enjoying learning about it. That's the important thing, don't you think?"

"Wow. That's cool," I said.

"Cool? I like that word," she said as she walked to the back bedroom.

Emma and I wandered outside and sat on the small stoop just outside the living room door as we pondered what we should do with the rest of the afternoon. There was a fair amount of the day left to enjoy. I suggested we go back to the tree house, as it was still fairly new to me and deserved further investigation. She said she liked that idea and went inside to get some snacks to take along. She grabbed two bottles of Mountain Dew from the refrigerator and some Oreo cookies, and put them in a bag. Then, we made our way across the backyard, down the road, and up the access road to the large maple tree.

"Here. Hold this," Emma instructed as we approached the maple tree. She handed me the paper bag, and started up the ladder rungs. When she was mid-way up, she reached down and I handed it back to her. Upon reaching the opening in the deck floor, she gently tossed the bag up and crawled through. I quickly made my way up next and joined her. I was beginning to get the hang of this climbing thing.

Once again, I was amazed by how great the views were from up there. I could see the entire airport, including the restaurant and office, the various hangars, and the runway. Things were fairly busy today and gave us plenty to observe as we sat on our high perch. A plane sat at a fuel pump, while another taxied out to the end of the runway. As the afternoon wore on, several planes took off or landed, one after the other. Emma was very good at identifying each type of plane as it flew past.

The area directly below us was a large, grassy field where several planes were parked. The nearest structure to us was the large turquoise hangar only a few hundred feet away. Nothing appeared to be happening at that hangar today, though. Its two huge front doors were closed, and no one came or went.

"I wonder why the airport is named Gatewood Airport," I mused, munching on a cookie. "Shouldn't it be called Kingwood Airport or Fishers Airport, or something like that, since Uncle Forrest built it?"

"Gatewood is a family name," Emma explained. "My mom told me Uncle Forrest didn't want his own name used. That's all I know."

"Really? If I built an airport, I think I'd put my own name on it. The Vanessa Airport. Doesn't that have a nice ring to it? That'd be so funny, especially since I'd never fly," I said, giggling.

"There're a lot of women who fly, you know," Emma remarked. "The chief flying instructor at the airport is a woman. She taught Buzz, Uncle Forrest, and a bunch of other people to fly. She's my mom's instructor, too."

"Wow. That's cool," I said. I liked the idea of a woman doing something that was traditionally thought of as something only men did. I was looking for something like that for my own career some day, but flying probably wasn't it.

We sat on the edge of the deck whiling away the lazy afternoon. It was unlikely anyone knew we were there, which made observing the world below especially enjoyable. It was fun watching people who don't know they were being watched, like being a detective on an undercover assignment. We opened our sodas and sipped them as we took note of every movement at the airport.

After a while, a large plane circled overhead. After my flying experience with Buzz, I could tell that he was lining up his approach to land. This one was much larger than the other planes that landed earlier that afternoon. It glided down the runway, past the refueling area, and then followed a small taxiway to the turquoise hangar. It stopped just outside the large doors, and cut its engines. A red "S" in a circle was painted on its tail, just like the marking on Pete Scaggs's DC-3. But since Pete told Buzz he was flying to Vegas in his own DC-3 this morning, I didn't see how it could be the same plane.

"Is that Pete Scaggs's plane?" I asked Emma. "I recognize the red 'S' on the tail. But isn't he supposed to be Vegas?"

"Yeah. I think you're right. It's definitely a DC-3 and has the same markings," Emma observed.

"That's weird. How could that plane be back here so soon?" I wondered aloud. "It must fly really fast. Or maybe he never went to Vegas. Houston's a lot closer. Maybe he really went there."

"Okay, so what if he didn't go to Vegas?" Emma countered. "Maybe he just said that he was going there to look like cool in front of Buzz. What's the harm in that?"

"Oh, nothing. I just think it's odd he lied about where he was going, that's all," I replied.

A white panel truck that was idling near the restaurant drove over and stopped beside the DC-3. The back door of the plane opened and steps lowered to the ground. A man came out and greeted the guy from the truck, and they walked to the back of the truck and opened its two rear doors. I studied the man who came out of the DC-3. It was a little too far to see him clearly. It wasn't Pete because he wasn't big enough, but it could have been his friend, Ralph.

"I'm glad we finally have something to watch on this side of the airport," I said. Emma nodded in agreement.

The men pulled out of the back of the truck what looked like crates, and began stacking them next to the steps to the plane. The crates were light colored, with lots of small holes in their sides. They were large and heavy enough that both men were needed to unload them from the truck and carry them over to the plane. The men worked quickly and methodically, taking each crate out of the truck and stacking it on top of the others by the plane.

"Wonder what's in those crates?" I pondered as I watched the men work. I squinted and tried to see what was printed on their sides. I could tell there was something written on them, but I was too far away to make it out.

"Maybe it's food," Emma suggested. "You know, baked things, like donuts! Mmm."

"Silly. It has to be something that needs air," I concluded. "Why else would there be holes in the sides?" Trying to guess the contents of the crates was like trying to solve a riddle, and it was fun.

"Only living things need air, right?" Emma asked.

She made a good point, but *what* living things would be in crates? There was no way to know.

About half an hour later, the men finished unpacking the truck and closed it up. Then the driver jumped inside the vehicle and started it up.

Backing up quickly to turn around, he accidentally bumped into the crates, causing the top one to fall to the ground. It landed on its side, and to our great surprise, released several small dark creatures that slowly walked out from beneath the crate's broken lid. I could see their tiny dark forms silhouetted against the light-colored surface of the concrete pavement.

"Whoa!" I exclaimed. "What're *those*?"

"They look like they could be turtles, don't they?" Emma suggested.

I watched the truck driver and the other man scurry around picking up the creeping things. One-by-one, they placed them back into the broken crate.

"They look a little larger than standard turtles, but I can't tell," I answered, standing and trying hard to see. "Sure would be handy to have binoculars. We could really see what's going on if we had a pair of those."

"I'll go get them," Emma exclaimed. "Be right back!"

Before I could blink, she shimmied down the rope and was on the ground running home. I kept a watch on the men as they continued their task of corralling whatever those things were. They had almost completed their task and were loading the crates onto the plane, when Emma reappeared with a pair of binoculars hanging around her neck. She was huffing and puffing by the time she crawled up onto the deck next to me.

"I thought I'd never find them," she said excitedly. "I had to get Luke to help me. He had them out in the barn. He'd been watching a hawk or something."

"That was fast!" I said admiringly. "But it's too late, I'm afraid. Whatever they were, they're all picked up now."

"Let me see," she said as she raised the binoculars and began fiddling with the knob to focus them. She studied the scene, and then declared, "I think I see one of those crawl-y things sitting by a crate. Yep! It's a turtle all right. Here. See for yourself."

She handed the binoculars to me. I looked down and zeroed in on a dark form sitting by a crate. The men hadn't noticed it yet. It definitely looked as though it could be a turtle. It had a speckled back I'd never seen on a turtle before, but had the customary rounded back of a turtle. It was also a larger than the run-of-the-mill turtles you see down by the creek.

"It sure could be a turtle," I agreed, lowering the binoculars. "What a funny thing to load into a plane. A bunch of turtles. Why would Pete Scaggs carry turtles on his plane?"

"People carry all sorts of weird things on planes," Emma reasoned.

"I know, but. . . .Wait a minute! Didn't you say there were turtles on the ghost plane?" I asked. "And, that they were unusual turtles, too?"

"You know, now that you mention it, that's right," Emma agreed. "What a weird coincidence."

"What's with all the fancy turtles in planes around here?" I asked, looking through the binoculars again.

"Let me look again," Emma said, reaching for the binoculars. I handed them to her and she studied the scene. "I think I can make out the words on the side of one of those crates. It says. . . Scaggs Construction!" she shouted gleefully. "I'm confused. Do they belong to Pete's construction company? Take a look."

I put my hand out to take the binoculars from her, but they slipped out of my hand and fell out of the tree, striking several branches on their way down.

"Oh, no!" Emma cried, looking over the railing at the binoculars on the ground below. "My dad's going to kill me if those are damaged."

Just then, one of the men working at the plane stopped what he was doing and looked in our direction. He must have seen or heard the binoculars fall to the ground. Or maybe one of the lenses reflected the glint of the sun as it fell, and caught his eye. He stood motionless, searching for us.

"Don't move," I whispered to Emma. "I think one of those guys saw the binoculars fall. If we don't move, maybe he won't see us."

"So?" Emma said. "We're not doing anything wrong. Why does it matter if he sees us?"

The man called to his partner and pointed toward us. They peered intently in our direction for several moments, as if trying to zero in on our precise location.

"I don't know, but it's creepin' me out that they're staring and pointing over here like that," I said. "I wish they didn't know we're up here."

"I agree. They almost look like they think we're trespassing, or something. Why should they care if we're up here?" Emma said in a low whisper. "Do you think they can see us?"

"I don't know. Let's sit as still as possible just in case they can't," I replied softly.

"But I need to go down and pick up the binoculars," Emma complained.

"Just wait a little bit," I cautioned. Emma frowned, but didn't move.

The men eventually turned away and resumed loading the plane. I was relieved they gave up concerning themselves with us. Finally, one of the men drove the van away. The other man walked up the steps into the plane and closed the door. Seconds later the two large engines fired up and its propellers began rotating, and the plane taxied out to take off.

"I guess we can move now," I said to Emma.

I had hardly taken a breath through the whole episode. I was glad to be able to finally stand and stretch my legs. Emma immediately scurried down the rope and picked up the binoculars from the grass where they'd fallen and examined them closely.

"Whew!" she said, rubbing dirt and grass off the lenses. "They look okay. I don't think they're damaged." She put the cord around her neck and patted them reassuringly.

"Good," I shouted down to her. "They're going to come in handy. Let's come back again tomorrow and be sure to bring them. I want to watch those guys some more. It's fun to try to figure out what they're doing." I quickly collected our trash and climbed down the ladder.

"Sure, it's fun, I guess, but Mom says people don't like it when you watch them," Emma offered. "That's probably why those guys acted weird."

"If they have nothing to hide, they shouldn't mind, should they?" I countered.

"I think you've watched too many spy shows on TV. Do you think you're Agent 99 on *Get Smart* or something?"

"I'd prefer to think of myself as Honey West," I replied, laughing. "I loved the *Honey West* show. She was tall and had that cool black leather jump suit, and was hands down the slinkiest TV female detective there ever was."

"You're too much!" she replied, shaking her head.

We occupied ourselves on the way back to her house with ranking the best TV female detective or secret agent of all time. I stuck to my guns with Honey West. Emma said she really liked Emma Peel from *The Avengers*. I said that was only because she and Emma Peel have the same first name. She claimed she never even noticed that. I didn't believe her.

CHAPTER EIGHT

Unidentified Flying Objects

When we entered Emma's house, the evening news was in progress on TV, although no one appeared to be watching. The news reports were mostly about the Vietnam War. The news announcer said China had just agreed to give North Vietnam a huge amount of financial aid for the Vietnam War, and that the United Sates had just sent over an additional 45,000 soldiers. "To Sir With Love" sung by Lulu was playing on the radio in the kitchen. Only Emma's older sister, Margret, appeared to be in the house. She was in the bathroom in front of the mirror taking giant brush curlers, the size of small cans, out of her hair.

"Hi, you guys!" Margret called to us when she heard us enter. "What have you been doing?"

Margret was about twenty, slender, and had long, dark blonde hair that fell to the middle of her back. She wore her bangs long to just above her eyes, the way high-fashion model Twiggy and many other British fashion icons did. She was wearing a short, lime green dress with long sleeves that belled at the elbows, and an owl pendant on a long chain. She also had on white, textured knee-highs and brown leather flats with a t-strap near the toe and a French heel. I thought she looked very stylish and very Carnaby Street, as they labeled her style in the trendy fashion magazines.

"Buzz took us up for rides in his Cub," Emma reported, walking to the hallway outside the bathroom. "Even Vanessa went up," she added, looking back at me.

"Good for you, Vanessa," Margret said, still working on her hair. "Everyone around here flies, you know. Now you're in the club."

"I wouldn't say that exactly," I replied. "I'm still a bit of a nervous flier."

She teased the hair at the crown with a small narrow brush, and then smoothed the outer hair over the teased hair so that it was higher than the sleek hair around her face. I was fascinated, and observed closely so I could pick up some styling ideas for myself.

"You look pretty. Are you going out?" I asked, changing the subject.

"Wendy and I are going down to Broad Ripple to hear the Fifth Wheel band play at the Patio," she said as she gave her hair a good going over with hairspray.

Wendy was Daniel's older sister. She was about the same age as Margret and lived across the street with Daniel and his family.

"*Those* guys again," Emma exclaimed. "The way you follow them around, I know you've got to have a crush on one of them."

"I'll never tell," Margret said playfully, turning off the light and walking into the hallway. "If you must know, I have a crush on *all* of them!"

"Hey! Where is everyone?" Luke shouted as he slammed the screen door and walked into the house. "When's dinner? I could eat a horse."

"Dad's bringing White Castles home for dinner tonight," Margret replied as she walked to the bedroom she shared with Emma. "So, better not eat a bunch of junk before he gets back, or you won't have room to inhale your usual zillion sliders."

"That sounds great. I just hope he brings enough for me," Luke answered. He plopped down at the dining room table with a *Richie Rich* comic book and began turning its pages.

Margret emerged from her bedroom holding a small green handbag. "Okay, you guys. I'm off," she said cheerfully. "I'm crashing over at Wendy's tonight, so tell Mom when she gets back from her walk."

"Have fun hanging out with the hippies in Broad Ripple," Luke teased without looking up. "Just don't get caught with any doobies those potheads might give you."

"Very funny," Margret returned. "You know that's not my scene." With that, she walked out of the house and drove off in the family's red 1962 Chevy Bel Air sedan.

After an hour later, Uncle Evert rolled up the driveway in his blue Ford Econoline van. He walked into the house holding two large white paper bags filled with little blue-and-white boxes containing the trademark White Castle square hamburgers.

"Mmm! I smell onions! Must be time to eat!" Luke exclaimed as Uncle Evert placed the bulging bags on the dining room table, causing a stampede to the table. "Let's eat!"

Aunt Louise and Lars came into the dining room just as Luke, Emma, and I sat down at the table. Uncle Evert passed orange plastic dinner plates around the table, and carefully stacked the tiny hamburger boxes onto a platter in the middle of the table. I took one of the boxes and slid out the hamburger. After only two or three bites, I had consumed it.

"That was good," I said reaching for a second. "We don't get these very often at my house."

"Well, when you're out here, you're well fed," Uncle Evert said. "These are all-American."

"Yeah, all-American," Luke repeated, talking with his mouth full. "Like the Beatles and the Jaguar XKE."

"Those are both British, not American, genius," Lars replied dryly.

"They are?" Luke answered. "Okay. Like the Rolling Stones and Porsche, then."

Lars began to correct him again, but just shook his head and kept eating. After the last White Castle was consumed, we cleaned up the dishes and the boxes strewn across the table. Then, Emma retrieved what remained of a big bag of Oreos from the kitchen pantry. As she, Luke, and I sat at the table eating them, the screen door opened and Randy Lampert trudged up the steps into the house.

"We're eating Oreos. Sit down and help yourself to some," Luke offered.

Randy fell into the chair that Uncle Evert had just vacated, and reached into the bag, pulling out two cookies.

"Hi, Vanessa," Randy mumbled, not making eye contact with me as he pulled a cookie apart.

"Hi, Randy," I answered.

"Are you guys going over to the UFO launch across the street tonight?" Randy asked. "I heard someone say it was tonight."

"What are you talking about?" Emma asked.

"Buzz is going to launch a UFO after it gets dark. He launched one before, and it really flies," Luke explained.

"You mean UFO — — as in unidentified flying object?" I asked with disbelief. "How is he able to make a flying saucer? You must be pulling my leg."

"You'll just have to go over and see. We're all meeting in Daniel's front yard at about 8:30 or so," Luke explained. "They're supposed to call us when they're all set up."

"Yeah. That's why I'm here," Randy added. "I want to see it. Should be cool. You ought to come too, Vanessa. I mean. . . .if you want to, that is."

I wasn't sure if they were spoofing me, or not. I was intrigued that Randy thought I ought to go over. Why me in particular? I looked at Emma to see if she thought we should go over, and she shrugged, which I took as an affirmative.

"Why not?" I replied half-heartedly.

"Great!" Randy said, smiling shyly.

After finishing our cookies, Emma and I walked outside to wait for the call to go to the launch. It was a beautiful summer evening. The lightning bugs were beginning to fire up their tiny orbs of light as darkness fell, and I enjoyed watching them fly all over the yard. It wasn't long until the phone rang. Moments later, Luke emerged from the house with Randy following close behind.

"Daniel just called. They're getting ready to launch. Let's go!" Luke said enthusiastically. He charged across the yard down to Allisonville Road as if going off to battle, as Randy, Emma, and I followed.

Daniel and Buzz were standing in their yard as we walked up. The yard bordered along the access road where the tree house was, with the airport just beyond. Buzz was putting the finishing touches on a contraption that didn't look remotely like a UFO. It consisted of two, two-foot-long strips of wood tied into a cross on which they had glued birthday candles side-by-side along the entire length of both strips. A clear plastic dry cleaning bag was taped to each of the four ends of the wood strips. That's all there was to it.

"Okay, this is the trick," Buzz explained. "You've got to light all of the candles as quickly as you can without burning a hole in the dry cleaning bag, or letting the first ones you light burn down too quickly. Otherwise it won't fly."

Suddenly I heard Jim's voice in the distance. He ran up the access road toward us. "Is this Cape Kingwood?" he called out as he approached.

I braced myself. There was no reason to panic. Still I felt flustered, and was glad it was dark enough that he couldn't see my face. I hadn't expected to see him tonight, and had to steady myself.

"We're just doing the countdown. You haven't missed anything," Luke informed him.

"Hi, everyone," Jim said. He shot me a quick smile, which I returned. "Is that it? Will that fly?" he asked, looking down at the sticks and candles as Buzz continued tinkering with them. "I know you know what you're doing. Just asking."

"Sure. It's simple physics," Buzz stated. "The hot air from the candles collects in the bag, and then it lifts and takes off. All you have to do is keep the sides fairly wide open so the candles get enough oxygen to burn. That's all there is to it."

"I'll help you light the candles if you want," Daniel volunteered, kneeling over the UFO.

"Okay. When I say go, start lighting those on that end as quickly as you can, and I'll start lighting these on this end," Buzz said, handing a book of matches to Daniel.

Buzz and Daniel squatted down over the candles as the rest of us huddled around them and watched. As the tiny candles were lit, one-by-one, it was amazing how brightly they burned when there were so many of them. The bag started to bulge as hot air collected inside. Luke stepped in to hold the bag upright. Finally, when the bag was fully inflated, Buzz gave Luke a nod to let it go.

The bag slowly drifted up into the air. It was amazing. Up, up it went, higher and higher. It was bright gold with the light of a hundred little candles burning brightly. In seconds, it was soaring higher than the tallest of the trees standing along the access road. It continued flying upward for a while, and then drifted toward the airport.

"Is it okay to fly over the airport like that?" Randy asked, looking worried.

"It should be okay," Buzz answered, watching it closely. "It should keep going over the airport to the fields just south of it, and then the candles will burn out and it'll harmlessly come down. That's what it did the last time."

We stood in the grass watching the UFO silently float higher and higher as it gained momentum. When it was well over the airport, we ran to the chain-link fence to get a better look. It was pretty neat, I had to admit.

"Pretty cool, isn't it?" Jim remarked, walking up next to me.

"Uh, yeah," I stammered. "Cool."

When it had almost reached the airport's refueling area, a sudden change in the direction of the wind caused the device to change its flight path. It drifted toward a row of parked airplanes tied down in a grassy area near the turquoise hangar and began descending, even though many of the candles were still burning. Down it went, slowly at first, and then it really dropped quickly. It appeared the UFO was going to land on the wing of one of those planes with its candles still lit, which would surely cause serious damage.

All of the boys bounded over the chain link fence in an instant and ran toward the crashing contraption. Emma and I were right behind them. We had almost caught up with them when an airport security car with flashing red lights came speeding down the runway toward our group.

"Run back over the fence!" someone shouted. "Go back! Hurry!"

I turned with everyone and ran back as fast as I could. I tripped, but got to my feet and managed to reach the fence. I couldn't seem to get my footing to climb over, though. The rubber soles of my tennis shoes had gotten slippery in the dewy grass, and I slipped each time I tried to make the first step. My frantic desire to get over didn't help, either. The more hurriedly I tried to climb, the more I failed.

"Wait for me!" I shouted in panic as the bright lights of the security car approached. I could see the shadows of everyone else, including Emma, already on the other side, running across Daniel's front yard. "Hey, you guys! Wait for me!" I shouted again.

"Oh, it's always something with you, City Slicker, isn't it?" Luke shouted in exasperation, turning to come back. "If we get arrested, it's *your* fault!"

"I'll help you," Jim called as he ran back to the fence and bounded over.

"No, I'll help her," Randy said, running over to the fence.

"I've got this, Randy," Jim replied. "Go on up to the house."

"No, *I've* got this!" Randy insisted, jumping down to the ground next to me. "Here, let me help you." He took my arm and steadied me as I put my shoe into one of the holes in the fence and stepped up.

"Here, let *me* help," Jim said, taking my other arm.

"What're you doing? I'm helping her. Go back to the house," Randy ordered.

"No, *I'm* helping her," Jim replied curtly, still holding onto my arm. "You got it now, Vanessa?"

"Get away from here," Randy said loudly as he pushed Jim's arm away.

"Hey! Watch that!" Jim said angrily. "Who do you think you're pushing?"

"I said get away from her," Randy repeated.

"Hey, you guys. It's okay now," I replied. "Look. I'm fine now."

I took a second and then a third step and quickly climbed over to the other side. I felt foolish I'd been so clumsy. They didn't seem to notice or care what I was doing, however.

"Watch your tone," Jim said to Randy, ignoring me. "Or else."

"Or else what?" Randy said, leaning defiantly toward him.

The two boys stood glaring at each other as I ran across the yard to Daniel's house. They were oblivious about me, and were caught up in their angry conversation. Why were they arguing? Surely, there had to be more to their tense exchange than wanting to help me, but I didn't know what.

The security guard stopped his car at the edge of the pavement and slowly walked over to Jim and Randy who'd argued so long they'd failed to get over the fence to safety. He shone his flashlight in their faces as he approached. I reluctantly turned around and came back to the fence to face the guard with them. I wanted to run, but it didn't seem right to do that.

"So, what's going on here?" the guard demanded. "What do you kids think you're doing?"

"We were just trying an experiment with something we saw in *Popular Mechanics* magazine," Jim answered politely. "We meant no harm, sir. The wind just blew it in the wrong direction."

"What is it you had in the air over there?" the guard continued, shifting his gaze and the beam of his flashlight toward the parked planes. I looked toward the planes, too, searching for the UFO or the sign of a fire, but didn't see anything. The candles must have burned out. None of the planes was damaged as far as I could tell.

"Just some sticks and birthday cake candles, sir. Nothing dangerous," Jim explained. "We didn't mean for it to come over to the airport property."

"Well, you kids were pretty reckless, wouldn't you say? You could have damaged one of them expensive planes over there. I'll bet your daddies wouldn't like paying a bunch of money to fix the damage you caused, just because you kids wanted to have some fun on a summer night, now would they?" the guard lectured.

"No, sir," the boys said in unison.

"You could have set one of them planes on fire. Did you think of that before you launched that contraption?" the guard continued. "No, siree, I sure bet you did not. I ought to turn you in for trespassing and damaging private property."

"But we didn't exactly damage any private property, did we, sir?" Jim replied. "Meaning no disrespect, sir," he added quickly.

"Well, you're darned lucky you didn't," the guard replied. "Are you all guests of the Kingwoods here?"

"Yes, sir. We are," Jim answered.

"It's a darned good thing Mr. Kingwood's such a fine man," he said. "I'll let you go with a warning tonight. But you kids have to be more careful in the future. You understand?"

"Yes, sir. We will," Jim confirmed dutifully.

After he let the boys go, the security guard walked over to the parked planes and walked around, searching through the grass with the beam of his flashlight. He must have been checking to make certain whatever was left of the UFO wasn't going to harm anything.

Randy and Jim climbed back over the fence and the three of us walked silently back to Daniel's house. I sensed Randy and Jim were still at odds with each other for some reason. I was confused about what was going on. Were they possibly fighting over me? That didn't seem plausible, and would mean Jim still had feelings for me. Was that possible? Oh, how I hoped so! I gazed at Jim as we walked along and felt the old feelings returning. He'd been very gallant to come back to rescue me and risk getting in trouble. That was the kind of person he was, and one of the reasons I couldn't get over him.

CHAPTER NINE

Hearts Apart

When we entered Daniel's house, everyone was standing at the windows watching us. They were very eager to learn what had happened when we were detained by the airport security guard.

"He just asked us a bunch of questions," Randy said in a surprisingly matter-of-fact way.

"Yeah. He asked us if we were visiting over here, and I told him that we were. That seemed to impress him, and he let us go," Jim added.

"I was never so scared!" I said. "I wasn't sure how I was going to explain to my parents why I was in jail."

"Listen, City Slicker," Luke scolded. "If you're planning on participating in these adventures with us in the future, you're going to have to do better scaling fences and getting the heck out of Dodge when the situation calls for it. What happened out there, anyway?"

"I don't know," I started. "I tripped and then my foot got caught in the fence. Thank goodness Jim came back to help me." Turning to Jim, I added, "I don't know what I would have done if you hadn't come back."

Jim gestured that it was nothing. Then, remembering that Randy had also helped me, I turned to Randy and added, "You too, Randy."

"I need to be going," Randy muttered, walking to the door and slamming it behind him. He disappeared down the driveway.

"What's with him?" Luke asked.

"He's a bit of an odd duck, isn't he?" Jim said.

"Sorry it didn't work like it should have," Buzz apologized, looking down at the charred and wax-coated remains of the UFO sitting on the table near the door. "I think the bag must have split or something. That would cause the UFO to lose altitude quickly and crash like it did."

"Is that it on the table?" I asked.

"Yeah. I grabbed it and ran," Buzz said. "I thought it best to remove the evidence."

We all had a good laugh. I watched Jim and wondered if he'd come over to speak to me. Didn't what just happened back at the fence mean anything to him? Instead, he stood with the guys as they examined the remains of the UFO and rehashed the details of the launch. He seemed totally disinterested in me. After a few minutes I could see there was no reason to hang around, so Emma and I left. I secretly hoped I'd hear him come through the door after me once he realized I was gone, so I walked slowly as we made our way down the driveway. But my fantasy didn't come true, and he didn't follow.

"Why are you walking so slow?" Emma asked, a little annoyed.

"Am I?" I replied. "I didn't realize." I picked up my pace.

"I saw Randy go back over the fence to help you," Emma said as we walked up the gravel driveway to her house. "Maybe he likes you."

"What are you talking about?" I replied, surprised by her remark.

"Don't tell me you don't know. I think Randy has a crush on you," Emma said. "Why else would he go back to help you and risk getting in trouble?"

"I don't know. I'm sure I mean nothing to him," I insisted.

At least that's what I hoped. I had to admit that I didn't understand what had just happened between the two boys. Randy was a nice enough guy, but he wasn't my type. It made me uncomfortable to think he might have feelings for me. There was no way I could reciprocate. After giving it some thought, I concluded that Emma was must be wrong. Randy just didn't seem the type to be interested in romance — — with anyone.

Lars was lying on the couch reading *Time* magazine when we got home. I could see the cover and it featured drawings of the recent race riots in Detroit. The TV was on, but he didn't appear to be watching it.

"Well, the terrible twosome has returned," he teased as we entered. "What have you been up to this fine evening?"

"Nothing," Emma answered flatly. Lars lowered the magazine and looked at us with skepticism.

"I was almost arrested by the security guard at the airport!" I blurted out. Just as soon as I did, I regretted it. Emma scowled with disapproval.

"I see," Lars replied. "In other words, just a typical evening." He resumed reading and said nothing further about it, much to my amazement.

It was late and it had been a long day, so I was ready to go to bed. Emma must have been pretty tired, too, because she lay down on the bed after she changed into her pajamas, and fell fast asleep.

The next day was a typical Friday morning. I must have slept a little later than usual, because Emma was already up when I opened my eyes. The Beatles' *Rubber Soul* album was playing on the record player; I could see the album cover sitting on the floor in the living room. Whoever put the album on must have decided I'd slept late enough. "Michelle" was the song playing when I walked into the dining room. I sat down next to Emma, who was eating a bowl of Cheerios.

"You're a sleepy head today," she said. She was already dressed for the day in blue jean shorts and a light blue knit top. Her blonde hair was pulled back in a loose pony tail.

"Running from the law makes me sleepy," I replied, yawning.

"Shh! I don't want my parents to hear anything about last night, so don't say anything. Okay?" she instructed.

"What about Lars? Will he say anything?"

"No, he's trustworthy," she replied. "Lucky for you!" she added. "What do you want to do today? Would you like to ride bikes over to Northern Beach and go swimming?"

"That sounds great," I agreed. I had packed the cute turquoise polka dot swimsuit my mother purchased for me earlier in the summer at L.S. Ayres in Glendale. It had several rows of small ruffles around the hips, which helped to give my slim figure some curves.

"Well, get dressed and put your suit on under your clothes and we'll go," she said.

After I finished dressing, I found Emma outside poking around the workroom in the garage.

"The tires on the bikes are a bit low," she said, clanging around in boxes and moving things on shelves. "Luke should notice that and fill them, but he never does. Aha! Here it is!" She picked up a tire pump and walked out of the workroom.

Emma had already pulled the bikes out of the barn. Both of them were boys' bikes with the characteristic middle bar, which was okay with me. I'd had plenty of experience riding my brother's bike. She knelt down and unscrewed the cap on the tire valve and connected the pump and began pumping, stopping occasionally to judge the firmness of the tire. After she had filled all of the tires, we were ready to go. We decided that I'd ride the taller bike, and she'd take the one that had the slim seat and racing-style handlebars.

"Why do boys think this kind of bike is so sexy?" she asked as we rode down the driveway to the street. She looked uncomfortable leaning so far forward the way racing handlebars require. "Totally silly. And the seat's uncomfortable, too."

"I agree. That tiny seat is killer, even with the extra padding we girls have in certain places," I joked.

We rode along 106th Street, and then turned and rode down Eller Road. It was a pretty day and I enjoyed riding, especially since it hadn't gotten too warm out yet. There weren't many cars on Eller Road, so that made it especially pleasant, even though the gravel road surface was dusty. It was fun to allow my bike to speed up as we flew down one of the small hills along the road, and then let the momentum carry me up the hill on the other side. Suddenly, though, while speeding down one of those hills, disaster struck and my front tire blew, almost throwing me off my bike. I hit the brakes and was just barely able to stop without crashing. Emma circled back to see what had happened.

"That was a close call," I gasped. I hopped off the bike and checked out the shredded tire. "I think this tire's a goner."

"Yep. Sorry about that," Emma agreed, studying the situation. "I had no idea it was in such bad shape. You're lucky you weren't thrown off. That could've been bad."

"You're telling me. I guess I'll just have to walk it back to the house," I said, looking back at the long stretch of road we'd just traveled.

"How about if I ride back and get Mom to come pick you up?" she suggested. "I think she's still home. We can put your bike in the trunk, and she can drive us over to Northern Beach. That way, we won't have to miss out on swimming."

That seemed like a good idea. So, Emma took off for her house, while I slowly walked my bike back the way we'd just come. Insects and birds darted from the tall weeds in the fields along the side of the road as I trudged along. I continued making my way, and hardly saw another person or car, except for a pickup truck that honked hello as it passed. Suddenly, I heard a voice from behind.

"Well, fancy meeting you here," he said. I turned and saw it was Jim! He was out on his bike. He stopped and got off and walked it up to me. "What on earth are you doing? Tire problems?" he asked, looking down at what remained of the flattened tire.

"Oh, hi," I said. "What are you doing along here?"

"I'm on my way to work at Northern Beach. I saw you walking and thought you might need help. So, I turned around and rode up here to see. What happened? Your tire blow out?" he asked, kneeling down to get a better look.

"Yeah. Emma's gone back to the house to get Aunt Louise and the car," I replied. "I think this tire's had it."

"Oh, that's rough," he said.

He smiled that warm smile that was so endearing. Why did he have to be so cute? I felt self-conscious talking to him. For the first time, I sensed he might feel self-conscious about me, too. Up until that moment, I thought I was the only one struggling to make sense of our relationship. Maybe he was, too.

"Hey, um, I'm kinda glad I ran into you this way," he began. "I mean, not with a blown tire, but alone. I've been hoping to run into you."

"Really?" I replied. "Why?"

"'Cause I've wanted to talk to you about why I've been acting different toward you," he said. "You must have noticed."

"You don't owe me any explanation," I answered coyly. I wanted to know, but I wasn't about to let him know that. I resumed walking my bike up the road.

"Oh, Vanessa. You're such a funny girl," he said, chuckling. He started walking also. "Wait up, will you? Don't be so blasted headstrong."

"You'd better go. You're going to be late for work," I said, continuing to walk.

"Stop. Stop," he said, grabbing the handlebars of my bike. "Just hear me out, okay?"

"Look. I know about Monica," I said, turning toward him. "There's nothing more to say, is there? So, just run along. I'll be fine."

"You're wrong. There's a lot more to say," he insisted, looking directly into my eyes. "I meant what I said about my feelings for you when we were together in June. Monica and I had already been spending some time together back then, but we weren't going steady or anything. Even so, I had no business getting involved with you the way I did. I guess I. . .it's just that you. . .well. . .you have this certain quality I've never known in a girl before, and I guess I just forgot about Monica and got lost in the moment with you."

"I wish you'd stop," I said. "I really don't want to hear this."

"Okay, I'm almost finished, and then I'll stop. Monica's a really nice girl. She's in my class at school and we have a lot in common," he continued.

"Okay. I get it. She's in your class and the two of you are a couple. End of story," I said curtly.

"I owe it to her to continue with her and see where it goes. I've more or less made a commitment to her. Not officially, but you know, emotionally. I'm really sorry if I've hurt your feelings. I didn't mean to, Vanessa. Not you of all people. I'm sorry if I did. Really I am," he said.

He looked and sounded sincere, as well as a little troubled. I knew enough about Jim to know it wasn't his style to be a player and date more than one girl at a time. Even so, it hurt me to hear him speak so fondly about Monica. I knew he was showing integrity to stick by his commitment to her, but deep down, I didn't care. I wanted him for myself. I wanted him to be emotionally committed to me, not to her.

"Okay. Got it," I said softly. "Now I've got to go."

"Wait. Wait," he said. "One more thing." He looked down and paused.

"Yes?" I asked impatiently.

He looked up into my eyes as though he were looking straight through me. "The problem is — — — she's not you," he said finally, almost in a whisper.

I couldn't bear to hear this, and abruptly resumed walking as fast as the damaged tire would allow my bike to go. Jim dropped his bike in the weeds and ran after me. He grabbed my arm and I let go of my bike. Almost as if it were a choreographed dance between us, he pulled me up toward him and kissed me. The kiss was both passionate and sweet, and revealed a depth of feeling that stunned me. His vulnerability broke down my barriers, and I wanted him to kiss me again. Instinctively he did, with a slow, sensuous kiss that was wonderful. We stood silently for a moment, leaning into each other with our arms entwined, allowing the moment to flow over us. Then the spell was broken, and he stepped away from me.

"I. . .I shouldn't have done that," he said. "I'm sorry. Gotta go." He ran back to his bike, picked it up, and hurried away, almost embarrassed.

I stood speechless and a bit breathless. What was *that* about? What did it mean? He made it clear he was with Monica now, so it had to mean nothing more than good-bye. But it didn't *feel* like good-bye. As I watched him ride down the road, I was more confused, and more smitten, than ever before.

CHAPTER TEN

Sizing Up the Competition

*A*unt Louise and Emma arrived moments later. I was glad to see them pull up in the Bel Air. I wasn't getting very far walking the bike back to the house, especially after that interruption. I took a deep breath and collected myself. I hoped they didn't see what had just happened with Jim.

"Hey. Was that Jim Sparks standing here talking to you?" Emma asked as she got out of the car. "We saw someone with you as we were coming down the road. Was it Jim?"

"Yeah," I said. I walked the bike around to the back of the car and lifted it into the trunk with Aunt Louise's help.

"What did he want?" Emma asked.

I could tell that she wanted to know about the status of my relationship with him. I didn't mind telling her about my feelings for him generally, but I didn't want to reveal anything more, especially not the kiss. An encounter like I just had with Jim meant too much to me and was private. I decided, for now, anyway, not to disclose anything to her. Especially not in front of Aunt Louise.

"He just said hi and asked if he could help," I replied. "I told him you guys were on your way and I was okay. So, he left."

"Is that *all*?" she asked, drawing out her question and smiling slyly.

"Yes. That was *all*. Why? What else should he have said?" I answered, making a silly face.

"Oh, nothing, I guess," she said, looking away, disappointed.

I was glad the interrogation was over, for now anyway.

Northern Beach Swim Club was in a park that bordered the White River, with lots of grassy areas and large shady hickory, elm, and maple trees. It consisted of several park buildings built in the 1920s when the park was first established. Some of the buildings were open-sided picnic shelters. One of them was the pool house, which is where we were headed.

Aunt Louise pulled into the park and drove back to the pool and stopped. After we said goodbye to her, we made our way into the old structure holding the towels she'd given us. Our flip–flops flapped against our heels as we approached the young man who collected an entry fee of twenty cents per person at a window inside. We paid, passed through the area that housed the showers and lockers, and then headed outside to the pool.

The pool was shaped like a giant kidney bean, lined with rough brown concrete full of lots of little pebbles. It had three or four six-foot water sprinklers made from ordinary pipe out of which water continuously rained on swimmers. The best thing about the pool was the two water slides which stood in the middle of the pool, each curling twice before depositing swimmers into the water. Kids were constantly scurrying up the ladders to the tops of the slides, and then flying out below with gleeful yells and a loud splash.

Emma and I placed our towels on two unoccupied pool chairs, pulled off the street clothes we wore over our swim suits, and jumped in. The water was warm, despite being shaded in one section by an old maple tree.

I stood in the chest-high water and looked around for Jim. He had just told me he was on his way to his job at Northern Beach, and I knew he worked in pool maintenance, so it was likely I'd see him there. I didn't know exactly how I'd feel running into him now, but I desperately wanted to just the same. I scanned the entire area, shading my eyes against the sun glistening off the water, but didn't see him. I was disappointed, but relieved in a way. I decided to focus my mind on other things.

"I think Mom got another letter in the mail today about the foreclosure," Emma said out of the blue, splashing her way through the water over to me. "She seemed really bummed out after she read this one particular letter. She wouldn't tell me what it said, but I knew from her reaction that it had to be about the foreclosure."

I didn't know what to say. It appeared the foreclosure of the farm was moving down the road to what would be an unbearable conclusion. If only we could find a way to prevent it from happening. I felt guilty brooding over my romantic concerns when more important things like the security of her home were weighing heavily on my cousin's mind.

"It's all right," Emma continued, staring at the ripples on the water as if hypnotized. "If only I weren't just a kid. I've tried to think of something to do to fix this, but it's too complicated for me to figure out. If I were an adult, I bet I could."

"Maybe we should go back to the wishing tree when we get back to your house," I suggested, smiling.

Emma let out a small laugh. "Yeah. I wish I had the same confidence in that tree that my mom does." She slapped the surface of the water with her hand, and then added, "Oh, well. Let's have fun today, and try not to think about it."

She and I swam and played in the pool and slid down the curly water slide several times as the morning wore on. I enjoyed myself thoroughly and had so much fun that I forgot about almost everything else. I perfected my cannonball dive, and Emma worked on diving off the low diving board. It was wonderful being so carefree.

Then, everything changed. A girl I suspected was Monica Calhoun entered the pool area with two girlfriends. It was hard not to notice her as she made her entrance from the pool house. I'm sure just about everyone did, especially the men. I stood in the pool and watched her with rapt attention. I finally got to see what the competition looked like, and it wasn't encouraging. She was short, with sleek dark brown hair that fell straight to her waist. She wore a red two-piece swim suit that she filled out well, and a gold chain necklace with a gold heart that I assumed Jim had given her. She was very tan, and moved with the confidence of a beauty pageant contestant. I hated to admit it, but she was quite pretty.

"That's Monica!" Emma whispered loudly to me as she hurriedly bobbed over through the water. "You know. . . THE Monica."

"Yes, I thought so," I replied. "I think I saw Jim talking to her at the Rainbo roller rink the last time I visited you."

She and her friends strolled over to three pool chairs, spread out their beach towels, and sat down. Then they took tanning lotion out of their straw totes and slowly, and methodically, slathered themselves with it.

"She's very tan," I observed glumly. "Not like me."

"So what?" Emma replied emphatically, being ever the supportive friend. "You're a redhead. It's not your fault you don't have the kind of skin that gets a tan. Come on. Let's continue playing and forget about her."

But I couldn't take my eyes off Monica. I obsessively watched her every move as Emma and I continued taking turns with the slides and practiced our pretend water ballet. I was curious to learn more about this girl who'd stolen Jim's heart. I noted that she and I couldn't be more different. Not only physically, but in style and attitude, also. She seemed perfect —-— but perhaps a little too perfect. There had to be a catch somewhere. At least my jealous heart hoped so.

Monica and her friends spent the afternoon chatting and reading fashion magazines, and didn't appear at all interested in getting in the water. Occasionally, a boy or some foolishly brave older guy worked up his nerve to casually walk by her and attempt to strike up a conversation. Each time, she ignored him or shooed him off. It was curious to watch each attempt take its inevitable course as each would-be suitor was rebuffed.

"Those poor suckers," I muttered, shaking my head.

"We should go," Emma said, breaking my focus. "I think it's just about time for Mom to pick us up."

"Yes. Okay," I said, bobbing to the edge of the pool.

I pulled myself up on the side and stood up. Looking down at my turquoise polka-dot one-piece suit as it dripped water all over the walkway, I wondered if I looked as sexy as Monica did. I loved my suit and thought it was pretty cute. But it was certainly not as sexy as a red two-piece. I guess I knew the answer to my own question.

We quickly gathered our things, ran through the pool house, and trotted out to the parking lot. We found Aunt Louise waiting patiently in her car. Emma managed not to say anything about Monica during the ride home, and I was grateful for that. When we got to the house, Daniel was standing outside near the screen door.

"How are you, Daniel?" Aunt Louise said as she walked by him on the sidewalk. "What are you doing out here? Why don't you go inside?"

"I'm waiting for Luke," he said. "He ran back inside to get some comic books. We're going over to Joey's to trade them. There's a comic book swap at his house today."

"I see," she replied, opening the door and going inside.

As Emma and I passed Daniel to enter the house, he took a couple of steps away from the door and motioned for us to come over to him.

"What is it?" Emma asked impatiently, shivering in her blue suit. "Whatever it is, hurry and tell us. I want to get out of this wet suit."

"Okay, okay. I'll make this quick," he began. "I went over to the airport this morning and walked around the area near the big turquoise hangar, and I found this." He pulled out a crumpled piece of paper from inside that fringed suede jacket he always wore.

"What's that?" I asked, gazing down at the paper in his hand. "A receipt for something?"

"I think so. It says five hundred dollars is payable for — and I quote—*pressure treated lumber (ten e. box t.)*," he read. "I thought about it, and I think the 't' must be an abbreviation for turtles, and the 'e' for eastern."

He appeared excited and looked at me with his eyebrows raised in a questioning expression as if to gage my reaction, but I was a totally confused about what he was trying to say.

"So?" Emma snapped. "It has something to do with someone buying a bunch of lumber. I'm getting cold. See you later."

"No, wait. Almost done," Daniel continued. "There's such a thing as Eastern box turtles. I read in *National Wildlife* that Eastern box turtles are endangered and close to extinction. Bad guys are making money by illegally by smuggling them disguised as other things."

"Like treated lumber?" I asked.

"Bingo!" he exclaimed, raising his hand as if to ring a bell.

"So, you're saying the 'ten e. box t.' means ten Eastern box turtles?" Emma asked.

"Right" he said. "The paper says the money is owed to S. Builders. The 'S' could stand for Scaggs, don't you think? This could mean that Scaggs is smuggling and selling Eastern box turtles."

"Hmm. Maybe you've got something there," I said, nodding. "I don't think we've told you that Emma and I saw some men loading crates onto Pete's DC-3 yesterday. They could hold these turtles."

"What? Where?" Daniel asked.

"It was parked right outside the turquoise hangar," Emma explained. "The plane had the 'S' markings, so it had to be his plane."

"What makes you think they had turtles in them?" Daniel asked.

"One of the crates tipped over and a few crawled out," Emma recounted. "We saw them through my dad's binoculars."

"There you go!" Daniel exclaimed. "This receipt doesn't refer to pressure treated wood. No, this is for a crate of Eastern box turtles. That has to be it! He's got to be a smuggler."

"Wait a minute you guys. Aren't you a little getting carried away?" Emma cautioned. "You don't know for sure that that paper refers to turtles, and even if it does, they could be legal. Wouldn't Uncle Forrest and the other people around here know if Pete was doing something illegal like that? I think Vanessa's got you infected with the detective bug. I'm going inside now."

At that moment Luke came flying out the door holding five or six comic books.

"You guys look serious. What're you talking about?" Luke asked. "Wait! Don't tell me." He paused dramatically. "I don't care what it is," he continued abruptly. "Come on, frontier boy. Let's go to Joey's before all of the good comics are gone."

"Hold on," Daniel said. "If Mr. Scaggs is smuggling Eastern box turtles illegally, he might have also stolen Bobo to smuggle. There's a black market for black spider monkeys, you know, just like there is for these special turtles. It'd be easy. No one inspects any of the planes that come and go through this airport."

"Oh, for crying out loud. Are you still harping about Bobo?" Luke berated. "Dude, let it go. He's gone. Get your dad to buy you another monkey so I don't have to hear about this again. Problem solved. Now, let's go." He began walking down the driveway.

"Go ahead and I'll be there in a minute," Daniel stalled. "I've got to do something first."

"Okay. Have it your way. Just don't come crying to me if all of the *Thor* comics you love so much are gone by the time you get there," Luke yelled over his shoulder.

Emma went inside. I was eager to go inside and change out of my wet suit, too, but Daniel seemed to want to talk, so I stayed put.

"I saw Pete Scaggs' DC-3 land on my way over here. You can't miss that oversized 'S' painted on its tail. We could go over and watch him from the tree house, and maybe get more stuff on him. Who knows? We might find Bobo," he proposed. "It's worth a shot. I don't care what Luke says. I don't want just any monkey. I want Bobo."

"Sounds okay to me," I said. "I'll go inside and change."

Emma came through the door just as I was about to enter. She'd changed back into her shorts and shirt already. Her blonde hair was extra curly from still being wet.

"What's going on?" she asked.

"Daniel and I are going over to the tree house. Want to join us?" I asked. "I'll be right back."

"Oh, no," Emma said, looking at Daniel. "What are you guys doing now?"

"You'll see. Go get the binoculars, will you?" Daniel replied.

"Sheesh!" she said, rolling her eyes. "You guys are killing me." Despite her reservations, she turned and marched back into the house to get them.

CHAPTER ELEVEN

The Stakeout

*E*mma, Daniel, and I walked to the access road and climbed up into
the tree house. I was glad I'd become somewhat nimble maneuvering up and down the tree. I felt almost like one of the characters in the
Swiss Family Robinson movie about a family shipwrecked on an uninhabited island. They built a magnificent, multi-level house in an enormous
tree, and navigated around it with ease. My confidence was growing, and
I decided one of these days I might even try the rope elevator. For now, that
was out of the question.

"What's *that?*" Emma cried out, recoiling as she stood at the door of
the tree house.

I rushed to the door and looked inside. A dead possum lay in the middle of the floor. My guess was that someone found it lying alongside the
road and carried it up there as some sort of prank. Looking around,
though, I realized this was more than a harmless stunt. The small table had
a leg broken off and was thrown up against a wall, and the chair was
smashed into pieces strewn around the room.

"Oh! The poor thing," I said, turning away after seeing the dead animal. "Who would do such a thing?"

"I don't know," Daniel replied, his face red with anger. "It sure didn't
get here by itself. I'm going to tell my dad and brothers about this.
Whoever did this won't get away with it."

"How will you ever know for sure who did it?" I asked.

"I don't know, but somehow I will!" he declared forcefully. "You
guys can stay outside, if you want to, while I clean this up."

I gladly waited on the deck with Emma as Daniel ran up to his house and returned with a burlap bag and gloves. When he marched into the tree house with them, he was a man on a mission.

"Hey, you guys! Come here and look at this," he shouted from inside after the possum was in the bag. He looked agitated.

Emma and I dutifully stepped inside. Daniel pushed the door closed, and on the back of it were the words, "Stay Away," in red paint. It sent a shiver through me when I saw it.

"Who do you suppose did *that*?" Emma blurted with surprise.

"I don't know, but this whole thing is creepin' me out. Maybe we should go back to your house, Emma. I don't think it's safe to be up here," I suggested.

"I just don't get it," Daniel said, shaking his head. "It took Buzz and Lars weeks to build this. If someone wanted to vandalize it, they could have done it then. But no one ever touched it or even moved a plank of wood. Why start now?"

"Hey. Do you remember those guys the other day working down at the turquoise hangar?" I reminded Emma. "They looked up here and acted strange. And, yesterday when you dropped the binoculars, those workmen seemed very curious about us up here."

"Yeah, I remember that," Emma answered. "Are you saying you think those men had something to do with this?"

"Maybe," I replied, nodding. "Like you said, sometimes people don't like being watched. Especially if you're Pete Scaggs and have something to hide."

"Yeah, could be. Or maybe it was some kids playing a practical joke?" Emma added.

"All I know is that someone is trying to intimidate us," Daniel said.

"Well, it's working," Emma declared. "Let's go." She walked out on the deck and started to crawl out to the rope.

"No, wait!" Daniel commanded. He looked more serious than I'd ever seen him. "This is *our* tree house. We can't let whoever did this take it from us. Especially if it was Pete Scaggs. I'm staying right here and do what we came to do. Are you with me?"

A look of determination and defiance flashed in Daniel's eyes. Emma and I exchanged glances. To be honest, I didn't want to stay. The atmosphere was spoiled now, and it wasn't fun to be there. Still, I couldn't let him down, even if I did feel uneasy.

"Okay, I'll stay," I said.

"Me too, I guess," Emma muttered reluctantly.

"Good. That's the spirit!" he replied, ignoring our obvious lack of enthusiasm.

He climbed down and carried the burlap bag with the dead possum back to the barn. By the time he returned, Emma and I were already sitting on the edge of the deck observing Pete Scaggs' DC-3 parked outside the turquoise hangar.

"See? I told you I saw his plane here," Daniel said, sitting down beside us. "Did I miss anything?"

"Not really," Emma replied. "A man came out to the plane from the office and then walked back to the coffee shop. I don't think it was Pete, though. He was too skinny. That's about it."

"Well, let's keep watching," Daniel said. "We've just got to get the goods on that scumbag. I'll catch that crook if it's the last thing I do."

It seemed that having Bobo stolen and the tree house vandalized were direct assaults on Daniel's world, and he wasn't going to tolerate it. He took the binoculars from Emma and carefully studied the scene below. After he completed his initial check, we each took turns looking through them. As the minutes passed and nothing happened, I began to realize it would take patience to wait for something significant to occur.

Finally, a man walked out of the restaurant to the DC-3, climbed inside, and emerged moments later carrying a large box. The box appeared to be heavy, judging from the way he carried it. He took it to the large hangar doors, slid them open, and went inside. He reappeared moments later empty-handed, locked the doors, and walked back to the airport office.

"Wonder what *that* was about?" Daniel asked. "My dad told me this morning Pete's company has leased the entire hangar. That means he's the only person who can use it."

"That's convenient for Pete, don't you think?" I observed. "He can do whatever he wants to in there, and no one will be around to see."

"Yeah. I bet that's why he leased the whole thing," Daniel said, looking through the binoculars. "I wonder if Bobo's in there. He might be, if he isn't already on his way to China. I'd like to go down to that hangar right now and rip those doors open and get him out of there."

"Did you tell your dad you think Pete stole Bobo?" I inquired.

"Nah," Daniel said, handing me the binoculars. "I don't want to tell my dad anything until I have all the goods on that monkey-napper. I don't think he'd believe me otherwise. He and Pete go way back, and Dad actually thinks Pete's a good guy. Can you believe it? I don't think he'll ever think anything bad about Pete until he has solid evidence otherwise. So, that's what we've got to get — — solid evidence."

The three of us sat lined up along the edge of the deck watching for the slightest development below. We continued our vigil for quite some time, but nothing out of the ordinary happened. As the minutes continued to tick by, Daniel grew more and more restless.

"I'm going down there," he announced finally. "This is my chance to look around the plane while that guy is off telling tall tales in the coffee shop. I haven't seen anyone else around, so he's got to be the only person to keep track of."

"Are you sure you should?" I cautioned. "He could come back any moment and catch you."

"I won't go inside," he said. "I just want to look around outside. They can't object to me walking around my own father's airport, can they?"

"Okay. But be careful," I warned. "Promise me you won't go inside that plane. Okay?"

He nodded in agreement. Even so, I felt anxious about this. Someone had left a strong message for us today. It could have been just some kids playing a practical joke. But maybe Pete Scaggs knew we were watching him and was warning us to back off. After all, this tree house wasn't completed until last week. Now that we could hang out here, Pete had an audience, and I bet he wasn't too happy about that. He didn't strike me as a man to mess with.

Daniel climbed down, walked to the chain link fence, and climbed over. It was a short walk through the grass to the tarmac where the DC-3 stood. He walked along one side of the plane looking up at the windows. He circled around to the plane's nose, and then walked along the other side to the door in the back. He paused at the base of the steps and looked up at the open door. Then to my surprise, he climbed up the steps all the way to the door as if to go inside. He stood teetering on the top step, peering inside. I held my breath. He was on a private property now and was playing with fire.

Meanwhile, two men appeared in the door of the restaurant talking. One of them was a big man who looked as though he could be Pete. Neither of them looked in the direction of the plane, which was fortunate for Daniel. If they had, they surely would have seen him standing on the steps. I jumped to my feet and tried to signal Daniel, but he didn't see me waving my arms from so far away.

"Stand up and wave your arms with me. Quick!" I urged Emma. "Maybe the two of us doing this will catch his attention."

"I don't think he's looking up here," Emma said, waving frantically next to me.

Emma was right. Instead of retreating, Daniel appeared to go inside the plane. I couldn't believe it. *Get out, get out!* I repeated anxiously over and over under my breath.

The men began strolling slowly toward the plane. Daniel re-emerged from the plane and ran down the steps, which fortunately faced away from their approach. He darted across the grass with the speed of a gazelle to the fence and bounded over, almost in a single leap. He continued on to the maple tree and scrambled up to us. The men continued talking and walking in a slow gait as they made their way to the DC-3. It appeared they hadn't noticed him. Daniel was lucky this time.

"*What* were you doing going inside that plane?" Emma scolded after Daniel crawled up on the deck. "You just about gave me a heart attack!"

"Yeah. I thought you promised you were just going to look around outside," I said. "I was really worried. Those men have been standing outside the restaurant for several minutes and could have seen you."

Daniel took several deep breaths, then smiled.

"Look at this," he said proudly, still panting. He reached inside his fringed jacket and pulled out something like looked like a small dog collar.

"What's that?" Emma asked.

"It was lying on the floor just inside the door," he began. "It'd been kicked off to the side. I was able to reach in from the top step and snatch it."

"A dog collar? What's so special about a dog collar?" Emma asked, taking it from him. She turned it around and examined it.

"That's just it. It's not a dog collar," Daniel explained excitedly. "It's *Bobo's* collar. I should know. I bought it for him at a pet store in Chicago when I was there with my dad. It has a jeweled blue *B* glued to the back. See? There can't be two of these in the world."

"Did he have it on the day he disappeared?" I asked.

"Yup, he sure did," Daniel said, his eyes fixed on the thin band of blue mesh material. "I never took it off him except to give him baths."

"Wow. So, I *did* see Bobo in that window," I said, taking the collar and studying the distinctive letter on it. "I just knew it. I knew it!"

"The evidence is piling up. The noose tightens on Mr. Scaggs," Daniel declared. He looked more upbeat than he'd seemed in a long time.

"Yes, indeed," I agreed.

"Now all we have to do is find Bobo," Daniel added, looking hopeful. "I wanted to go all the way inside and look for him, but I didn't have the nerve. I called for him a couple of times, though. I didn't hear anything. Even so, I know we're getting closer to finding him."

I gazed at Daniel as he handled Bobo's collar so tenderly, and felt sorry for him. He sorely missed his pet. I nodded in agreement, but wasn't as optimistic about finding his beloved Bobo as he was.

CHAPTER TWELVE

A Close Call

The man who looked like Pete climbed into his plane while the other man unlocked and slid open the two large hangar doors. Moments later, the plane's two engines suddenly came to life, coughing clouds of exhaust as the propellers turned. Then the large plane slowly rumbled forward into the hangar and stopped. It appeared they were putting it to bed for the night.

"If I could just get in there, I could check out the hangar and that plane all at the same time," Daniel said, intently watching the action below. You could sense he was just aching to do just that.

"Don't be silly," I said. "It'd be far too dangerous."

Suddenly, I heard Luke's signature peacock call, "Heyeric! Heyeric!" coming from Allisonville Road. I looked out the tree house window and saw Luke walking toward us carrying something that looked like comic books.

"I thought I'd find you knuckleheads up there," Luke teased, looking up at us as he approached. "Ever since Buzz finished that oversized birdhouse, it's become your favorite hangout."

"Come on up," Daniel beckoned, looking down over the railing. "We've got some interesting stuff to show you."

"Nah. You come down here. I'm headed home to get a meal," Luke insisted. "By the way, you missed a really good comic book swap while you were up there having a tea party with the girls all afternoon."

"Wait! I'm coming down. You'll eat your words when you see what I found!" Daniel said excitedly. He quickly lowered himself through the hole in the deck and climbed down.

Emma and I followed. Daniel showed him Bobo's collar and described all of the details of his daring inspection of Pete's DC-3. As we all walked back to Emma's house, we also filled Luke in on all the details of how the tree house had been vandalized.

"Dude, you've got to be careful," Luke said, shaking his head. "A tough guy like Pete Scaggs is probably packing heat."

"You mean he might be carrying a gun?" I asked. That hadn't occurred to me.

"What if he is? Would he shoot a kid like me, just because I looked inside his fancy plane?" Daniel asked. "He'd have a lot of explaining to do to my dad if he did."

"Yeah, and your dad might thank him!" Luke said, laughing. "But seriously, if this Scaggs character has money at stake, there's no telling what he might do if he thinks you guys are interfering with his plans. He could make it look like an accident and no one would be the wiser. You've seen how the bad guys do it on *The Naked City*, haven't you?"

"What've *we* done?" Emma protested. "We haven't done a thing to him."

"Except spy on him," Luke continued. "He must know by now that you're up in that tree house looking down at what he's doing over there. Maybe he doesn't like that."

"Why should he care what we see, unless he has something to hide?" I asked.

"Oh, no. Miss City Slicker, junior detective extraordinaire is back at it again, eh?" Luke moaned.

"I'm just using my intelligence to put the pieces of the puzzle together," I said, not backing down. "Is that such a crime?"

Before Luke could answer, we were interrupted by the voices of Uncle Evert, Lars, and Aunt Louise having a heated conversation in the dining room as we approached the house. We immediately stopped talking and listened as we stood on the walkway.

"I mean it," Lars stated emphatically. "I'm not going back to Bloomington next semester, and that's all there is to it. It's a waste of time. IU's just not right for me. I plan on sitting out the next semester to decide what I want to do next."

"A college education is never a waste of time," Uncle Evert insisted. "If you need to change majors, do it. Find out what it is you want to study, and complete your degree. You've already got two years under your belt, for goodness' sake. Why not see it through and get your degree?"

"You know, dear, if you drop out of school, you'll lose your college deferment, and you'll be called up for active duty," Aunt Louise added.

"That's right. I wonder if you'll feel cut out for the Army when you're slogging through the steamy jungles of North Vietnam," Uncle Evert pointed out. "You'll wish you were back in the scholastic jungles of Indiana University, I guarantee you."

The Vietnam War was raging. Filmed reports of the war were on all the TV news programs every evening. It was an unpopular war, and becoming active duty was a real concern to many young men of a certain age. Those who dreaded the possibility of being drafted hoped to qualify for a deferment so they didn't have to go. Being enrolled in school was one of those deferments, so many boys stayed in college for that very reason. It would be unthinkable to drop out, unless you were forced to, because you'd be subject to the draft almost immediately.

"I don't care," Lars answered with defiance. "If they tell me I have to go to 'Nam, I'll go to Canada or figure something else out." He stormed to the back bedroom and slammed the door.

"I'm not going to lose the farm and my eldest son all in the same year," Uncle Evert shouted after him. "You're going back to school, and that's all there is to it!"

"Is Lars going to Vietnam?" Emma asked softly, looking worried.

"No," Luke reassured her. "They have this conversation all the time. It doesn't mean anything. He'll go back to school when the time comes. I'd bet my coin collection on it."

"I hope you're right," I said. "He sounded pretty determined to drop out."

"Of course, I'm right. But what did Dad mean about losing the farm? That was a weird thing for him to say," Luke asked, looking puzzled.

"Oh, darn it," Emma said with a start. "I think I left the binoculars up in the tree house. Do you think they'll be okay until the next time we go over?"

"Better go get them right now, little sister," Luke urged. "Dad'll kill you if someone takes them. From the sound of things, nothing left up there is safe from being taken or trashed."

"I'll go with you if that helps," I volunteered.

"There you go. You have company. Now, run along and fetch," Luke said playfully.

Emma looked unhappy, but she began walking through the yard to the path, so I followed. We crossed Daniel's lawn and went up the access road. She ran ahead and was already up on the deck when I got to the tree. I didn't see any reason to go up, so I stood in the grass below and waited for her to come back down.

"Just think, we could outfit this place to make it real cozy," she yelled down. "You know, install a barrel to catch rain water, and a pulley to bring up food and other things we need." She was off in a Disney fantasy of tree house domesticity.

"Yeah, sounds good. Did you find the binoculars?" I shouted impatiently. "What's taking you so long?"

She didn't answer, and I didn't hear or see her walking around. What was she doing?

"Come on. Let's go. Hey! Are you up there?" I called again.

When she still didn't respond, I stepped out into the middle of the access road to get a better look. The road was used only rarely. I'd personally never seen a vehicle on it. But this evening, out of nowhere, a large sedan suddenly came roaring up from Allisonville Road creating a large cloud of dust as it gained speed. I stepped back onto the grass to let it pass. Just as I did, the car left the road and drove into the grass heading straight at me. By the time I realized the car was about to hit me, it was almost too late to react. Fortunately, I jumped back and fell behind the tree, just as the car roared past, missing me by only inches. If not for the tree, the car probably would have struck me.

The car continued speeding up the access road and then turned into a small driveway leading onto the grounds of the airport. It was gone as quickly as it had appeared. I remained splayed out on the ground in a state of shock.

"Vanessa! Vanessa!" Emma called as she slid down the rope to the ground. "Are you okay? Oh, my gosh, that was close. Are you okay?"

I collected myself, stood up, and swept away the grass and small sticks from my clothes and hair. My glasses were a mess. I took them off and wiped the lenses clean with my shirt.

"Are you hurt?" Emma asked again.

She looked me up and down with a concerned look. I shook my head no, that I was okay. I was too stunned to speak.

"Who *was* that?" she asked indignantly. She looked toward the airport for a trace of the car, which was now long gone. "We've got to find out who that was and report him. It looked like he intentionally steered right for you, as though he deliberately wanted to hit you."

"I know," I said, still feeling emotionally wobbly. "He could have killed me!"

It seemed strange the car appeared out of nowhere and drove so fast and so recklessly. It was difficult to accept the possibility that someone wanted to hurt or kill me. Why? Surely that wasn't the case. But it was too much of a coincidence that it left the road bed and drove through the grass straight at me. I took stock of my arms and legs and appeared to be fine, with no broken bones or sprains. I was just badly shaken.

"Did you get a good look at the driver? Did you recognize him?" Emma asked.

"No. I didn't have a chance to see anything," I replied. "Did you see the car?" I was hoping she had.

"Yes, I'm sure can describe it," Emma said with the confidence of a mother identifying her child.

"Great! Describe it to me," I said eagerly.

"Well, it was a big sedan, a few years old, with four doors. And, it was blue, or maybe green. No, it was greenish-yellow," Emma began. "Come to think of it, it might have been dark blue."

"Good job," I said sarcastically. "That should give the authorities enough to go on. If they're psychic, that is."

"Gimme a break. I was up in the tree and couldn't see so well," she said with an apologetic shrug.

"Oh, don't worry about it. It doesn't matter. Let's go. Did you get the binoculars?" I asked.

"Gosh darn it," she exclaimed. "I got excited and forgot them. I'll go back up and get them. Now, you stay out of the road this time and watch carefully for cars. Okay?"

CHAPTER THIRTEEN

Ice Cream and Warm Nights

When Emma and I arrived back at her house, Luke was bouncing in and out of the kitchen in his usual hyper way, coaxing Uncle Evert to hurry as he warmed hamburgers and Kraft macaroni and cheese on the stove.

"I'm starving," Luke said. "Can you please hurry?"

"Take this bread to the table and get out of my kitchen, will you?" Uncle Evert ordered, handing him a plastic sleeve of Colonial-brand sliced white bread. Luke dutifully grabbed it and recklessly tossed in onto the dining room table.

"Hey — — what happened to *you*?" Luke asked as I walked up the steps into the kitchen. I must have looked all done in.

"Vanessa was almost hit by a car!" Emma answered excitedly. "She was standing in the grass under the tree house waiting for me, and a car swerved off the access road and steered right at her."

"Are you hurt?" Uncle Evert asked with a concerned look. He looked me up and down.

"No. I'm all right," I answered. "Just shaken up a little." I walked slowly into the dining room and sat down.

"You say a car swerved off the access road?" Luke asked, sitting down beside me. Uncle Evert stood in the kitchen door listening.

"Yes. Almost as though the driver was aiming at her on purpose," Emma continued. "Can you believe that?"

"Well, kinda," Luke began. Emma shot her brother a stern look of disapproval. "Okay, okay. No jokes. Did you get a good look at the car?"

93

"No. All I remember is that it was big," I replied, trying hard to remember. "It all happened so fast."

"I think it was greenish-blue, or navy maybe," Emma recalled. "From a distance it looked maroon-ish even."

"Thanks, Sherlock, but could you narrow it down a little?" Luke taunted.

"I was up in a *tree* when it happened, for goodness' sakes!" Emma protested.

"I suppose that means you didn't get a license number, either?" Luke replied.

"Okay, everyone calm down," Uncle Evert said, gesturing with his hands. "These things happen. We're just sorry that it happened to you, Vanessa, but we're very glad you're all right. I probably should call the sheriff. This should be reported. There might be a dangerous drunk or criminal on the road." He started to walk toward the phone in the living room.

"No, please don't. Not on my account, anyway. I'm sure it was just an accident," I said quickly. I didn't see any reason to get things stirred up. Besides, how could they track the car? Neither Emma nor I remembered the color, make, or any distinguishing detail of the car.

"Well, okay, if that's how you feel," Uncle Evert replied, changing course. "How about if we eat and think about it?"

"Sounds good," I replied, forcing a smile.

As Emma and I were clearing the table after Luke, Uncle Evert, Emma, and I ate, Lars emerged from the back bedroom. He was clearly dressed for a special occasion. He wore an orange dress shirt, dark brown slacks, and a beige sport coat with stylishly wide lapels trimmed with dark brown top-stitching. His dark hair was combed neatly, and he sported dark brown patent leather shoes with trendy square toes and boxy heels.

"What the heck are you all decked out for?" Luke asked, making a face. "You look like you're going to a funeral."

"I'm going to Starlight Musicals to see *Kiss Me, Kate*, if you must know," Lars answered dryly.

"Isn't that based on a Shakespeare play?" Luke asked. "Yes, folks. A musical *and* a Shakespeare play combined into one. Talk about a double snore! I'd rather watch the grass grow."

"Unlike *some* family members, I enjoy getting a little culture every now and then," Lars quipped.

I had heard of Starlight Musicals. It was an outdoor theater located on the campus of Butler University in Indianapolis where Broadway touring companies, headlined by TV and movie stars, performed in the summer.

"Well, don't be out too late," Uncle Evert replied. "I always worry that your Corvette is a magnet for trouble when it gets late."

"Lars, why don't you have something to eat before you leave?" Aunt Louise coaxed, walking into the dining room. "At least have a little macaroni before you go. I believe there's still a little left on the stove."

"Thanks, but I'm meeting friends at the Tee Pee before the show, and I'll eat there," Lars answered. "Well, good night, family."

He walked outside, and not long after, I heard the low rumble of his Corvette engine as he drove away.

"The Tee Pee," Luke said, sighing. "I just love that place. Girls in sexy outfits bring food to your car on a tray. All you have to do is turn on your headlights when you're done eating, and they come right back and take the tray away. Where else can you get cute girls to come to your car on command like that?"

"Are you calling those long, blue woolen slacks and white blouses those girls wear sexy outfits?" Uncle Evert asked.

"Well. . .," Luke said, smiling slyly.

"You're just a horny teenager," Emma said with disdain. "You sound like a pervert."

"I have a healthy libido, that's all," Luke said, puffing out his chest. "Nothing wrong with that, is there, Dad?"

"Talking about drive-in restaurants has given me an idea," Uncle Evert said. "How about if we help Vanessa forget about what happened this evening by going to the Dairy Queen in Noblesville? What do you say?"

That was a great idea, and I was all for it. Emma and I hurriedly finished cleaning up the dishes so we could go. Just as we put the last clean dish away, the screen door slammed and someone stomped up the steps.

"Hello everyone," Randy said, walking into the kitchen. He had on his usual dirty jeans with the torn knees and faded brown t-shirt. He was unshaven and looked as though he'd camped out last night.

"Hey, Randy," Luke said. "Change of plans. We're going to the DQ instead of shooting bottle rockets."

"Oh. Okay," Randy said. "Hi, Vanessa."

Randy looked at me with a goofy expression that made me uncomfortable. Emma's words earlier about his crush on me preoccupied my thoughts. I politely returned the greeting, and then made a beeline out of the kitchen. I didn't want to do anything that might accidentally encourage him.

"Did you hear? Someone tried to run Vanessa down today. She got away from them, though," Luke reported. "It wasn't you, was it? You'll have to aim a lot better next time if it was."

"What? Someone tried to run you down?" Randy exclaimed. He peered at me intently through the smudged lenses of his glasses. "Where?"

"On the access road near the tree house," Luke continued. "You sure it wasn't you?" Clearly, Luke was jesting, but Randy didn't appear to understand.

"Of course not!" Randy protested loudly. "I'd never hurt a person as authentic as Vanessa."

Luke gave out a chortle. "I don't have a clue what you just said," Luke laughed. "Authentic? I could think of some other adjectives to describe her."

I must admit that I was stumped by his use of that word. What did it mean? The screen door slammed again, and Daniel trudged up into the house still wearing his fringed jacket.

"What are you all doing?" Daniel asked. "Want to shoot some fireworks?"

"We're going to Dairy Queen, Daniel," Uncle Evert said, walking back into the room. "You boys are welcome to join us. Those who are going, let's go, shall we?"

We all walked outside to the van and climbed in. Luke took his usual position in the front passenger seat. Randy and Daniel were good sports and took the seats in the very back, leaving the middle seats for Emma and me.

"Everybody in?" Uncle Evert asked, looking over his shoulder at us. "Okay. Dilly Bars and Mr. Misty's, here we come!"

He started the engine and drove north toward Noblesville. I pushed open the window next to me and allowed the refreshing evening air to blow in and toss my hair. It was the only thing to do on a warm evening like this in a vehicle without air conditioning. We traveled on for about five miles, and finally arrived at the south end of town.

We passed Kenley's Supermarket and several blocks consisting of small older frame houses and cottages. Finally, the iconic red-and-white Dairy Queen sign appeared directly ahead on the corner of Pleasant and South 10th Street. Uncle Evert turned into the small parking lot adjacent to the small white building and turned off the motor.

"You kids get yourselves whatever you want," he said. He reached into his pocket and handed each of us two quarters. "Enjoy yourselves."

We eagerly piled out of the van and sprinted to the outside window to place our orders. A high school girl on the other side wore a white t-shirt with the Dairy Queen logo across the chest, and a white baseball cap with the same red and white logo across the crown.

"What're you going to have?" she asked, looking bored.

"I'll have a medium vanilla cone," Emma replied. "How about you, Vanessa?"

"She'll have a banana split and a large Coke!" Luke boomed from behind me.

"No. Just a medium vanilla cone," I told the girl. "That's all."

"So, you want a banana split, a large Coke, and a medium vanilla cone?" the girl repeated. "Will that be all?"

"Just a medium vanilla cone. That's all. No banana split and no Coke. He was just being funny," I explained. The girl rolled her eyes, and then stepped away to get my order.

Emma already had her cone and was licking its edges when the girl returned with my cone and handed it to me. Emma and I strolled behind the building where several picnic tables were set up to sit while you enjoyed your treat. It was a busy evening, but we managed to find an empty table and sat down. A crude sound system was rigged up with a single speaker sitting in a screened window at the back of the store, and "Baby Love" by the Supremes filled the air as we took our seats. Randy and Luke soon joined us with their large milk shakes. Daniel followed with a chocolate sundae. Uncle Evert got a soda and then opted to go back to the van, where he sat in the driver's seat with the door propped open and read the paper.

"Girls don't usually eat ice cream," Randy stated, stirring his milk shake with his straw. "Makes them fat."

"Well, I don't need to worry about that," I replied. "One little ice cream cone won't hurt me."

"Are you implying my cousin is fat?" Luke asked playfully. "'Cause I'm still trying to figure out what you mean by that 'she's so authentic' comment you made before, and I can only handle one challenge at a time."

"I'm just trying to be helpful," Randy answered with a shrug. "Girls are usually concerned about their weight, that's all. I just thought. . . ."

I shook my head. Randy was certainly a strange boy. Fortunately, I wasn't as worried about being fat as I was about not being as curvy as some other girls my age. I was trying to process Randy's remark, when I noticed Jim and Monica walking up to the order-taking window. They were holding hands and so engrossed in each other that they didn't see us.

"Oh, look. There's Casanova," Luke remarked with a smirk. "Ever since he got involved with that Monica he never has time to do anything. He's always tied up doing stuff with her."

"Yeah. Some women are good, and some are bad," Randy said, looking at me as he sipped his shake. I assumed he'd placed me in the good category, but it was hard to tell. All I knew was that I was authentic.

"You said it," Luke replied. "She's sucking the life out of him, like some kind of love vampire. I've got to figure out a way to break them up for his own good. That's all there is to it. Friends don't let friends date love-parasites."

"Luke!" Emma chided. "That's not nice."

"Well, I think she's really pretty," Daniel said out of the blue. "Jim sure is a lucky man."

Emma kicked Daniel under the table. "What'd I say?" Daniel blurted, frowning at her. She gestured for him to be quiet, which he returned with a confused look.

By now, Jim and Monica had their ice cream cones. Jim scanned the picnic tables looking for a place to sit and finally saw us. It looked as though he suggested to Monica that they come over.

"Hey, buddy, what're you doing at an ice cream joint on a warm summer night?" Jim asked Luke facetiously as they strolled over to our table. He looked at me and nodded hello, and then did the same to Emma, Randy, and Daniel, while Monica looked off in the distance.

"Do you guys know my friend Monica?" Jim asked, gazing over at her and smiling.

She looked at us and half-heartedly said hello. She was wearing a white lace V-neck top which really showed off her tan, and tight-fitting red Capri slacks. The gold chain with the gold heart I'd seen her wearing at the pool hung around her neck, and she had her long black hair pulled back into a thick ponytail.

"Let's go sit over there," she said softly to Jim, pointing to another table.

"You can sit with us," Luke volunteered, gesturing for the rest of us to move down. "Come on, scoot down you guys and make room."

"No, we don't want to crowd you. We'll sit over there," Jim said. "We'll be fine."

"Okay. If you say so," Luke replied. "See what I mean?" Luke muttered after they'd walked away.

"Maybe they have private stuff to talk about," Randy suggested. "I'm kinda glad they didn't sit with us."

"Mushy stuff is all they have to talk about," Luke grumbled. "Just mush. She's ruining a great guy. It's a crime, I tell you. A crime!"

Jim and Monica sat at a table facing us, which was very awkward for me. I tried not to look, but every now and then I couldn't help myself, and I peeked over at them. They sat on the same side of the table, and held hands most of the time. He looked totally smitten and happy. I should be glad for him if I really cared about him, I reminded myself. But my jealousy made that difficult. Seeing them together made me realize how serious they were, and that devastated me.

"What? That's crazy!" Daniel shouted, pulling me out of my thoughts.

Daniel didn't know about what had just happened along the access road, and Emma was filling him in on the details.

"I could kill the guy who tried to hurt you," Randy said emphatically. "If I ever catch that guy, he'd better watch out!"

"Dude, chill out there, will you?" Luke admonished. "We're the Love Generation. We want peace, not war. Remember?"

"Doesn't it seem odd that all of these strange things have just started happening?" Daniel observed. "I'd say it all began with Bobo disappearing."

"Oh, no. Not Bobo again," Luke mocked. "Will you ever get over losing that darned chimp?"

"He isn't a chimpanzee!" Daniel replied indignantly. "He's a monkey. They're two different things, you dumb ape."

"Daniel makes a good point," I chimed in.

"That Luke's a dumb ape?" Daniel quipped.

Laughing, I continued. "No, that there've been several odd things —
— Bobo disappearing, the tree house being vandalized, the ghost plane,
that car almost hitting me. . ."

"Yes, and each one can be explained logically," Luke replied.

"How?" Daniel asked.

"Let's see," Luke began. "Bobo let himself out of his cage, for
starters. As for the tree house, some kids probably heard about it and
pulled that prank. And the car thing could have been some drunk taking
the access road as a short cut and not paying attention to where he was
going. As for the ghost plane, some pilot didn't pay his taxes and made a
run for it, or something like that."

"What about me finding Bobo's collar in Pete Scaggs' DC-3?" Daniel
asked. "How do you explain that?"

"I know you think there's only one collar in the world like that," Luke
answered. "But that collar was probably made in Japan by the dozens. Given
how many people have flown in that plane with Scaggs, there could be any
number of people with a small dog who accidentally left it behind."

"I don't know if I agree with your theories," I said. "I think there's
something more to it. How do you explain that I saw Bobo's face in
Scaggs' DC-3?"

"You said you weren't sure you actually saw a monkey that day,"
Luke countered. "And even if you did see a monkey, how do you know it
was Bobo?"

"And, as for that crazy car," I continued, ignoring Luke's rebuttal,
"what kind of short cut is that? I don't know that much about the layout
of the airport, but doesn't that road turn and enter the airport right next
to the hangar Pete Scaggs is using? Why would anyone else but Pete and
his men use it?"

"I don't know, but lots of people use it," Luke answered. "I don't
know why they do. They just do. Do you think Scaggs would go to all this
fuss over one little spider monkey? Sorry, it just doesn't add up."

"I'll get him!" Randy vowed with a wild look in his eyes. "How dare
he try to hurt you, Vanessa! I'll get him, I swear."

I had no idea a mild-mannered guy like Randy could be so hot-
headed. I guess it was kind of endearing that he wanted to protect me, but
at the same time his extreme zeal was a bit unnerving.

"Dude, I thought I told you — — daisies, not guns," Luke retorted. "Stay cool."

"I just know if I could get into that hangar and get a good look around, I could get the dirt on Scaggs and find Bobo," Daniel said. "His DC-3 is parked in there tonight. He usually has it up in the air someplace else. So this would be a good night to get in there."

"Then why don't you do it?" Luke suggested. "Your dad owns the airport. Just borrow a key and sneak in there. What're you waiting for?"

"That's just the problem," Daniel said. "If I got caught, and it got around that I broke in, no one would ever trust my dad or my family ever again to handle their planes. Dad and the airport would be finished. So I can't do that, even as much as I want to."

"I'll do it," Randy suddenly declared, looking at me through his crooked glasses as though he were gazing fondly at a new puppy. "We've got to stop that guy before he does something worse. If that's what it takes, I'm your man."

"Forget it. You'd be in big trouble if you got caught," Luke advised. "Your dad doesn't own the airport like Daniel's dad does."

"Yeah, well maybe so," Randy replied. "But sometimes you have to put yourself on the line to protect the people you care about."

"I think he's referring to you," Emma whispered. I gave her a nod that I'd already picked up on that.

"It would be breaking and entering to go in there. That's a felony," Luke pointed out. "This is the kind of handy legal knowledge one gets from watching *Perry Mason*."

"Sometimes the hangar side door is left unlocked by accident. What if it were unlocked and someone went in that way? Would that still be breaking and entering?" Daniel questioned.

"Well, it's been a while since I've seen defense attorney Perry Mason handle this kind of thing, but I think that'd just be entering without the breaking part. But that's still a felony," Luke replied. "On top of that, some of Scaggs' guys could be in there working or guarding the place. They might not like having you crash their party."

"I'm still gonna go there tonight and check it out," Randy declared. "If the door's open or unlocked, I'm going in."

"Okay. It's your funeral," Luke said.

"Please don't talk about funerals," Emma said, looking worried.

Randy straightened his shoulders and looked at me with a stalwart smile. I felt partially responsible for this poor guy doing something that could be dangerous and illegal, but I didn't know how to stop him. Daniel began briefing Randy on how the side door worked and other bits of information he might need to know for his cat burglar operation. Luke added his own two cents, of course. Randy became more and more pumped up as the plan was discussed. I hoped these guys knew what they were doing. But I knew they probably didn't. After all, they were just impetuous teenaged boys.

CHAPTER FOURTEEN

Secrets Are Hard to Keep

*W*hile the boys continued planning the hangar caper, I took a quick break and walked to the ladies room in the back of the Dairy Queen building. It appeared to be a one-person at a time arrangement, accessed by a door that had a wide, frosted-glass window tilted open over it. An older woman stood outside the door with her arms crossed waiting her turn to go in. She turned around when I walked up.

"Two girls are already in there," she advised me.

"Oh. Okay. Thanks," I answered.

I gazed at the tables, hoping to casually observe Monica and Jim without being detected. Unfortunately, I couldn't see their table from where I stood, which disappointed me. Inside, two girls chatted and gig-gled. The tiled walls of the restroom made their voices echo, and I could make out what they said if I concentrated.

"You're so lucky to have a boyfriend like Jim," one of the girls said. "He treats you so well, and he's so cute. I wish I could find someone like him."

When I heard Jim's name, my ears perked up. *Was Monica in there?* I couldn't be certain.

"Yes, Jim's a nice guy, but nice guys aren't always the most exciting," the other girl answered.

"What? Aren't you happy?" the first girl asked.

"I guess I'm happy enough," the other girl answered.

"That doesn't sound too enthusiastic. Is there someone else? Come on, Monica. 'Fess up. I can tell you've got something to tell me," the first girl pried.

I gasped. One of the girls in there was indeed Monica! Was she really saying those things about Jim? I strained harder to hear as much as possible.

"No, not really, I guess," Monica answered.

"Come on girl, don't hold out on me," the other girl coaxed. "There *is* someone else, isn't there? Who is it? Gordon Lewis? Conrad Overman?"

"No, no. Oh, goodness no! Conrad Overman? Really. Give me a break," Monica scoffed.

"I don't think Conrad's so bad. But who then?" the other girl needled.

"Okay. I'm going to tell you something, but you mustn't repeat this to anyone. Promise? You have to really promise. Do you promise?" Monica demanded.

"Absolutely. You know you can trust me," the other girl vowed. "Come on. Spill it."

"Well, I don't know if I should," Monica teased, hesitating.

"Come on. *Tell* me!" the other girl pleaded. "I won't tell. Cross my heart."

"I wish she'd go ahead and tell her friend whatever it is, and then get out of there," the woman standing in line said to me, interrupting my concentration. "Other people need to get in there."

"I know what you mean," I stuttered in response. I really wanted to say, *Shh!! Can't you see I'm listening?* But that would be impolite, of course.

"Okay. Here goes. Vinny Shoals and I made out in the men's room at Clancy's Burgers," Monica confessed, giggling girlishly. "Can you believe it? It was so exciting! Jim would break up with me for sure if he ever found out. On top of everything else, he hates Vinny and thinks he's a low-life."

"Are you kidding me? Wow!" the other girl replied. "When did it happen?"

"Last week," Monica explained. "I went with Sally Johnson and Debbie Fowler to get a quick burger, and Vinny was at the restaurant with some guys he rides with."

"Vinny Shoals. He's got that big motorcycle, right? How'd you end up giving him the time of day?" the friend asked.

"I'm not sure. There's something dangerous and wild about him that excites me, I guess. And, he's so persistent and won't take no for an answer. I just can't resist," Monica continued. "Now, you promise you won't tell *anyone*. Right?"

"Right. Are you ever going to see him again?"

"I don't know. I met him at the Carmel movie theater a couple of days ago. He wanted to hang out in the back of the auditorium together, but I was with Debbie and it got too complicated. We've talked a couple of times on the phone since then, but I've been playing it cool," Monica explained. "I've got to keep Vinny under wraps for now. I'm not ready to let go of Jim."

"You're something else, Monica. I don't know how you do it," the friend said admiringly.

"I've got to get back to Jim now," Monica replied. "Remember your promise. Mum's the word. I mean it, Carol. I'd totally die if any of this gets out."

The two girls giggled, the door opened, and Monica and her girlfriend walked out. I stepped aside as they passed by. Neither girl gave me any notice. I'm not certain Monica even remembered having been introduced to me. From her demeanor, she had no idea she'd been overheard.

"At last!" the woman in front of me said as she hurried inside and slammed the door.

My head was dizzy and I was stunned at what I'd just heard. Monica had been unfaithful to *my* Jim. Or, should I say, to *her* Jim. How could this be? How could anyone be unfaithful to a wonderful person like him? Now that I had this information, what should I do with it? I didn't want Jim to be hurt. So, he should be told, shouldn't he? Didn't I have a duty to tell him? He'd probably thank me from the bottom of his heart. Then, he'd break up with Monica and come back to me. Yes, I should *definitely* tell him, I decided.

On the other hand, I remembered how lovingly he'd gazed at Monica at the picnic table tonight. He'd be crushed by this. So it must remain my secret. Yes, that was the right thing to do. Say nothing, and protect him. But if he ever found out I knew and didn't say anything, would he hate me? I couldn't risk that. So, I should tell him? Oh, this was too confusing and I didn't know what to do.

When I finally got into the ladies room, I was still debating with myself. When I returned to the picnic table, Randy and Daniel were gone.

"What took you so long?" Emma demanded. "You've been gone for hours."

"There was a line, and I had to wait," I reported. "Where did Daniel and Randy go?"

"Buzz gave them a ride. He dropped by for some ice cream on his way home, and offered to take them back to his house," Emma explained. "They were fired up to get there to plot their plans for tonight, and couldn't wait. I think Randy's pretending he's doing spy work, like Napoleon Solo on the *Man from U.N.C.L.E.* or something."

"I didn't go with them because I don't support Randy's crazy notion about busting into that hangar tonight," Luke said. "That boy would jump over the moon for you, Vanessa. You know that, don't you? He's one lovesick puppy. But don't feel guilty if he gets in trouble trying to defend you. You can't help it if you're a modern Helen of Troy."

"Oh, I just hate that word love!" I blurted out, exasperated. "Love screws up everything."

"Whoa! Where's this coming from?" Luke exclaimed. "You were a normal girl a few minutes ago. Normal for you, I mean. What happened in the ladies room?"

"I just overheard something I wish I hadn't. That's all," I complained.

I knew I was perilously close to revealing to Luke and Emma what I'd just heard. But I needed to talk to someone about it. It was too hard to keep it to myself.

"What did you overhear? Was it naughty?" Luke asked with a grin. "Was it hot? I hope it was steamin' hot. Give me all the details. Don't leave anything out."

"Oh, cut it out, you pervert," Emma scolded her sibling. "I think I saw Monica come out of the ladies room a few minutes before you returned. Was it something involving her?"

I looked over at the table where Monica and Jim had been sitting, and was surprised to see it empty.

"Did Jim and Monica leave, too?" I asked.

"Yeah. They left just a few minutes ago," Luke said. "Why? Does it have something to do with them? Did Emma guess right?"

"Yes. I probably shouldn't tell you, but I'll explode if I don't tell someone," I began. I wrung my hands and nervously pushed my hair back from my face.

"Well, what is it?" Luke pressed. "Come on! Tell it to Daddy."

I paused. "I heard Monica tell a friend that she made out with Vinny Shoals at Clancy's Burgers last week," I said quickly. *There, I had let it out of the bag.*

"What?!" Luke shouted, throwing back his head. "That tramp! I knew she was no good. No girl that good looking can be trusted."

"That's totally unfair!" Emma protested. "Plenty of beautiful women are perfectly trustworthy."

"Name one," Luke challenged her.

"Let's see. . . um. . . I know! Marilyn Monroe. She never cheated on Joe DiMaggio."

"As far as you know," Luke countered.

"Jackie Kennedy! How about her? She never cheated on President Kennedy," Emma offered.

"Yeah, but she should have, just to get even," Luke said.

"Hey, you guys," I interrupted. "Could we please get back to my dilemma? What do I do now? Should I tell Jim?"

"No. Definitely not," Emma stated with conviction. "You should stay out of it."

"I don't know," Luke pondered. "We men have a code to always watch out for the other guy. If we find out about something another guy needs to know, we tell him. And, vice-versa."

"Luke, promise me you won't tell him," I pleaded. "It would devastate him if he found this out. He really loves Monica. I could tell when I saw him with her tonight. Let me think about it first and decide what to do. Okay?"

"Yeah, okay, but she's a skank," Luke said. "I think he ought to know."

"Don't you want to rescue him and get him for yourself?" Emma asked. "If he knew about her and Vinny, he'd break it off with Monica for keeps. He'd be yours for the taking then."

"What? Don't tell me you're still in love with Jim. You're not, are you?" Luke demanded, looking at me with a questioning expression.

"No, don't be silly," I replied. "I care about him as a friend, that's all."

I studied Luke to see if he believed that whopper, and it appeared that he did. I was perfecting my ability to lie about my feelings, which I had observed from watching adults seemed to be a handy skill to have in this complex world. I was saved from further questioning when Uncle Evert flashed the van's headlights indicating it was time to head home. We threw our litter in the trash bin and strolled to the van.

I continued debating silently with myself all the way home about what to do. I finally concluded that I wouldn't tell Jim, because no matter how I sliced it, it just didn't feel right to be the one to burst his love bubble. So, I made up my mind that I'd never say a thing to him. He'd have to find out from Monica or from someone else. Not from me or one of my cousins.

Luke fiddled with the radio in his usual restless fashion most of the way back to the house. He finally tuned into a station playing "Your Cheating Heart" by Hank Williams, and settled on that. He turned around and flashed a devilish grin at me. I rolled my eyes and looked out the window.

CHAPTER FIFTEEN

Waiting for Disaster

*W*hen we returned to Emma's house, it was quiet and dark. Emma and I walked into the living room and plopped down on the couch. Luke walked to the window looking jittery. He nervously tapped the coins in his pocket with his fingers.

"I think I'll walk over to Daniel's house and see what the guys are scheming," he said finally. "Those dodoheads need supervising."

"Try to talk Randy out of this thing, will you?" I shouted to him as he walked through the kitchen to leave. "I don't want him to get in trouble on account of me." I was relieved Luke was going over to stop them.

"Women! They always screw up everything," he yelled back as he disappeared down the driveway.

"My brother isn't very progressive, I'm afraid," Emma said apologetically. "He was born in the wrong century."

"Yes, he would have made a great Viking," I observed. "As a modern man, he's a bit out of his element." Emma nodded in agreement, and we both smiled.

"Oh, I feel jumpy," I continued, sighing. "What's on TV? Maybe if we watch a show it'll take my mind off of things."

Emma walked to the TV and turned it on. *Nightmare Theater with Sammy Terry* was just starting on Channel 4. The live show was on every Friday night and showed old horror movies. Sammy Terry, the host, wore a ghoul costume with a black cloak, white face paint, and large black rings around his eyes. At the beginning of each show, he emerged from a creaking casket. His sidekick, a spider named George, was about the size of a basketball, and bobbed up and down on a cord over his head. Sammy was pretty hokey, but I didn't care. It was the only program that showed old horror movies, and he was endearingly home-grown.

Tonight, Sammy showed the 1957 movie *The Blob,* starring Steve McQueen. It was about a teenaged boy and girl who witness a jelly-like blob from outer space devour several townspeople. When they try to alert the adults, no one believes them. Finally, when the blob consumes a bunch of people in a movie theater, it's almost too late to save the town. The climax occurs in a classic diner in which the two teenagers are trapped by the blob, which has grown as large as the diner, having snacked on most of the town's inhabitants by then.

"That blob is kind of a silly looking monster. Too jiggly, like a giant Silly Putty," Emma remarked.

"Yeah, and Steve McQueen looks way too old to be a teenager," I noted.

"Why don't the adults in these movies ever listen to the kids?" Emma asked. "A lot of problems would be solved if they did." She furrowed her brow and appeared to be deeply considering the issue.

"I know. Just like in real life," I added.

The blob was finally frozen by fire extinguishers and flown by the Air Force to the North Pole and dropped off. Then, a giant question mark appeared on the screen. I guess we were supposed to wonder if the blob will thaw out some day and resume rolling around eating people.

"Fire extinguishers? Really?" Emma scowled. "I think it would have been neater if it was blown into a million little pieces by rockets or atomic bombs." She made a face and we laughed, which felt good.

Margret arrived a little later. She said she was picking up some fresh clothes to take over to Wendy's where she was staying for the night. She put a Herman's Hermits record album titled *There's a Kind of Hush All Over the World* on a stack of albums next to the record player on the floor in the living room. She said the album had just been released and was very popular. I took note of it because I really didn't know that much about popular music, but wanted to so I could be cool like her.

"Are you guys watching Sammy Terry?" Margret asked as she walked past the TV. "You guys crack me up with your horror movies and ghostie-things. If you want to see a good movie, we should go together sometime to see *To Sir, with Love,* which just opened. Sidney Poitier is in it. I saw it last night with Wendy, but I'd go back to see it again with you guys, if you're interested."

"That sounds great!" Emma replied enthusiastically.

"Isn't that the one about a bunch of British teenagers in an inner-city high school?" I asked.

"Yes. They have those beautiful English accents. I could listen to them talk all day. Well, gotta' go. You guys have fun." With that, Margret left.

There wasn't much on TV, so Emma turned it off. It was late and I was sleepy. I changed into my pink pajamas, and then crawled into the bed in Emma's room. The day had been long and eventful, and I was ready to go to sleep.

"Wonder what the guys are doing?" I mused out loud as I lay there. "I'm kinda worried that Luke hasn't come home yet. That could mean something bad has happened."

"It doesn't mean anything," Emma replied, yawning. "He's probably hanging out at Daniel's house watching TV and doing guy stuff."

"I hope so," I answered.

Just then, I heard the distinctive sound of Luke's heavy steps walk up the stairs into the kitchen. It sounded as though he went straight to his bedroom and slammed the door.

"Okay. Luke's home," I said. "I think I'll go ask him what happened." I started to get out of bed.

"Nothing happened. I told you those guys are all talk, no action. If something'd happened, he'd have made a beeline straight in here to tell us, you can be sure," Emma insisted.

"Okay. You're probably right. Nothing happened," I repeated. "Boy, am I relieved."

I thought about getting up to go talk to him, just the same, but fell asleep before I could motivate myself to get out of bed.

The next morning I was awakened early by the ringing of the phone on the desk in the living room. Uncle Evert answered it, and I could tell by the tone of his voice that something serious had happened. When he hung up, all hell broke loose.

"Everybody on deck!" he yelled. "On the double!" He stuck his head through the curtains and repeated his command to Emma and me.

"Dad? What is it? I'm sleeping," Emma moaned.

"Get out here. Now!" he commanded.

"Uh, oh," I said, sitting up in bed. "This could be bad. I knew it. I just knew it."

"Evert, what is it?" Aunt Louise asked, running from the kitchen.

Emma and I sleepily walked out to the living room and sat on the green couch, while Uncle Evert pounded on Luke and Lars's bedroom door. After exchanging a few words with their father, the boys stumbled out looking totally confused and bewildered.

"What on *earth*, Dad?" Lars demanded. "I was out late last night, for goodness sakes, and it's early. What time is it anyway?"

"You can go back to bed, Lars," Uncle Evert said. "I don't need you for this right now."

"Well, thanks," Lars replied, making a U-turn to go back to his bedroom. "I just hope I can get back to sleep after this joyful little interlude."

"Sit over there with your sister," Uncle Evert instructed Luke, pointing to the couch. Emma and I made room for him, and Luke sat down. Then, Uncle Evert rolled the desk chair over and sat directly across from us looking very angry. Aunt Louise stood behind him.

"Dad, I'm tired. Can we have this little powwow later?" Luke asked. His tousled blonde hair fell down over his eyes.

"Don't be insolent. You're in trouble, mister," Uncle Evert warned. "Uncle Forrest just called to inform me that your friend Randy Lampert was detained last night by the sheriff after the airport security guard caught him trying to break into one of the hangars."

"What?" Aunt Louise exclaimed. "And, here I thought Randy was such a nice boy. I'm usually a good judge of character, too."

"Apparently, Randy had a couple of accomplices who climbed over the airport fence and got away," Uncle Evert continued. "The authorities called Uncle Forrest this morning and filled him in on the details. He got a confession out of Daniel, who said he was one of the two boys who got away. He wouldn't say who the other boy was. Do any of you know who he was, by chance?"

"Uh, oh," I said under my breath.

"Dad, I can explain," Luke began. "It was me. Okay. There I confessed. But I was there trying to talk Randy out of doing what he was doing. Not to help him do it. I swear." He gave his dad a quick three-finger Boy Scout salute.

"What was Randy trying to do?" Uncle Evert asked.

"Some of us kids think Pete Scaggs is illegally smuggling endangered animals and using that hangar as his base of operations," Luke continued. "Randy was trying to get inside to get evidence. That's all. Not to steal or vandalize anything."

"What? That's preposterous!" Uncle Evert boomed, standing. "Pete Scaggs is a respected home builder and community leader. How on earth did you kids cook up such a crazy notion?"

"That's what I told everyone, but they wouldn't listen," Luke protested.

"Exactly *who* wouldn't listen?" Uncle Evert asked, peering at Emma and me.

Emma and I proceeded to tell Uncle Evert about all of the suspicious activities and sightings we'd experienced, including the animal collar with the *B* on it, and the suspicious invoice Daniel found. Uncle Evert explained away everything, just as Luke had done before. I even reminded Uncle Evert about the car that almost ran me down along the access road. With every argument we had, he had a logical counter-argument.

"But what about that invoice Daniel found?" Emma persisted. "It said Eastern box turtles right on it, didn't it? How do you explain that?"

"Did it ever occur to you kids that the phrase 'ten e. box t.' on the invoice Daniel found might mean 'ten each box transported' and *not* 'ten Eastern box turtles'?" Uncle Evert pointed out. "The phrase describes a quantity of a component used in construction that's been shipped. You're not disputing that Pete builds homes, are you, and might need building materials?"

"Oh," I said glumly. I had to admit it was disappointing that the invoice didn't mean what I thought it did.

"Some men who work for Pete Scaggs caught Randy lurking outside the hangar side door. It was lucky for Randy that he wasn't *inside* the hangar or he could have been charged with burglary and trespass. He can also thank his lucky stars that Scaggs isn't going to press charges, and asked the authorities to let him go," Uncle Evert told us.

"Thank goodness," I said softly.

"But Randy's been grounded by his parents for at least one month," Uncle Evert clarified. "He can't leave his house except to go to band camp.

And he's only allowed to go to that because his parents have already paid for it."

"Poor Randy," Luke said, shaking his head. "Can you believe they're *making* him go to band camp? That's inhumane!"

"As for you," Uncle Evert began, looking at us sternly, "I'm prohibiting all of you from going over to the airport for one month. Got that? One month!"

"But why am I being punished?" Emma protested. "I didn't have anything to do with what happened over there last night. Vanessa didn't either."

"No, but you're all too fixated on Pete Scaggs. You're being grounded for your own good," Uncle Evert explained. "You need to do other things that don't involve the airport."

"One month?" Luke complained. "What about the air show tomorrow? I've really been looking forward to that. This is the first one they've ever had. I gotta go! Don't forget I was trying to stop Randy. I'm one of the good guys in this."

"Dad, ple-e-e-ease," Emma chimed in. "We've all been so excited about the air show. Can't you please make an exception for that and let us go?"

Uncle Evert looked at Emma and his eyes grew soft and forgiving. This was the first I'd heard of the air show, but it sounded like something I'd really like to see. Even though Uncle Evert didn't address me specifically, I knew that whatever punishment he doled out to Luke and Emma applied equally to me. I was concerned that he viewed me as a bad influence on them, especially because it was obvious I was the first of us to become suspicious of Pete Scaggs. I didn't like being on Uncle Evert's list of troublemakers. I held my breath and hoped he'd answer yes and let us go. If he said yes, not only would I get to see my first air show, but that'd mean he wasn't too seriously mad at us, and more particularly — — not at me.

"Well. . . okay," he agreed, finally. "You can all go to the air show tomorrow, but that's it. You're not allowed at the airport for one month after that. I mean it. No exceptions."

"Yay!" Emma shouted. "Thanks, Dad." She jumped up and hugged him.

"And since you're so bored that you had to make up this complicated story about Pete Scaggs to entertain yourselves, I'm going to give you some work to do that'll keep you occupied and out of trouble," Uncle Evert continued. He looked suspiciously pleased with whatever he'd cooked up for us.

"You can't be serious," Luke muttered.

"Oh, but I am. You will each pick up one bushel of fallen apples in the orchard out back. When you've completely filled your bushel, you can stop. Now get dressed and have some breakfast, and then get directly outside to work," Uncle Evert instructed.

The three of us moaned in unison. Picking up apples? Banned from the airport? I was due to go home soon anyway, so not going over to the airport again wasn't so terrible. I definitely had no plans to go up in a plane again. But could it really be that Pete wasn't doing anything illegal? I thought I'd put together a fairly convincing case against him. I'd have to think about it further before I gave up. Even so, there'd be no more snooping on airport grounds, and that was disappointing.

After a quick breakfast of Crispy Critters cereal, the three of us went outside and found empty bushel baskets stacked in the barn. We each grabbed one and headed to the orchard. The orchard consisted of two rows of four or five old gnarled apple trees located near the barn. It didn't look as though the trees were tended very well. The apples were small and full of worms. I took my bushel and started picking up the half-rotten apples lying all over the ground beneath the trees. It was humid, but fortunately not too hot out yet.

"This is all *your* fault you know, City Slicker," Luke grumbled as we worked.

"What are you babbling about?" Emma asked. She stopped working and frowned at him.

"All I'm saying is that this whole thing about Scaggs was Vanessa's idea. If she hadn't gone all Nancy-Drew-Girl-Detective on us, I wouldn't be in trouble with Dad right now. And, I wouldn't be out here doing this godawful chore, either," he complained.

"Oh, just be quiet and fill your bushel," Emma lectured. "You're in trouble because of what you did, and you have no one else but yourself to blame."

"It's okay, Emma. You don't have to defend me," I jumped in. "I thought I had put the pieces of the puzzle together, but I guess I was wrong. Sorry."

"I'm not going to call you City Slicker anymore," Luke declared out of the blue, stooping down to pick up another apple.

"Thank you!" I said. "I was hoping you'd stop calling me that." I was delighted he was finally giving up mocking me with that name. I'd tried hard to fit in and prove I was just like them, and *not* a city slicker.

"No, from now I'm going to call you Nessie, just like they call the Loch Ness Monster in Scotland," he continued dropping several small apples into his bushel. "Yes, sir. Good ol' cousin Nessie. Just the thought of her coming to visit makes tough men shudder in fear."

"Luke! That's not funny. Stop it!" Emma snapped at her brother. "Just shut up and get to work."

"Yep. From now on you're Nessie the Loch Ness Monster," Luke proclaimed with fiendish delight. "Nessie, Nessie, Nessie," he said over and over, punctuating each word by tossing an apple into his basket as he said it.

I sighed, and continued plucking rotten apples out of the long grass.

CHAPTER SIXTEEN

The Spirits Speak

We continued picking up apples for what seemed like a very long time. To break up the tedium, every so often Luke threw an apple against a tree just to watch it break apart on impact. Just when my bushel was filled as far as I could fill it before it was too heavy to carry, a visitor arrived.

"Hello, everyone. What's this crop-picking thing you're doing?" Jim asked, strolling up across the grass. "I must say that I've never seen you work so hard, Luke. You must be getting paid pretty well for this."

My heart stopped. I was totally unprepared so see him, and felt unattractively sweaty and unkempt.

"Hi, buddy!" Luke replied, straightening up to greet him.

"I didn't mean to interrupt you," Jim said. "I thought you said to come over before I went to work. I can come back later this afternoon if that's better."

"No. I'm just about finished," Luke replied. "This is my father's idea of not sparing the rod to save the child. In other words, we got in trouble with him this morning, and now he's making us work like field hands to make amends."

"Uh, oh," Jim replied. "What'd you do *this* time?"

"I'll fill you in when we go inside," Luke said. He dropped one last small apple into his basket. "There. I'm done. What Dad thinks is full, and what *I* think is full, may not be the same thing. He'll just have to accept my interpretation of the term."

"Hi, Vanessa," Jim said. "You too, Emma. Are you both in trouble like Luke?"

"Hey. Her name's not Vanessa anymore. Didn't you hear? She wants you to call her Nessie from now on," Luke instructed. "As in Nessie the Loch Ness Monster. Go ahead. Try it."

"Vanessa's too beautiful a name to do that to it," Jim protested. "Why don't you grow up and stop tormenting your poor cousin?"

I gazed up at his tan face and looked into his hazel eyes. His dark hair was highlighted with light streaks from long hours in the summer sun, and framed his face as he looked down smiling at me.

"It's my job to torment people. Haven't you figured that out? All right. I'm done here," Luke declared, rubbing the dirt off his hands. "Let's go inside and I'll show you those comic books I got yesterday."

Luke marched off toward the house, leaving his bushel in the middle of the orchard.

"'Bye, ladies," Jim shouted as he followed.

"Don't let him get to you," Emma said when the screen door had slammed shut behind them. "Jim'll be okay, no matter what happens with that hussy. Guys like him are never heart-broken for long."

"I know," I agreed. "I'm not too worried about him, really. I was just thinking about how lucky Monica is, and she doesn't even know it! I'd give anything to have him look at me the way he looked at her at the Dairy Queen last night."

"What we need is to have some fun. I have an idea. Let's play a game," she said eagerly. "I know just the thing. I got it for Christmas, and I've wanted to check it out for a long time. Come inside and I'll show it to you."

We left our bushel baskets in the orchard and walked back to the house. Emma went into her bedroom and emerged holding a black box with the image of a mysterious blue shrouded figure on the top. Large white block letters spelling O-U-I-J-A were printed under the figure.

We sat down at the dining room table, and she opened the box and slid out a beige board with stylized letters and numbers printed on it. The words "yes" and "no" appeared in each of the upper corners, the alphabet appeared in two semi-circles across the middle, and numbers one through zero and the phrase "good-bye" were printed across the lower part. She also slid out a beige, heart-shaped plastic instrument with a circle cut out in the middle.

"It says here in the instructions that this plastic thing is called a planchette," she said, reading the box lid. "You place it down on the middle of the board and all of the players place their fingertips lightly on it. Then, you ask a question, and it moves on its own and spells out the answer."

"What? It moves on its own?" I asked, picking up the planchette and examining it. "How does it do that? Does it have batteries or something?"

"No, the spirits move it. They do! Really," she said, looking very sincere. "Let's try it out and you'll see."

"Okay. Sounds goofy, but I'm willing to give it a try," I replied. I had to see this in action.

She placed the planchette on the middle of the board, and then we placed our fingers lightly on it.

"Spirits, are you here?" she asked solemnly.

I looked down and stared at the planchette, waiting for it to move, but all it did was remain in the middle of the board where she'd put it.

"Maybe the spirits aren't here," I suggested after a few moments. "Maybe they sleep during the day, and only come out at night."

"Don't say that!" Emma chastised. "You're going to upset them, and then they won't speak to us. People say this always works, so please try harder." She closed her eyes, and then repeated softly, "Spirits. . . are you here?"

We sat silently and patiently held our curved fingertips on the planchette, but it still didn't move. My arms began to tire holding the awkward pose necessary to keep my fingers lightly on the device. I was just about to give up and call it quits when it began to move. Slowly at first, and then it swooped up to the upper left hand corner of the board and stopped abruptly over the word "yes."

"Look! Look! The spirits are here! The spirits are here!" Emma shouted excitedly. "It answered yes."

"Come on. *You* did that," I insisted. "'Fess up. There's no way that thing moved like that by itself."

"I did not. Honest! The spirits moved it. Honor bright," she said. She looked me straight in the eye and appeared genuine. I wasn't totally convinced, but didn't press the point further.

"Okay. Now that we know they're here, let's ask some good questions," Emma chirped happily, placing her hands back on the planchette. "What should we ask?"

"How about the name of the spirit?" I suggested. That seemed simple enough.

"Okay. Spirit, what is your name?" Emma asked in a low voice.

We stared at the planchette with our curved fingers resting along its edges. Nothing happened for several moments. Then, it slowly moved to the "F," and then to the "R," the "E," and finally, to the "D." Then it moved back to the middle of the board and stopped.

"That spelled Fred, didn't it? Is that your name, spirit? Fred?" Emma asked.

The planchette shot up to the "yes" in the upper left hand corner of the board and stopped.

"Fred?" I repeated. "Shouldn't it be something more exotic, like Mordecai, or Nicodemus, or Venetia?"

"Shh!" Emma admonished. "Fred can hear you. If he's insulted he won't communicate with us."

"Who's Fred?" Luke asked, walking into the room with Jim following behind. He looked at the table and pointed to the Ouija board. "What the heck are you guys doing with *that* thing? Don't tell me you're doing hokum in here. You'd better put that thing away. We don't want any homeless spirits looking for a home to come live with us, and that's what we'll get if you play with that thing."

"Go away and leave us alone," Emma scolded. "This is none of your business. Go hunt for gophers, or whatever. Just go away."

Luke pulled out a chair and sat down. "No. This looks more interesting. Come on, Jim. Let's see what's going on here. It might be fun."

Jim complied and sat down in the chair next to me. He pulled his chair close to mine so he could see the board. "Is that a Ouija board?" Jim asked. "I've heard about them, but I've never seen one before. You're supposed to ask it questions, aren't you?"

"I've got a question for it," Luke said, leaning toward the board.

"You've got to put your fingers on the planchette first, dummy," Emma said. "Like this." She placed her fingers on the device, and then Luke, Jim, and I followed suit.

It felt good to be so near Jim. We were practically touching shoulder-to-shoulder as we leaned forward to reach the planchette. I wondered if he really needed to sit as close to me as he did, but I didn't mind. He gazed at me and smiled, and appeared to be having a good time.

"Okay. Now that we have our fingers all dainty-like on this plastic thing," Luke began, "I want to ask the spirits if the St. Louis Cardinals are going to win the World Series this year."

"That's a dumb question," Emma chastised, abruptly pulling her hands off the planchette. "The spirits don't answer questions like that."

"Why not?" Luke asked, feigning ignorance. "Don't the spirits know everything there is to know? Well, I want to know. I might want to bet on the game."

"I've heard you're supposed to ask it questions about life," Jim said. "Such as whether you'll get married, or how many children you're going to have. Stuff like that."

"Those sound like sappy chick questions," Luke ridiculed.

"Fine. Then you can just go away and leave us alone," Emma said, scowling at him.

"Okay, okay. Don't get your pretzels in a knot," Luke returned. He placed his fingers back on the planchette. The rest of us did the same. "Here goes. Spirit, who here at the table has someone close to them with a secret?"

"His name is Fred," Emma whispered. "The spirit's name is Fred. You should show him some respect and use it."

"Shh!" Luke answered, holding his finger to his mouth. "You're not supposed to talk, are you? Won't that ruin Fred's concentration?" He smiled in a know-it-all way. Emma shook her head in disgust.

The planchette remained motionless for several moments, and then slowly moved to "J," then to "I," and finally, to "M." Then, it returned to the middle of the board and stopped.

"Jim? Did it spell *my* name?" Jim asked, with a look of surprise "Wow. That's weird."

"You can't fool the spirits," Luke said. "Someone you know must have a secret. Who can it be, I wonder? "

"I have no idea," Jim said, shaking his head. "I really don't. No one I know does anything they can't talk about."

Jim looked down at the board distrustfully as if it had suddenly come to life. I looked across at Luke and tried to catch his eye. I wanted to give him a look that would remind him not to reveal anything to Jim about Monica. The question he had just asked was treacherously close to spilling the beans. But he avoided looking at me.

"Well, then, let's ask Fred a few more questions," Luke continued.

"Okay. But I'm telling you. No one I know has a secret, unless it's you and you want to confess that you're moving this funny, heart-shaped thing," Jim said, laughing.

"Well. Let's just see," Luke said. "Fred, who has the secret?"

The planchette sat in the middle of the board, and then slowly moved to the letters that spelled "s-w-e-e-t-i-e."

"Sweetie? What does that mean?" Jim demanded. "This is all you, Luke, isn't it? You're moving that thing to say all of this. Well, very funny. Now let's go. I thought we were headed outside."

"No, sir," Luke said, holding up his right hand. "It's not me. Honest Abe. This is all the spirits talking."

"Oh, cut it out. Let's go to the creek like we talked about," Jim said. He appeared to be getting uncomfortable.

"Okay, but let me ask Fred one more question first," Luke said.

"Okay. But hurry and get it over with," Jim urged.

"Here goes. Fred, does Jim have a secret of his own?" Luke asked.

"Oh, cut that out," Jim moaned. He took his fingers off the planchette.

"Put your hands back there and let's hear Fred out," Luke insisted. Jim crossed his arms and looked disapprovingly at Luke. "You aren't scared about what Fred might say, are you?" Luke taunted. Jim slowly placed his fingers back onto the planchette. "That's better," Luke said. "Fred, let me ask you again. Does Jim have a secret?"

The planchette slowly moved to the upper left hand corner and stopped over the word "yes."

"So, you *do* have a secret!" Luke said. "I knew it! Man, this thing is better than a lie detector."

"Let's go," Jim said impatiently.

"Okay. Just one more question. Fred, is Jim's secret about a friend or someone he likes a lot?" Luke asked.

"What kind of question is that?" Jim grumbled. "If I can't figure out what you're asking, how can Fred?"

"Shh!"

Again, the planchette slid to the upper left hand corner and stopped over the word "yes."

"This is great!" Luke shouted.

"Okay. That's enough," Jim said, rising from his chair. "I'm out of here. I need to go to work soon anyway. Bye all," he said. He started toward the kitchen.

"Oh, come on. Take it like a man," Luke goaded as he followed Jim outside.

"Well, *that* was interesting," Emma said after they'd gone. "For a minute there, I thought Fred was going to tell him about Monica for sure."

"You mean *Luke*, not Fred——- right?" I said. "You do know that was all Luke's doing, don't you? This Ouija thing isn't real, and there's no spirit named Fred."

"I'm not so sure about that," Emma hesitated, looking down at the board.

"Well, anyway. About Luke. He got pretty close to telling, and I was anxious that he was going to," I said. "He promised he wouldn't tell Jim, and he'd better keep that promise. I'm counting on him to keep his mouth shut."

"What do you think about Fred saying Jim has a secret? Do you think it could be a secret about you?" Emma asked, still obviously preoccupied.

"Get real," I laughed. "Jim doesn't have a secret. Luke manipulated the board to say that. Besides, what kind of secret could Jim have about me?"

"You know. Maybe he still has a thing for you and wants to keep it a secret," Emma suggested. "He seemed real friendly when the two of you were sitting next to each other just now."

"I'm sure he doesn't care about me anymore," I said. "Besides, you're talking as though what the Ouija board says is real. It's just a game. One of us had to be moving the planchette, and it was probably Luke."

"I don't know," Emma said, thinking. "That planchette almost magically floated to those answers. I didn't feel anyone move it, did you? I think I'd feel it if someone had, especially if it was Luke. He's too rough to move something like that without feeling him do it."

I gazed out the dining room window and thought about what she was proposing. I had to be realistic. I was fourteen — — almost fifteen — — and Jim was sixteen. That was a big difference. I couldn't compete with an older girl like Monica who was his age. She was just too skillful at being enticing and alluring. I was just a skinny dork with almost no experience with boys. Maybe someday I'd know how to be more like her, but for now I was just too authentic, in Randy's words, for my own good.

My reverie was interrupted when I noticed Jim storming off outside. Moments later, Luke burst through the screen door and stomped up the stairs into the dining room, clearly agitated.

"I told you! Women ruin everything!" Luke shouted. "*Everything*!" He threw himself down into a dining room chair, crossed his arms, and frowned.

"What are you talking about? What happened?" I asked.

"I just told Jim the whole story about Monica, and he accused me of lying," Luke lamented. "Can you beat that?"

"What? You promised you wouldn't tell him!" I yelled. "How could you do that? You broke your promise to me. I'm furious with you!" I stood up, trembling with anger.

"Okay, okay. I don't need any more grief than I already have," Luke said, waving his hand dismissively.

I took a deep breath and struggled to regain my composure. "Tell me what happened," I said as calmly as I could after a few moments of silence. I needed to get the details from Luke, so I had to keep my temper in check, even though I wanted to explode at him.

"He wanted to know what had just happened with the Ouija board, and it just sort of slipped out," Luke began. "He said what I told him wasn't possible; that I was jealous of him having a girlfriend and was trying to ruin things for him. That I was immature. That what I said was a despicable thing to say about someone. He said he doesn't think he can be my friend anymore. I couldn't make him listen. He hates me now."

"Did you tell him that I overheard her talking to a friend at the Dairy Queen?" I asked.

"Yeah. He said either I made it up or you did," Luke answered.

"Me? Make it up?" I repeated. "You mean — — does he think I'm jealous and would do such a thing?" This was terrible. Now he'd never speak to me again, or even worse, believe in me. I never expected this. "You really fixed things, but good," I said angrily as I paced up and down the dining room floor.

"I know, I know. Cut me some slack, will you?" Luke said, running his hands through his tangle of curly blonde hair with an anguished look on his face.

I didn't know what to say. *What would Jim think of me after this?* As Emma put the Ouija board and planchette back in the box and tidied up the table, Luke and I rehashed his conversation with Jim. Both of us grieved the probable loss of our mutual good friend.

"Like I said," Luke murmured after a while, "women always screw things up."

"Oh, cut that out! It was a male spirit named Fred who tripped you up," I pointed out. "With a little help from a dumb human guy named Luke."

Luke looked over and scowled. "Women!" he grunted. "They're know — it — alls, too."

CHAPTER SEVENTEEN

The Strategy Session

*E*mma, Luke, and I were eating peanut butter sandwiches we'd made for lunch when my mother called. I'd been expecting her call, and dreading it because I wasn't ready to go home yet.

"I'll be out later today to pick you up," Mom said. "So be sure to have your things together. Okay?"

"Can I stay another day or two?" I asked. "I have things to finish here before I can leave."

There was no way I was going home until at least *something* was resolved. So far, not one thing had been settled. Not the foreclosure, or finding Bobo, or exposing Pete Scaggs and whatever he was doing — — and I was still convinced he was doing something illegal — — nothing. On top of that, my status with Luke had slipped from being City Slicker to Nessie Monster, and my status with Jim had slipped from possible-girl-friend to might-as-well-be-dead. Yes, without question, things were more messed up than ever.

"What do you mean you have something to finish?" Mom asked. "Are you and Emma doing crafts or something?"

It was too complicated to explain to her right then and there. For one reason, Emma and Luke were sitting at the dining table listening. So I didn't waste any time, and played my best card.

"The air show is tomorrow, and I want to go," I said. "All the cousins are going and so is everyone in Hamilton County, for that matter. You don't want me to be the only person to miss out, do you?"

"Okay, honey," she said after a brief pause to think it over. "Your father and I discussed coming out to the air show ourselves. You can stay until then, and we'll take you home afterward. So be ready to go just as soon as it's over."

We chatted a little longer, and then she said she had to get off the phone. I hung up and walked to the table and sat down. At this very moment, the radio in the kitchen played the melodic strains of "The Green, Green, Grass of Home" sung by Tom Jones, which I thought was an interesting coincidence.

"I know about the foreclosure, you know," Luke said out of the blue to Emma and me. We were alone in the house, so he must have felt it was safe to bring it up. "And I know you know about it, too."

"You do?" Emma asked, surprised. "I thought I was the only one besides Mom and Dad who knew. How'd you find out?"

"Dad told me yesterday when I rode with him to a quick appointment in Anderson," he explained. "He told me you know about it, too."

"I've been trying to think of a way to find the money to pay it off," Emma sighed, "but so far, I haven't come up with anything. Even Vanessa has tried to think of something to do."

"I know," Luke lamented. "I offered to sell my coin collection, but Dad said it wasn't worth enough to be of any help."

"I said I'd sell my jewelry, but Mom said the same thing — that it wasn't worth enough," Emma said wistfully.

The radio playing in the kitchen went to the mid-day news. The announcer said that the United States conducted a nuclear test yesterday at the Nevada Test Site, while the USSR did the same thing yesterday at its nuclear test site in Eastern Kazakh, USSR.

"Are President Johnson and Premier Brezhnev blitzed on weed, or something?" Luke exclaimed, turning his head to listen. "If this nuclear rat race keeps going the way it is, it won't matter whether we keep the farm or not. We'll all buy the farm, if you know what I mean."

"Oh, Luke," Emma said tearfully. "Don't try to be funny. This is serious. I don't want to have to move back to New Jersey."

"Don't worry. They can't get rid of the Larsson family *that* easily," Luke said defiantly. "They don't know who they're messing with." He held up his fist in a show of defiance.

"Well, I do, you big gasbag!" Daniel said, poking his head through the screen door. He entered the dining room, looking cheerful, as usual. "What's going on?" he asked.

I couldn't believe it. We were told that Daniel was grounded after what happened at the airport last night. How did he break free?

"Bro! Good to see you!" Luke exclaimed, jumping up and giving him a fist bump. "But does your father know you're over here? Aren't you grounded? Won't you get in trouble if he finds out you've flown the coop?"

"He knows I'm over here, and it's okay," Daniel confirmed. "I explained to him what happened last night — — that I was just watching and had no intention of going into the hangar with Randy — — and he cooled off a little. I'm banned from going over to the airport for a month, but he said I could go to the air show tomorrow, as long as I do chores for him."

"Pretty much the same here," Luke chimed in. "My dad was really angry. We're not allowed to go over to the airport for a month either, except to the show. Emma negotiated that for us using her fake tears. He even made me pick a bushel of apples in the orchard this morning. Totally unfair!"

"Don't forget Emma and I were out there with you," I added. "And we weren't even part of your band of hooligans last night."

"Hooligans, eh?" Luke mocked. "That sounds like a city slicker ten-dollar word."

"Hey. I want to tell you something," Daniel said, getting serious. "I heard those two guys in the hangar talking last night before you and I had to run when security arrived. You had already taken off for the fence. I waited to hear what they were talking about, and that's why I stayed and almost got caught."

"Cool. What were they talking about? Where they were going to go to pick up girls later?" Luke asked with a wink.

"Cut out the bull," Daniel said, still very serious. "They said they're going to load the plane with special cargo during the air show when everything's busy, and then take off as soon as the runway clears during the intermission."

"Sounds fairly routine. What else did you hear?" Luke said, feigning a yawn.

"I don't think you heard me," Daniel persisted. "They're going to load *special* cargo. During the show when no one will notice. *Special cargo*. Are you hearing me?"

"Okay," Luke answered dryly. "Still sounds routine to me. If I'm supposed to get excited about that, I think I must be missing something."

"You're definitely missing something, brainiac," I said. "If they have to use the show to distract people from seeing what they're loading on the plane, doesn't that raise suspicions?"

"Perhaps, but it's a stretch," Luke said. "I'm not trying to rain on your parade or anything, but I'm just not too jazzed by what you heard. My dad convinced me this morning when we had our little love chat that Pete's not up to anything remotely illegal."

"Well, this sounds suspicious to me," I said. "What did they mean by special cargo? Couldn't that mean exotic animals?"

"Nessie, there you go again. You really ought to volunteer to be a junior detective for the Indianapolis police department when you go home," Luke scoffed. "You're obsessed with this stuff! I need more to convince me, especially after Dad gave us good reasons for everything."

As if on cue, the phone rang. Luke walked over to the desk and answered it. His eyes became large with surprise when the person on the other end spoke. Emma, Daniel, and I became silent and listened in. Who could it be to cause such a reaction?

"Randy! Is that you?" Luke shouted into the phone. "Bro, what happened last night? I heard they caught you when you were almost inside the hangar. I thought you promised not to go there. What happened?"

I tried to piece together what Randy was saying based on Luke's responses, but Randy did most of the talking. When Luke finally hung up, I couldn't wait to hear what Randy had said.

"He said he couldn't talk long because his parents were real angry and would only let him make a quick call," Luke recounted. "He wanted to tell me that he never went inside the hangar. And, that just before Scaggs' guys grabbed him, he was able to get a good look inside through the side door."

"Yes? Go on. What did he see?" I asked, hanging on his every word.

"He said he heard a large bird, and saw two men handling a very large reptile that looked like a small dinosaur."

"A small dinosaur?" Emma repeated. "That's crazy. Dinosaurs don't exist anymore."

"What could he have seen?" I pondered.

"I don't know. A Komodo dragon, maybe?" Daniel suggested after giving it thought.

"Is that an endangered species?" Emma asked.

"Yes, I think so," Daniel answered, nodding. "Poachers hunt them for their skins, which is illegal. In fact, I think even buying and selling them alive is illegal." Daniel was an avid reader of *National Wildlife* magazine, and knew these things.

"So, why would Pete Scaggs have one in his hangar if he's just a home builder and not doing anything else?" I asked, driving home my point. "Did Randy see anything else odd or suspicious in there?"

"Not really," Luke said. "Except, that he thought it was strange there wasn't much more in there. No stacks of wood, or flooring, or stuff for building like you'd expect to see when the hangar is used to transport and store building supplies."

"I think we need to look into this," I suggested. I didn't like the idea of someone making money trading vulnerable animals. If I could stop it, it was up to me to do whatever it took.

"Oh, no. You're not channeling Nancy Drew again, are you?" Luke moaned. "You're *always* trying to catch the bad guys. Why don't you go back to playing with your Barbie dolls? You're a lot less trouble when your Barbie is chasing after Ken to be king of the prom."

"There could be a hideous, cruel crime going on your *own* backyard that exploits helpless animals close to extinction, and you mean to tell me you're just going to sit by and let it happen? Some he-man you are!" I shouted loudly with as much indignation as I could muster.

"Well, Nessie, how do you suggest we go about stopping it? We can't even go over to the airport now. No, I think we should just stay out of it. It's not our concern. I'd care a lot more if they were illegally smuggling guns or sex slaves. I could really get into that."

"Dad said we could go the air show," Emma pointed out. "We could look around while we're at the show, couldn't we?"

"Yeah, my dad will allow me to go to the air show, too," Daniel joined in. "That'd be the one time we could look around. If Bobo's still around, maybe we could find and rescue him before it's too late. I'd really like to try."

I nodded in agreement. We had a loophole to work with, and I, for one, was planning on working it. I didn't know how, but I would think about it between now and tomorrow and come up with a plan. Daniel looked so distressed about Bobo. We had to help him.

"By the way, Randy also asked about you, Nessie," Luke added, batting his eyelashes playfully.

"What?" I replied. "He did not. You're just playing with me."

"Yes he did. Pinkie swear. He asked if you're okay. I think he's worried someone will try to bump you off again. He just wouldn't be able to go on if that happened, you know. He's totally ape over you." Luke continued. I made a sour face to show my displeasure.

After learning about what Randy and Daniel heard and saw at the hangar, I was more eager than ever to go to the air show and look around. Unfortunately, it was almost a whole day away. I didn't know how I was going to avoid jumping out of my skin with anticipation until then.

"What are you kids doing in here on such a great day?" Uncle Evert asked, looking mildly surprised to see us in the house as he walked in from the barn. He seemed particularly surprised to see Daniel. "Daniel. I didn't think I'd have the pleasure of your company until at least Christmas, but I'm glad to see you. Does your dad know you're here?"

"Yes," Daniel replied. "I'm on probation, but he chilled out and said I could come over. He's cool with it."

"Glad to hear it," Uncle Evert replied. He looked through the desk for something, and then went back outside.

"What's gotten into you, dude?" Luke asked Daniel.

"What do you mean? Lay it on me, brother," Daniel replied.

"What's all this 'peace and love' talk you're using lately?" Luke asked. "Cut it out. It's getting on my nerves."

"I've been watching *Where the Action Is* on TV with Wendy, and picked up a few boss, hip words, that's all," Daniel explained. "I've been square for too long. I'm a groovy, far-out cat from now on."

"Well, cut the flower power talk or I'll send you way, way out!" Luke admonished. "You dig?"

"What an uptight square you are," Daniel whispered under his breath "Smell the daisies, and don't hassle me, man. Mellow out."

"What did you say?" Luke asked, turning slowly toward Daniel. "Do I need to set you straight with a five-minute treatment?"

"Uptight bourgeois," Daniel retorted. He seemed to know that the dreaded five-minute treatment was inevitable, because he darted from his chair and ran through the kitchen and outside without waiting for a further reply from Luke. True to form, Luke followed closely on his heels. "Make love, not war!" Daniel yelled as he ran, laughing. "Outta sight, dude!"

"There they go again," Emma sighed. "I really don't understand boys at all."

I walked to the screen door to see what was happening, and barely missed being hit in the face by an apple that whizzed by my head just as I walked outside. The boys slung them at each other fast and furiously. The apples in the bushel baskets we'd gathered earlier provided them with almost unlimited fire power.

Uncle Evert came around the side of the garage, clearly displeased with the mess they were creating. I decided it was best to get out of the way and go back into the house. Lars was now at the piano playing something classical that sounded beautiful, but complicated and difficult to play. I didn't even realize he was home. That was often the way it was here. Folks came and went, and half the time I had no idea where they'd been or where they were going.

"Well, I guess we won't be able to watch TV if Lars is going to play now," Emma said.

"At this time of day on Saturday," Lars said, raising his voice to be heard over the music, "all that's on is *Midwestern Hayride*, so you're not missing anything, trust me."

"I guess he's right. How about if we play a game instead? Or, we could go fish down at the creek," Emma suggested. "What do you want to do?"

As I pondered which option was the most appealing, the red Chevy Bel Air pulled up, and Margret and Wendy got out. They were both dressed in white blouses with large collars and long gathered sleeves, short skirts, and crocheted vests. You could easily see they were good friends and read the same fashion magazines. Each carried a light blue L. S. Ayres department store shopping bag, which caught my eye.

"Hi, you guys," Wendy said as she and Margret walked through the kitchen. "What're you doing?"

"We're not sure," Emma replied. "Did you guys go to Glendale? What'd you buy?"

"I picked up some green opaque hose. They're a new look," Margret said. "Wendy bought a long Vera scarf in red, white and blue. Very cool."

Margret took her shopping bag to her bedroom, and then returned to the dining room. "We saw a matinee screening of *Thoroughly Modern Millie* at the Carmel Theater this afternoon," she said. "You know, the musical with Julie Andrews and Mary Tyler Moore that takes place in the twenties. It was released a few months ago and we finally got around to seeing it. It was cute."

"Oh, yeah," I said. "I've seen some advertisements for it on TV. It looks really good. The flapper fashions Julie Andrews wears in it look like something you'd see in *Seventeen* magazine today." I loved that magazine and was always glad when my older sister bought one.

"I agree," Wendy said, sitting down at the table and crossing her legs. "Some really groovy fashion looks."

Margret went into the kitchen and returned with two cold bottles of Tab soda pop and handed one to Wendy.

"Thanks, sweetie. I'm so thirsty!" Wendy said, taking a large gulp of the beverage. "I didn't get my usual Coke at the theater. The soda fountain wasn't working. I ended up with just Twizzlers."

"You were gone an awfully long time to come back with just Twizzlers. I thought you'd gone to meet a new boyfriend," Margret teased.

"I wish! It took some time for them to declare the fountain a lost cause," Wendy explained. "On top of that, I was distracted by seeing two people having a secret rendezvous. I forgot to tell you about that, Margret."

"What? How do you know it was a secret rendezvous?" Margret asked.

"They made some effort not to be seen," Wendy said, taking another sip of her soda. "And, they were very, *very* cozy."

"Tell me more! This sounds intriguing," Margret urged.

"Well, I was on my way back into the theater and noticed the side exit door was open. They don't usually keep that open and I thought someone should close it. So, I went over to check it out. That's when I saw them."

"Who? Anyone I know?" Margret inquired. "What were they doing?"

"They had their backs to me and I couldn't see their faces. The guy had tattoos and long dirty-blond hair, and the girl was petite with long brunette hair," Wendy continued. "They were canoodling like crazy standing there in the open door."

"Uh, could it have been Monica Calhoun?" I inquired. It was a long shot, but why not ask?

"Is she the girl Jim Sparks is dating?" Margret asked.

"Yes," I answered softly. Did *everyone* know they were dating?

"I guess it could have been her. I've seen her at the pool at Northern Beach a few times, but I don't know her that well. This girl was about her size and appeared to be about the same age. Like I said, she had her back to me and I couldn't see her that well," Wendy said.

"What happened then?" I asked.

"Oh, when I figured out what was going on, I turned around and went back to my seat. It's not cool to spy on people in situations like that," Wendy explained. "Besides, I'd seen enough."

Poor Jim! If that was Monica, her treatment of him made me angry. He deserved to be treated so much better. To think he'd defended her character to the point of ending his friendship with Luke — — and me — — only a few hours earlier. I assumed the boy Wendy described was Vinny Shoals, the guy Monica talked to her friend about at the Dairy Queen.

"See? The Ouija board tried to warn Jim about her this afternoon, but he wouldn't listen," Emma whispered to me. "Didn't I tell you the Ouija board always works?"

I smiled feebly at my cousin and nodded. I honestly didn't know what to think.

CHAPTER EIGHTEEN

Stars and Gooney Birds

Wendy, Margret, Emma, and I took a quick trip down to Hook's Drugstore on 86th Street so Wendy could purchase some Tangee lipstick. She'd read in *Glamour* magazine that it goes on clear and then magically changes to your perfect lip shade, and she just had to have some. It was fun hanging out with the two older girls for a change. I enjoyed looking at the perfumes, pretty hair barrettes, and all of the other odds and ends at the drugstore. I finally settled on purchasing a necklace made of colorful candy pellets strung on an elastic cord that you could wear *and* eat. You had to give whoever invented that a lot of credit. It combined two of my favorite things — candy and jewelry.

Margret drove. We dropped Wendy off at her house and then made our way back to Emma's house. When we walked in, Aunt Louise was in her bedroom with several large cardboard boxes on the bed and floor. She appeared to be filling them with clothes, shoes, and other things. Lars was sitting in the living room watching TV, and Luke and Uncle Evert were at the dining room table reading.

Emma walked to the door of the bedroom and silently observed her mother's actions for a moment. "Mom, what are you doing? You look like you're packing or something," she asked timidly, as though she knew she wouldn't like the answer.

"Yes, that's exactly what I'm doing," Aunt Louise answered bluntly, not pausing from her work.

"Why?" Emma asked.

"We're going to have to adjust to some changes around here soon, so I thought I'd take the bull by the horns and start packing tonight," Aunt Louise explained.

"But I thought the foreclosure wasn't supposed to happen," Emma said, her voice cracking with emotion. "You promised you'd do something to make it go away. Now you're packing? What's going on?"

Margret walked over to Emma and put her arm around her shoulders.

"Come on, tell me. What's going on?" Emma asked loudly, almost shouting.

"Hey Sis," Luke said, looking up from his comic book. "Grow up, why don't ya? This is the real world. Life is tough. It's over. You can kiss this place good-bye."

Emma bolted like a shot through the kitchen and out the screen door, slamming it hard behind her.

"Real sensitive, you dumb lunkhead," Uncle Evert scolded, closing his book with a bang.

"Someone should go after her," Lars suggested.

"Oh for crying out loud," Luke exclaimed, rising from his seat. "I'll go."

I was already half-way outside following her. In the dark of the night, I couldn't see her at first. Then I spotted her in the distance. She was walking fast in almost a slow jog across the yard toward the old graveyard beyond the barn.

"I was just trying to toughen her up," Luke explained apologetically when he caught up with me. "You got to be tough in this world if you're going to get through it. You know?"

I didn't say anything, because I couldn't think of anything helpful to say. Luke was probably doing his best to cope with the reality of the foreclosure just as Emma was, only Luke's method was more outspoken.

"Emma! Emma! Wait up!" I shouted. "Please wait. I don't know the way out here in the dark as well as you do."

She didn't slow down, or at least it didn't seem as though she did. She kept up a pretty quick pace to wherever she was going. Luke and I followed her through the yard next to the barn and through the wooden gate. The grass was tall and already wet from dew. After we passed through the gate, the grass turned to tall weeds that were crunchy under foot and prickly as I charged through them.

"Where the heck is she going?" Luke asked, continuing his long, quick strides.

I wondered the same thing. I had to pick up my pace to keep up with him.

"Emma!" Luke shouted. "Cut it out, will ya? I was just playing with you. Don't be a big drama queen. Emma!"

"Get lost. Stop following me!" she shouted from the darkness. "I hate you!"

It wasn't long before we were near the edge of the small Civil War-era graveyard; it had once belonged to a nearby church that burned many years ago. It was odd that the graveyard was located in the middle of the farm, but there it was. It wasn't terribly large, having only thirty or forty graves, and was encircled by a wrought-iron fence with a small gate stuck half-open. I wasn't too happy about being almost in the middle of it at this time of night, even having Luke with me.

"Emma!" I shouted again. "Please stop, wherever you're going. It's too dark and creepy out here. *Please?*"

She passed the graveyard, then turned and headed toward the ridge of land that overlooked the oxbow in the creek that cut through the farm.

"Aha! I think I know where she's going," I said triumphantly. Her change in course reminded me of the morning Aunt Louise took us on a walk to give us a pep talk.

"Where?" Luke asked. "I think she's flipped her wig. The last thing I need right now is a sister in a straitjacket."

I diverted my eyes and tried not to look at the graveyard as we passed. It was only out of love for my cousin that I would ever be that close to a place like that at this late hour.

It was amazing how dark it was. I was accustomed to night like it is in the city where there's always a random light from a house or street light to punctuate the darkness. Out in the country there were no lights, and the sky and everything seemed darker.

"Stop following me!" Emma commanded angrily when we finally caught up with her. "I want to be alone. Vanessa can stay, but not you, jerk face," she said, raising her chin in defiance toward Luke.

"Oh, come on," Luke said as sweetly as he was capable. "I didn't mean to hurt your feelings. You know that."

"You don't care that we might have to move," Emma said, tears welling up in her blue eyes. "You don't care about anything."

"Yes, I do!" Luke protested. "Do you think I want to move? This is where I belong, but what's the point of cracking up if we have to move?" He gazed around, and then continued. "Why'd you come way out here, anyway? You could slip and fall into the creek from up here if you're not careful. Especially in the dark like this."

"I came here because this is where the wishing tree is," she said, looking up at the branches of the old sycamore tree next to her.

"What the heck is a wishing tree?" Luke asked, looking around.

"Mom told us that your wish will be granted if you ask this tree," Emma said. "I came to ask it to help us stay here."

"Oh, for goodness' sakes. Are you gullible or what?" Luke laughed, shaking his head. "No tree can grant a wish. You didn't buy that stuff she said, did you? You know how Mom is."

"I thought you were supposed to make her feel better," I whispered to him, hoping Emma wouldn't hear me. "Let her have the tree thing."

"Don't you think I *know* a tree can't grant wishes?" Emma declared indignantly. "I know that. I'm not a child."

"Then why'd you run out here in the dark like this?" Luke asked.

She looked at us and said nothing, appearing to grapple within herself to find an answer.

"I just wanted to believe that it could. I guess I just needed to believe," she said, looking defeated.

She seemed so sad. I didn't know what to say or do. Should I hug her? I didn't know, so I just stood there, trying not to take a false step that would cause me to slide down into the creek.

"Oh, little Sis," Luke said, walking over and putting his arm around her neck in the stiff way a basketball player puts his arm around a fellow player. "Even if we have to move, it'll be all right. We'll all be together, and that'll make it okay. Right?"

"Ugh," Emma said. "That's what bums me out."

"That's the spirit," Luke said, smiling. "See? You made a little joke. That's a good sign. You've come back from the looney bin and rejoined us here on earth."

"Oh, leave me alone!" she said, gently pushing him away.

"Be careful," he replied. "I might go overboard into the creek, and then you'd feel really bad again."

"No, I wouldn't!" she said, smiling. "That'd make me laugh. Hard."

"Sure, sure. So you say," Luke replied. "I'm not going to sacrifice myself to find out."

"Hey, you guys. Look over here," I urged.

I pointed to a large slab of granite or limestone positioned near us almost at the top of the ridge. It was just about a foot off the ground, and was long and flat making it a perfect bench. I sat on it facing in the direction of the creek.

"I bet there's a great view from here during the day when you can actually see something," I speculated.

"Hmm. Let me see," Luke said, sitting down next to me so recklessly that he almost landed on me. "You can see a lot from here, even at night. See? Look through the trees. You can see the reflection of the runway beacon over at the airport in the clouds."

He pointed at the sky in the direction of the airport. I narrowed my eyes to see what he meant and concentrated. I saw the slightest faint glow of light in the otherwise black sky.

"Oh, yeah," I said. "Now I see it."

"Is there room for me on that rock?" Emma asked, sliding down next to me.

"Let's be quiet and listen to the night noises," Luke said softly, gesturing for us to be silent.

"It's kinda creepy out here in the dark, all by ourselves like this. Maybe we should get back to the house?" I suggested. "Has Big Foot ever been seen out here in these woods?"

"Shh!" Luke commanded. "Be quiet and listen to the night sounds." He gazed around with a contented smile as though he were listening to a secret symphony.

I obeyed and stopped talking. It was surprisingly silent. You could hear the water babbling down below, even though it hadn't rained much recently. In the distance, an owl hooted to another. The air was very still, and not a leaf moved in the trees. I heard the sound of twigs snapping far down below. Was there a small animal making its way along the edge of the creek?

"Did you hear that?" Luke whispered. "I think there must be a raccoon or a possum down there coming out of the woods for a drink."

"As long as it's not a coyote coming to eat us," I joked.

"It's okay, City Slicker," Luke said. "You're not in danger." I was back to being City Slicker. Well, maybe that was better than Nessie.

"I just love nature," Emma sighed. "I hope I always live among trees like this, no matter where I live."

"Yeah," Luke said in a rare pensive moment. "The pioneers had it made. No concrete. No streetlights. No automobiles. Just this."

We all grew silent again. I relaxed into the moment, and enjoyed our high perch and the calm of nighttime in the woods. There was a lot to be said for a moment like this, sitting with my cousins listening to nature. I looked up at the stars and the silhouettes of the trees outlined against the deep blue sky. There was a special feeling to this place, I had to admit. Maybe Aunt Louise knew more than we gave her credit for.

But the tranquil moment didn't last long. Suddenly, a large plane flying so low that it barely cleared the treetops buzzed directly over our heads. It seemed to come out of nowhere. The roar of its engines and the glare of its bright running lights startled me, and I almost fell off the rock. It was flying so fast that it took only a few seconds to cross overhead and disappear beyond the trees in the direction of the airport and out of sight.

"What the heck?" Luke shouted, ducking instinctively. "That guy's flying too low, especially at night. What's he thinking? He could hit one of these grand old trees, or a power line, and crash right on top of us!"

"Where's he going? To the airport? Are planes allowed to land at the airport at night?" I asked.

"Yeah, they can, but it's not optimum. You could get in trouble because there isn't that much light over there, and it's difficult to judge your approach unless you're really experienced," Luke said. "Maybe he's flying in for the air show tomorrow. If he flies like that, though, he won't survive to make it to the show."

"That looked like a DC-3," Emma said. "Wasn't it?"

"Yep. It was a gooney bird," Luke confirmed. "Good job, little Sis. You've got what it takes to be a plane spotter."

"What's a plane spotter?" I asked.

"Don't ask," Emma said. "It's a military thing."

"Why did you call it a gooney bird?" I continued. "I thought you said it was a DC-3."

"That's what the military guys used to call the DC-3 during World War II because it looks like one," Luke explained.

"That's a weird thing to call it. Why was it flying so low?" I wondered out loud.

"I don't know," Luke answered. "Maybe the pilot's drunk. Or . . ."

"Or, what?" I persisted.

"Or, maybe he doesn't want to be detected on radar," Luke speculated. "If a plane flies really low, it can't be picked up on radar. The radar gets confused between what's a plane and what's stuff on the ground."

"Does the airport have radar at this time of night?" I asked.

"No, but the big airport in Indianapolis could track it on their radar at this time of night unless it flies really low, like I said," Luke explained. "Their radar extends this far north."

"Why wouldn't the pilot want to be picked up on radar at the Indianapolis airport?" I asked. "Isn't it safer to be on radar so you don't crash into another plane?"

"I guess that would depend on whether the pilot is more concerned about safety or about flying undetected," Luke reasoned.

"Pete Scaggs has a DC-3, right?" I asked.

"Right, Nancy Drew. Are you going to make something out of this, too?" Luke teased.

"Not necessarily," I answered. "Just tucking it away in my brain. But that plane *could* have been his gooney bird, right?"

"Oh, here she goes again," Luke said with a sigh. "Maybe yes, maybe no."

"He might have reason to take the risk of flying so low if he was carrying illegal cargo and didn't want to be picked up on radar, correct?" I continued.

"Maybe. I guess we'll never know for sure," Luke answered. "C'mon you guys, it's late. Let's go back to the house before Mom and Dad think we've all drowned in the creek." He stood and stretched.

"Okay. I feel a little better now," Emma said, standing. "I'm ready to go back and face the boxes. Only, stop saying we're moving, 'cause we're not. Got that?"

"Whatever it takes to keep the men in white jackets from taking you away, Sis," Luke said, smiling.

I nodded to Emma and she managed to return a half-hearted smile. If she and Luke ended up moving, we might not have another night to sit together on that rock ever again. That thought made me sad. Something had to happen to change things. But what?

We carefully made our way in the dark back down the ridge, past the graveyard, and through the field behind the barn to the house. Emma and I hummed the melody of "Up, Up and Away" by The Fifth Dimension on the way back. I think it did us all good to visit the wishing tree tonight, even if we didn't hear any answers coming from its lofty branches.

CHAPTER NINETEEN

Things Are Always Clearer at Midnight

*A*s Emma, Luke, and I approached the house upon returning from wishing tree, I was startled by seeing the silhouette of a man standing in the shadows near the screen door. He stood just out of the range of the plume of light descending from the old light fixture perched over the door. It seemed odd he was loitering there, and we all slowed our pace cautiously as we walked up.

"Who's that?" Emma whispered nervously to me.

"Daniel! Is that you there?" Luke called out. "Why are you outside? Why don't you go inside?"

"It's not Daniel. It's me," Jim stammered, stepping into the light. "I. . .I thought I'd drop by to talk to you. . . if you have time, that is."

He had both hands in his pockets, and there was an air of urgency about him.

"You mean me?" Luke asked as we walked up.

"Yeah, you," Jim answered, taking his hands out of his pockets.

"Is everything okay?" Luke asked.

"Sure. Sure. I just need to talk to you about something," Jim pressed.

Emma and I went on inside and left the two boys alone. I was dying to know what urgent matter had caused Jim to drop by the house so late. I lingered just out of sight in the kitchen attempting to overhear their conversation, but couldn't make out much. I berated myself for behaving in such a sneaky way, but continued eavesdropping anyway. They finally walked out into the yard, thwarting my sleuthing, so I gave up and walked into the living room.

Aunt Louise's bedroom door was closed and there were no packing noises coming from there, so I assumed she must have given up and gone to bed. Uncle Evert wasn't around either, so he'd probably gone to bed, too. Lars was planted on the couch watching a big, splashy Hollywood musical on TV. I walked over and sat down next to him, preoccupied with thoughts of Jim. I didn't notice what was on TV until a scene with Marilyn Monroe caught my eye, bringing me back from my thoughts.

"What movie is this? That's Marilyn Monroe, isn't it?" I asked.

"It's *Gentlemen Prefer Blondes*," Lars answered, his eyes fixed on the TV screen. "Marilyn and Jane Russell are gold-digging night club singers looking for rich husbands on a cruise ship from New York to Paris."

I was just in time to see Marilyn perform "Diamonds Are a Girl's Best Friend" in a strapless pink ball gown surrounded by male dancers in tuxes.

"Oh, yes. I've seen this movie before," I replied. "I love it."

"Why are beautiful women so shallow? Why don't they look for men with brains and personality, instead of money? Or make careers in something besides modeling, like podiatry or taxidermy?" Lars asked.

"I wish you guys would stop talking so I can hear this song," Emma complained. She walked over to the TV and turned up the volume, and then returned to her seat in the chair with the carved serpent arms that everyone called the dragon chair.

Just then, the screen door opened and Luke stomped up the steps into the house. I looked over hoping to see Jim with him, but he was alone.

"Nessie Monster," Luke said in a high pitched, playful voice. "Mr. James Sparks would like to speak to you outside. If you can spare a moment for the likes of him, that is."

"Mmm. . .," Lars said, slyly smiling. "Sounds as though there's intrigue a-brewing."

"What is it?" I asked, quickly rising from my seat. I was both happy and surprised that he wanted to see me.

"Nothing," Luke replied. "He just wants to talk to you for a second. So, be a good little Nessie Monster and go outside." As I passed by him, he whispered, "Monica's history. Don't act like you know."

I nodded in understanding. My heart smiled. I knew it! Jim must have found out about Monica and Vinny. That was fast work, indeed. I took a deep breath and straightened my hair.

Jim was standing at the edge of the cement apron just outside the screen door when I walked outside. Now that he was in the light, I could see that he had on new jeans and a neatly pressed, light blue button-down shirt; the kind of clothes a guy wears on a date. His dark hair was combed neatly and fell across his forehead just perfectly. When he was clean and pressed like this, he looked even better, if that was possible. I was strangely nervous, and had to suppress my excitement and be cool.

"Hi, Vanessa," Jim said. "Thanks for coming to see me."

"Of course," I replied. "Is something wrong? You seem upset or something."

"Monica and I broke up tonight," he blurted, looking down dejectedly. "I found out she was seeing someone else behind my back. Luke was right all along. I guess you knew it, too."

I stood in silence. I didn't know what to say. Then, he continued.

"I came by to apologize to Luke for all the mean things I said to him when he tried to warn me about her. I want to apologize to you, too. I guess I was blinded by love. I didn't want to believe she was all the things he said."

"I'm so sorry," I said, reaching out to touch his arm gently. "Are you going to be okay?" I tried to look into his eyes, but he avoided my gaze and looked off into the distance.

"Oh, yes. I'll be okay," he said. He suddenly looked directly at me. My heart melted when his handsome eyes met mine. They revealed a vulnerable sadness that was unusual for him. It made my heart break.

"What can I do to help?" I asked softly.

I took a small step toward him. It was the only encouragement he needed. He reached out and drew me into his arms and held me tightly. He kissed my cheek softly, then placed his head on my shoulder. His strong arms almost completely enveloped me. I buried my cheek into his chest and closed my eyes. I detected the faint scent of his Canoe cologne that made the moment even sweeter.

We lingered in an embrace for several seconds. I didn't want to be the first to pull away, so I continued holding him, enjoying being able to show the feelings I'd hidden for so long. After a while, he looked down and took my hand.

"I need to confess something. I said things about you to Luke that I regret. I said you made up bad things about Monica because you were jealous. I'm sorry about that, I really am. I should have known a person like you wouldn't lie. Besides, it was totally idiotic of me to think you'd be jealous." His eyes revealed a combination of guilt and regret.

I pondered what to say. Since he brought it up, this seemed like a good time to tell him how I felt. He probably already knew. But I was afraid if I actually put my emotions into words, our friendship might be ruined, or he'd laugh at me. Still, I had to let him know. I had to be brave and say what was in my heart. This seemed like the time to do it, so I went for it.

"I *was* jealous. Terribly jealous," I confessed. "You must know how I feel about you, Jim. I care about you — a lot. I'd never make up a story like that — a story that would hurt you so viciously."

"You? Jealous?" he repeated. "I don't believe it."

Before I could say another word, he leaned down and kissed me. It was a long passionate kiss. I'd never been kissed quite like that before, even by him. Perhaps it was triggered by his ardor for me, or maybe it was fueled by pain and a damaged ego. Whatever the motivation, it was a wonderful kiss. I felt as though I were soaring, and I forgot everyone and everything else. I wasn't even self-conscious about whether I was beautiful or alluring enough for him. I was too swept away to think about anything at all. I didn't even care if anyone saw us. I was simply going to claim this moment for myself and enjoy it. Time stood still as we shared the tenderness.

"You must think I'm a real cad to break up with Monica, and then come here and be with you like this, all in the same evening," he said, pulling away slightly to speak.

I gazed into his eyes. The dead look he'd had only minutes before was replaced by the vital and happy demeanor I'd always known him to have.

"No. Not at all. It's okay. I understand," I reassured him. At that moment, I didn't care why he kissed me. That was how thoroughly smitten I was.

"Let's find a place to sit down and get away from this light," he said, squinting at the bright bulb over the door where insects were swirling in chaotic flight. "These moths are driving me crazy."

We walked hand-in-hand, our fingers entwined, to the yard behind the garage. A small bench made from a split log positioned under an elm tree made a perfect place for us to sit. We settled down and he put his arm around me. I sat close and snuggled against his broad chest.

"Look at those stars up there," he said, peering skyward. "Just think of all the people through the ages they've looked down on, just like us. They must wonder why people down here keep making the same mistakes, over and over, century after century."

"There's nothing wrong with making mistakes, as long as we learn from them. Right?" I asked. "That's what I've always been told, anyway."

"Yeah, I guess so," he agreed, his voice becoming melancholy again. "Maybe that's the human condition, you know? To keep hoping to get whatever it is we desire, even if it's futile."

"If we weren't persistent, though," I observed, "we'd never get what we want. Don't you think?"

At that moment, I was feeling pretty good about the pay-off for my own perseverance. Here I was nestled against the boy of my dreams after waiting so patiently. Jim didn't seem as sold on the concept, though.

"Right!" he said with forced enthusiasm. "What is it that you desire, my dear Vanessa?"

At that moment, I could think of only one thing — him! But I would never be bold enough to say it.

"I don't know," I said, blushing. "How about you?"

"Well, let's see," he said, pausing to think. "When I was younger, I wanted to grow up to be a professional baseball player."

"That's great!" I exclaimed. "Who knows? Maybe someday you will."

"Nah, I don't think so," he said, looking off into the distance again. "I worked hard at it. My dad even paid a guy to help me work on my game, and sent me to some baseball camps. But I never got to the level to be able to play professionally someday. I finally figured that out and gave up. It's okay, though. Learn and move on, I always say."

"There'll be another dream take its place, right?" I suggested, trying my best to put a positive spin on things.

He looked at me and smiled. "Yeah, but try to convince my dad of that."

"What do you mean?" I asked.

"Oh, you know. The usual parent stuff," he began. "Dad had his heart set on seeing me play ball professionally. He took it hard when he could see it wasn't going to happen. I don't think he'll ever forgive me. He doesn't say it, but I feel it. That bothers me — a lot."

"I'm sure he's still very proud of you," I said, totally meaning it. "I mean, you're a great person, Jim. I'm sure he knows that. He must!"

Jim let out a quick laugh. "Oh, who knows? Why am I boring you with this stuff, anyway? What is it about you, Vanessa? I spill all my secrets to you, and you always make me feel better. That's why I have such a yen for you." He leaned down and kissed me playfully on the nose.

After that, we sat quietly on the bench, huddled together and being near. Every now and then he'd give me a soft and gentle kiss. It seemed natural to be with him, and I was uncharacteristically relaxed. He was everything I wanted in a boy, and, at last, he wanted me. He needed me, and I wanted to give him the love I had in abundance. I wanted to rid him of the sadness Monica had caused. The happy stars in the clear, dark sky danced over our heads as the minutes ticked away and we traded secrets and laughed. I didn't want this moment to end — —ever. If only it could be that way.

"Well, I should be going," he said finally. He looked at me and grinned, his handsome eyes twinkling. "After one more kiss, that is."

He wrapped his muscular arms around me and gave me one last kiss. It seemed to go on and on. It was a special moment. Until Luke butted in, that is.

"Oh, cut the mush!" Luke shouted scornfully, standing at the corner of the garage looking at us with his arms crossed disapprovingly. His loud voice startled me, and Jim and I broke apart.

"What are you, a perv?" Jim chided. "Go away and stop watching us, you degenerate."

"Can't I leave the two of you alone for a moment? You're behaving like two horny teenagers at a church picnic," Luke scolded. "Now get away from my cousin, you masher."

"Okay, okay. Hold your fire. I was just leaving," Jim reassured. "Vanessa's good reputation is untouched."

"Hey. Don't forget the air show tomorrow. You can go with us if you behave. If not, we'll have to send you back home," Luke reminded him.

Jim rolled his eyes, and then took my hand and kissed it. It was a sweet gesture and made me giggle. "'Til tomorrow, my sweetness," he said.

He walked over to his bike propped up against the side of the garage and got on. I waved good-bye as he rode down the driveway. He waved back and blew me a kiss, and then disappeared into the darkness. Elated, I turned to go back into the house. Even though I'd just said good-bye, I couldn't wait to see him again tomorrow. I didn't know how I'd be able to calm down enough to sleep. All I wanted to do was replay our time together, enjoying thinking about each moment.

"You should be careful, Nessie," Luke warned as we walked back inside. He seemed uncharacteristically serious. "You shouldn't fall too hard or too fast for that guy."

"Why?" I asked. "He's a good person, isn't he? He's your best friend, after all."

"Sure. He's the best of the best," Luke affirmed. "But he just broke up with what's-her-face. He told me about how it went down, and it was pretty brutal. He's on the rebound, and might not even realize it. I'd hate to see you get hurt, even if you *are* a city slicker."

"Aw. You old softie," I said, gazing at him fondly. "I appreciate your concern, but I can handle myself. I'll be careful, I promise."

"Okay. That's all I ask," he replied as we trudged up the steps together into the kitchen. "My little sister almost went looney tunes tonight. I can't handle my cousin going mental with a broken heart all in the same evening."

"I'm really touched by your concern," I said, patting his shoulder playfully. "Deep down — really deep — really, *really* deep — you're kind of a good person, aren't you?"

"Oh, cut the mush," he said. "Save it for lover boy on the bike."

I laughed and squeezed his arm affectionately.

CHAPTER TWENTY

The Run-Up

T he next morning was another beautiful late-summer morning. I awoke to the distinctive sounds of Johnny Rivers singing "Secret Agent Man" on the radio in the kitchen. By the time he got to the lyric "Swinging on the Riviera one day/And then layin' in the Bombay alley next day," I was wide awake. Once again, Aunt Louise, or someone, had determined that the best way to get everyone out of bed in the morning was to play rock 'n' roll music as loud as possible.

I didn't get out of bed right away, though. I lay there for several minutes daydreaming about the wonderful time I'd had last night with Jim. I was so delighted to know he still had feelings for me. Feelings for skinny, dorky, undeserving *me*! And they were strong and passionate emotions, too. I shrugged off Luke's warning that Jim was on the rebound. I knew Jim, and I could tell he was genuinely attracted to me, just as I was to him. Yes, there was no question about it. Life was very good this morning, and I was happier than I'd ever been.

I finally climbed out of bed and shuffled out to the dining room table. Emma was already there in her pajamas paging through a *Richie Rich* comic book. Margret walked out of the kitchen and placed a large plate of hot biscuits and a jar of grape jelly down in the center of the table.

"There you go. Eat up you guys," Margret said. She was dressed in a long blue quilted robe. Her dark blonde hair was wrapped around curlers the size of cans of peas. In fact, it looked as though that's exactly what they were.

"What on earth's in your hair? Something out of the garbage can?" Lars asked as he walked over to the piano.

"I read in *Glamour* magazine that if you wrap your hair around empty vegetable cans, it will come out smooth and straight. So that's what I'm doing." She patted one of the cans in her hair playfully.

"Not to mention your hair will have the faint smell of succotash for days after," Luke joked, entering the room. "Mmm. Peas and corn. Sexy!"

"Very funny. Eat your biscuits and be quiet," she admonished, frowning disapprovingly.

"Hey, Liberace," Luke yelled to Lars as he began playing. "What time does the air show begin?" I was glad he asked, as I was very anxious to get going. "You're helping out over there, aren't you?

"Uncle Forrest told me that a precision parachute jump opens the show at about one o'clock," Lars replied. "I'll be heading over a little before noon. My services aren't required before then." He turned back to the keyboard and resumed making music.

"Well, that's when I'm going over, too, then," Luke said, grabbing a biscuit.

I ate a few biscuits, and then hurried into Emma's bedroom to select my wardrobe for the day —a yellow A-line skirt with a brown-and-yellow-striped mock turtleneck. Something special for a special day. Then, I went to the bathroom and pulled my long hair up into a ponytail, and slipped on a tortoise-colored headband. After applying some pink Yardley lip gloss and a little mascara, I was ready to go.

We had almost three hours to kill before noon, and I was impatient for the time to pass. I didn't know when Jim would arrive. I was so eager to see him that I was a little jumpy, and looked for him to appear every time I heard the slightest noise outside.

"Do you want to go fishing?" Emma asked. "We can walk down to the creek and get away from everyone until it's time to go over to the show."

"Sounds fine, but won't I get dirty if we go down there?" I asked cautiously.

"Good grief! You're such a city slicker," Emma complained. I shrugged. What could I say? I'd gone to some trouble to look pretty today, and I didn't want to ruin it. "I know a clean spot where we can sit. Don't worry," she added.

She ran into the kitchen and grabbed a half-eaten bag of Colonial-brand white bread to use as bait, and we walked outside. Just then, a small plane flew low over the house headed to the airport. As the morning wore on, the frequent buzzing noise of other small planes flying in for the show, together with the sound of traffic building up on Allisonville Road, created an atmosphere of excitement.

We grabbed two fishing poles out of the garage work room, and then took off toward the creek.

"Are you okay?" I asked as we walked along. She had seemed oddly distant all morning. "Are you upset or mad about something?"

"You should know," she grumbled, looking straight ahead.

"What? I don't know. What do you mean?" I asked, totally confused.

"I was with Luke in the kitchen last night watching you and Jim through the screen door," she said, sounding upset.

"Okay. So?" I coaxed.

"Well, you two looked pretty chummy. *Real* chummy, as a matter of fact," she continued, finally making eye contact with me.

"Yeah. He and I are friends again. Don't you approve? I thought you liked him," I said. I really didn't understand what her beef was about.

"It's just that. . . I just want to know. Are you and Jim a couple now? Because, if you are, everything will change, and I can't handle that," she lamented.

"What're you talking about?" I asked. I stopped and we faced each other. "Look. I have no idea if Jim and I are a couple or not, but even if we are, nothing will change between you and me. Nothing. We'll always be friends, no matter what. Even if you end up moving back to New Jersey."

"Yes, it will. Things will change. You just wait and see!" she exclaimed. "You'll want to be with him all the time, and you'll never want to hang out with me and do the stuff we used to do together. You won't be my best friend anymore. I know how it goes."

"Your. . . best. . . friend?" I repeated slowly. I was touched that she called me that. "We'll still be best friends no matter what, and I promise to keep doing stuff with you. You're stuck with me, I'm afraid. Okay?"

"Are you sure?" she asked, her brow furrowed.

"Yes. No matter what," I pledged with a sincere smile.

"Okay," she agreed, reluctantly. Then, turning toward me with a pleading look, she added, "Please don't grow up too fast, Vanessa. I don't want either of us to grow up yet. I like being a kid. Don't you?"

I laughed. "Silly. I'm only fourteen going on fifteen. I'm still a kid and so are you. We've got lots of time left to be kids, don't we? I'll refuse to grow up if you will."

"I'm goofy, I know," she said, laughing self-consciously. "It's just that when I saw you with Jim, I felt that you were changing, that's all."

"Not a chance! I have a feeling I'll be immature my whole life," I replied. We laughed and hugged, and then resumed our trek.

Emma led me to a fallen sycamore tree suspended over the creek where we could fish. She situated herself on the massive trunk first, and then I stepped up and gingerly scooted onto it, making certain I didn't snag my yellow skirt on its rough surface. We rolled the bread into little white dough balls to use as bait, and dropped our lines in the water. The movement of the ripples hypnotized me, and I daydreamed about Jim as I stared down into the green depths of the creek.

It was funny how different the world looked to me today. The sound of the water flowing in the creek, the puffy white clouds in the sky, the soft breezes of the summer morning — everything seemed more vivid and alive. This was the first day of the next phase of my relationship with Jim, and I was so glad it had finally arrived. This was a perfect day, and all was very well with the world. I was definitely high on life, and it felt great!

"Poor Randy. I bet he's in big trouble with his parents for what he did last night. That guy sure has a major crush on you," Emma said out of the blue.

"Oh, no he doesn't," I replied firmly. "He doesn't because I won't let him, and that's all there is to it."

"Ha. Well, I don't think you can do much about it," Emma laughed. "Before he met you, I felt his eyes watching me all the time. Now he's *your* fan club. You'll just have to face it. You're a nerd magnet!"

"Cut that out!" I said, jostling her shoulder. She almost lost her balance and fell into the creek. We giggled uncontrollably about it.

After about an hour or so, Emma and I decided to call it quits and go back to the house. It had to be nearly time to go to the show. I didn't catch anything, which was thoughtful of the fish. Emma caught one or two little ones, which she quickly threw back.

The Beatles song, "The Yellow Submarine" had played over and over in my mind the whole time we were at the creek.

"What's that tune you're humming?" Emma asked as we strolled along.

"What? Am I humming?" I asked. I knew I heard it in my mind, but didn't realize I'd been humming it.

"A sky of blue, a sea of green," she said, smiling.

We laughed, and then sang the song at the top of our lungs as we continued on our way.

When we got back to the house, Uncle Evert was standing near the door hosing down a folding chair. He seemed especially glad to see us when we crossed the yard dragging our fishing poles.

"There you are!" he exclaimed. "Lars and Margret have already gone over to the show. Margret wanted to be there early with Wendy while the rock band sets up. You know what groupies those girls are. Your mother and I are about to go over ourselves."

"Has Luke left yet?" Emma inquired.

"No, he's inside with Randy and Jim," he answered, dropping the hose and turning off the spigot. "Randy's parents are letting him go to the show, too. He just got here. Have fun and I'll see you over there," he said as walked toward the barn with the chair.

Jim! I couldn't wait to rush inside to see him. I was about to open the door when he surprised me and walked out. It was good to see him. Although he appeared refreshed, he was more reserved than he'd been last night. He didn't exude the welcoming demeanor I expected. Emma hurried inside, leaving us alone.

"Hi. Are you excited about the show?" I asked, grinning like a fool.

"Uh, Vanessa, I have something to tell you. Could you walk over here with me for a minute?" he asked, taking my hand and guiding to the large elm tree where we'd sat together last night. I braced myself and looked into his handsome eyes. Was something wrong?

"Monica called me this morning. I want you to know I didn't call her. She called me."

"Oh, my gosh!" I blurted. I sensed my happy world was about to be turned upside down.

"And, she asked me to. . .well, we talked things over. . .and. . .she said she was sorry. She asked. . . .well, I agreed. . . to give her another chance. . ." He was stumbling all over himself.

"Just stop," I snapped. "I got the idea, and I can't believe it." I turned to walk away, but he gently grabbed my arm and pulled me toward him.

"Please stay. Just. . .stay," he pleaded. "I need to discuss this with you. This is hard for me, you know. I care a lot about you. The last thing I want to do is hurt you."

"Then why is it that's what you're always doing?" I asked. "Now please let go of my arm so I can go inside."

"Look. I wouldn't be doing this if I wasn't concerned she might do something drastic if I don't give her a second chance."

"Something drastic? Like what?" I asked. I had to hear what this girl had cooked up to lure him back.

He let go of my arm and took a deep breath. "You know. . .She might hurt herself. I could never forgive myself if something unthinkable happened to her on account of me."

"Did she say she'd hurt herself?" I asked.

"No, but she was pretty upset," he explained.

"What did she say *exactly*," I asked, looking him squarely in the eyes.

"She was a mess. She said she wouldn't be able to go on if I broke up with her," he said. "I'm not exactly sure what she meant by that. Maybe it meant nothing, I don't know. I just know I can't leave her when she feels like she does right now. I need to try to work this through with her so she's not as emotional if we split up again."

If we split up again? That didn't sound very promising for me. From what I observed about Monica, she was experienced when it came to relationships. She didn't seem the type to harm herself, but I understood he had to be careful. His sense of duty and honor were admirable, but now I realized he had feelings for her that he just couldn't shake. He'd have to figure this out for himself without interference from me. There was no way I could change his mind about her. All I could do was let go and move on, for his sake and mine.

"So, you're going to go back with her, even though she cheated on you?" I asked sarcastically.

"Oh, that. She explained that she didn't really cheat on me," Jim explained. "She said Vinny was chasing her all over town, and that she was doing her best to give him the cold shoulder. He's not the sort of guy she'd ever be interested in, I guarantee you."

I stood speechless, looking at his handsome face filled with conflicted feelings. If he wanted to believe her, so be it.

155

"I hope you'll both be very happy," I managed to choke out, and turned abruptly and walked into the house.

There was nothing more to be said. I was devastated. I was certain I'd never be happy again. Not ever.

CHAPTER TWENTY-ONE

The Air Show

When I entered the house, my heart was beating wildly. I knew my face must be beet red. I couldn't believe it. Jim had sucker punched me right in the heart. . . again! I sat down at the dining room table, not hearing anything or anyone. I was in a state of shock. A wave of sadness washed over me. I had crashed from the highest high to the lowest low in a matter of only a few hours. I'd been given only one short morning in which to bask in the joy of my rekindled relationship. Just one crummy short morning. Couldn't the fates have allowed me to live in a fool's paradise for just a little while longer? Life was totally unfair. Monica didn't want him, not like I did. I was sure of that, but what could I do about it? I wanted to cry, but didn't dare. Not in this small house; not in front of all these people.

Randy was on the couch going through a small stack of comic books. He looked different somehow. He was clean shaven, and wearing a plaid, short-sleeved button-down shirt tucked into clean jeans that weren't ripped or too large. His dark blonde hair was combed, and he wore lace-up shoes instead of the heavy military boots he usually wore. I wondered if he was trying to impress someone, and hoped it wasn't me.

"Hey, Vanessa!" he greeted me when he saw me. I smiled and nodded.

I had to keep it together so he and the others would have no clue about what had just transpired between Jim and me. After a moment or two, I heard the screen door close and Jim walked slowly into the house, passed me, and took a seat in the dragon chair. He appeared to take great pains to avoid looking in my direction. What would become of us now? It would be painfully awkward to be around him, that's for sure. To conceal my dismay, I sat with my eyes cast down at the red gingham plastic table cloth covering the table.

"Everything okay?" Emma inquired, emerging from her bedroom.

"Sure," I answered half-heartedly.

She gave me a funny look, and I forced a weak smile to discourage any further questioning. She looked as though she was about to say something when Luke bounded out of his bedroom wearing a brown and cream color-blocked bowling shirt with the name "Ernie" embroidered in yellow thread over the chest pocket.

"Don't I look gorgeous? I'm ready to go now," Luke announced, proudly striking a pose with his fists on his hips.

"What are you wearing? We're going to an air show, not a bowling tournament, you jug head," Jim teased, shaking his head.

"I know. This is the closest thing I have to a uniform, and I believe this occasion calls for one," Luke declared. "I think I look rather stylish, don't you?"

"Who's Ernie?" Emma asked. "I think you should give that shirt back to him, whoever he is."

"I snagged this gem at Goodwill when I was there with Dad a few weeks ago. Whoever Ernie is, he must have been a darned good bowler, because he certainly had excellent taste in clothes," Luke replied, fondly stroking the front of his shirt.

"You're not seriously going to wear that thing today, are you?" Jim taunted. "You'll never be able to show your face in school again. You know that, don't you?"

"Heck yes I'm wearing this today," Luke answered. "Isn't this the era of individualism?"

"Hey, enough about that stupid shirt. Do we have a plan for today?" Emma demanded. "Luke, you agreed to try to help those helpless animals, so don't try to back out."

"I'll do whatever you want," Randy volunteered without hesitation, sitting up straight as if being called on in class. "Just tell me what you want me to do, and I'll do it."

"Shh! What if Mom or Dad walks in here and hears you," Luke warned, looking over his shoulder toward the door. "Keep it down, will you?"

"I think we should go straight to the hangar and look around first thing," I suggested. "If it's open, we can walk around inside with the other visitors, and no one will notice us. If we could get our hands on a camera, we could even take photos of anything suspicious we find."

"Margret has a Brownie camera. I'm sure she'd let us borrow it," Emma volunteered. "I don't know if it has film in it or not. It's been a long time since anyone used it. I'll go look for it." She ran to her bedroom.

"I could sneak aboard Scaggs' DC-3 and look around," Randy suggested.

"Whoa. Don't go all Napoleon Solo on me," Luke cautioned "You might run into some evil guys on that plane, and then you'd be toast. It'd be your second offense, and they might send you to Sing Sing this time."

"I agree with Luke," Jim said calmly. "It's too dangerous for anyone to go aboard that plane. That's totally out of the question. Are we all agreed on that?"

"Okay," Randy muttered. He appeared disappointed, and slouched back in his seat.

"You've got no disagreement from me," I said. I thought of myself more as the brains of the operation.

"Okay. I've got it!" Emma said, emerging from the bedroom swinging the boxy brown camera from its short wrist cord. "I checked and it has film in it."

"Okay, let's go, shall we?" Luke said enthusiastically. "Enough talking."

Luke, Emma, Randy, Jim and I walked outside and crossed the yard to the path down to Allisonville Road. I did my best to avoid walking anywhere near Jim. I needed to keep my distance from him right now, and he seemed to want the same thing. I thought I noticed Randy and Jim keeping their distance from each other, too. I still didn't understand what the friction between them was all about. There was no doubt that we were a quirky little group.

As we walked south along Allisonville Road, long lines of vehicles were already slowly moving bumper-to-bumper in both directions waiting to turn into the airport. Homemade yard signs directed cars to park in long columns on the large grassy area near the large hangar on the south side of the airport. We walked along the shoulder of the road, and then crossed between several stopped cars and scurried through the parking lot to the gate and walked in.

"We're going to catch up with some guys, so we'll see you later," Luke announced once we were inside. "Ciao!"

"Wait a minute," I protested. "What about our plan to investigate the hangar? Shouldn't we walk over there and do that first thing? There's no telling how long it'll be open."

"Gosh darn it," Luke complained. "Can't we have some fun first?"

"Luke, you promised," Emma said sternly, glaring at him.

"Tsk, tsk. If you keep frowning like that you'll get wrinkles," he mocked.

She was about to ramp up her chastisement, I could tell, when Jim interrupted. "I'm okay going over there now if the girls want to," he volunteered. "Why don't we do that now and get it over with? What do you say?"

Luke surrendered, and turned and silently made his way through the crowd in the direction of the hangar as Emma, Jim, Randy, and I followed. Cars and pickup trucks were parked everywhere — along driveways, taxiways, runways, and on the grass. Several small planes that had flown in earlier were parked in the grass wing-to-wing on the far side of the runway. A small stage was set up near the large hangar, and four guys with long hair were setting up sound equipment. People were walking every which way. It didn't look like the same sleepy airport I'd known.

"Look at this!" Uncle Forrest exclaimed, walking up behind us so energetically he might have just downed six cups of black coffee. He was tall and lean, with an expressive face and thick brown curly hair. He was dressed up more than usual in a white, short-sleeved dress shirt, dark slacks, and slim dark necktie. "Can you believe this turnout? There must be two thousand people here already, with more pouring in!" I could see the excitement in his eyes behind his dark-rimmed eye glasses, and sensed his satisfaction that the event was turning out to be a success.

"This is our first air show, and after all the flak the neighbors gave us trying to prevent it, it's really going to happen!" he said with heartfelt excitement.

A plane suddenly flew high above the runway, and one-by-one five people jumped out from an open door in the back. The sky-divers immediately maneuvered themselves into a circle holding hands as they plummeted down. After a moment or two in position, they broke the circle and pulled their rip cords, allowing their white parachutes to open and yank them upward, and then let them slowly drift back to earth. A roar of appreciation rippled over the crowd as people cheered and applauded.

"It's time for the show to begin!" Uncle Forrest said. "Those are the precision skydivers that open the show."

A man with a clipboard rushed up to him, and the two hurried away.

"Ladies and gentlemen!" an announcer's voice suddenly boomed over speakers positioned around the airport. "Give the Indianapolis Skydivers a big hand! The Indianapolis Skydivers!" The sound of hundreds of clapping hands reverberated in the clear summer air.

Moments later, Buzz's Piper Cub went roaring by just a few feet above the runway, and then made an abrupt ninety-degree turn and flew straight up into the air. It flew so high that it seemed impossible for it not to fall back to earth. At the top of the climb, the pilot — who wasn't Buzz, but someone introduced by the announcer as George Stevens — put the plane into a corkscrew dive and spun around and around until it was only a few feet above the runway. Then he leveled out upside down and flew over the heads of the crowd so low that I thought I could see his smiling face as he passed over me.

"My goodness. I didn't think that plane could do that!" Uncle Forrest exclaimed, his eyes fixed on the bright yellow vintage plane. "I had no idea George was going to do that when he asked if he could borrow the Cub for the show. I sure hope he knows what he's doing. I'd hate to have an accident out here today. That'd ruin us!"

I hoped so, too! I'm certain I'd be emotionally scarred for life if that were to happen. But George, whoever he was, seemed to know what he was doing, and all went well. He flew the Cub behind a row of trees and out of sight for a few seconds as though he had crashed, only to pop up unexpectedly and make a large loop. Each stunt elicited gasps and loud cheers from the audience. To think I had flown in that very plane only a couple of days ago! I couldn't imagine having the nerve to fly like that.

Jim, Luke, Randy, Emma, and I continued weaving through the crowd, making our way slowly toward the hangar. Occasionally we paused to watch the show whenever Luke insisted on it. When we passed the restaurant, I noticed Pete Scaggs smoking a cigar with a group of men on the patio. He wore a fancy, light-colored sport coat, mirrored aviator sunglasses, and dress slacks. He was the kind of man who wore his shirt unbuttoned one button too many over his barrel chest and large gut. His flashy dress and large stature made him easy to spot.

"Look," I said to Emma. "Isn't that Pete Scaggs over there?" I nodded in his direction.

"Yes, that's good ol' Pete Scaggs," Uncle Forrest interjected, walking up behind us in his usual high-energy fashion. "He's allowing us to use his DC-3 for a skydiving act later on. Eight skydivers are going to jump out of it with colored smoke in their backpacks. Should be really something special to see. Very good of him to let us use his plane for that."

Good ol' Pete, eh? Uncle Forrest rushed over to Pete and vigorously shook his hand and patted him on the shoulder. It appeared they were good friends. Why did everyone but me think Pete was such a great guy?

"Hey, you guys," Daniel said, darting out of the crowd toward us. "I was hoping I'd find you. I'm running some errands to help out my dad, but I'll be done soon. I can meet you over at the turquoise hangar later on if you're still planning to go there to look for Bobo. You are, aren't you?"

"No problem," Luke confirmed. "Nessie is insisting we march over there first thing. We're going there right now."

"Groovy!" Daniel said, making a peace sign with his first two fingers. He rushed away through the crowd.

"What on earth is wrong with that boy?" Luke asked, shaking his head. "That hippie thing he's doing lately has got to stop."

Jim chuckled. "Right on, but you should mellow out there, dude," Jim advised. "Peace and love, you know. Not war."

Luke grimaced, and we resumed our trek through the crowd. We passed Patsy, the waitress, outside the restaurant standing at a table selling hot dogs for ten cents each and Cokes for a nickel.

"Hi, you guys," she said cheerfully as she handed a patron a hot dog. "Can I get you something?"

"No. We're just walking around looking at stuff. How's it going?" Luke asked.

"These hot dogs are selling like crazy. Mrs. Kingwood has to cook them fast to keep up," Patsy answered. "I hope we don't run out. How's it going, Randy?" she asked, smiling coyly at him.

Randy appeared surprised that she addressed him. "Cool show," he answered in a fairly disinterested tone.

"Yes, it is," she replied energetically. "If you want, I'll give you a hot dog for free, Randy. It'll be our little secret. I'm sure Mrs. Kingwood won't mind. She said I could eat as many as I want."

"He doesn't have time to eat right now," Luke interrupted. "Besides, we don't want to be part of any air show graft."

"Okay. I'll be here when you get hungry," she replied good-naturedly. She resumed her duties placing a hot dog in a bun and handed it to the next patron.

"Dude, I think you have a little fan club there," Luke said to Randy as we continued walking.

"What are you talking about?" Randy asked, looking bewildered.

"Never mind, son," Luke said, slapping him on the back. "Come back and talk to me when you hit puberty."

The pilot landed the Piper Cub and there was a momentary lull in the action. The rock band that had been setting up on the small elevated stage near the large hangar played "Hang On, Sloopy." About twenty or thirty teen-aged girls in mini-skirts and long hair were clustered in front of the stage swaying to the music and mooning over the musicians. Wendy and Margret were among them.

"My sister's as obsessed with those guys as she is with the Beatles," Luke lamented. "Emma, promise me you'll never go nutty for rock musicians like those girls."

"If you ask me, I think the lead singer's kinda cute," Emma whispered to me, and then giggled.

We finally got through the most crowded part of the audience and followed the paved taxiway to the turquoise hangar. The hangar's two large doors stood wide open. Only two or three people were walking around inside. I was excited as we approached. At last I'd see what was in there.

"Okay, we're here," Luke declared. "Let's go in there and look around real quick so we can go have fun like everyone else."

"Let's do it!" I said enthusiastically. This was finally my chance to satisfy my curiosity.

I rushed inside. The space was actually larger than it appeared from outside. The metal trusses holding up the roof were so high that the sound of our footsteps made the kind of echo you only hear in extremely large, empty spaces like cathedrals or museums. I scanned around the building looking for boxes, cages — —anything incriminating. But the hangar was almost completely empty, except for a forklift parked in a corner and a couple of stacked airplane tires. There was no separate office or storage room to investigate, just one large space that I could easily see from where I stood was virtually empty. I was deflated. My plan to find a clue came crashing down around me. This was becoming a day of disappointments! I didn't want to give up, though, and stubbornly walked around with my eyes focused down at the floor looking for any telltale item. The others milled around looking bored and anxious to leave.

"Are you satisfied? Can we leave now?" Luke groused. "I think you've turned up a big ol' goose egg here, Nancy Drew."

"I can't believe it," I said with disbelief. "There's nothing in here. Nothing at all. But Daniel said he overheard those men say they were going to load the plane and fly out during the show. Load the plane with what? Maybe he misunderstood them. He must have. What a bummer."

"You win some, lose some," Randy said, looking sympathetic.

"Wait! Randy, didn't you tell Luke on the phone that you heard a large bird and saw two men handling a very large reptile that looked like a small dinosaur in here?" I asked.

"Well, yeah," Randy replied slowly, as though he thought he was going to be in trouble if he answered in the affirmative. "I thought that's what I saw and heard. I don't know. I only got a quick look. It's not fair to hold me to that."

"Calm down there," Luke said. "It doesn't really matter what you and Daniel saw or heard Friday night over here. That was two days ago, and there's nothing here now. I've done my duty. So, I'm going back to the show."

"Well, okay," I agreed reluctantly. "But I think I'll stay and look around in here some more." I wasn't ready to give up.

"It's a free country," Luke answered. "But let's agree on a couple of things before we split up. If any of us gets in trouble for *any* reason, the safe house is the tree house, and the call for help is the peacock call. Everyone got that? Tree house—peacock call."

"What do you think could happen?" Emma asked, looking worried.

"Nothing," Luke replied. "Who'd mess with any of us with all these people standing around? I just think we should have a plan so we're all set and there's nothing to worry about. Just call me Mister Careful."

"Why the tree house?" I inquired.

"I don't know," Luke replied. "It's nearby and easy to get to, and not everyone can get up there easily. Certainly not someone hefty like old Pete Scaggs. And, even if someone did manage to get up there, you could always zip down the rope elevator and get away before they had a clue where you went."

We all nodded in agreement. It was probably best that the boys went on their way and left Emma and me to look around alone. Jim and I had barely looked at each other the whole time we'd been at the show. It couldn't have been more uncomfortable to be with him in this small group. It might be better for a number of reasons if the boys weren't around. Jim was distracting me, and I'd be able to concentrate better if he left with Luke and Randy.

"Okay, girls. Don't forget to enjoy the show," Luke reminded us. "There's more to life than detective work, you know."

With that, Luke, Jim, and Randy walked out the hangar and down the narrow taxiway toward the crowd, leaving Emma and me behind. Judging from their brisk pace, they were eager to be on their way.

I turned and looked back at the hangar's interior as though it were a gigantic puzzle. There *had* to be a clue in there somewhere, but where was it?

CHAPTER TWENTY-TWO

Peacocks and Hyacinths

Emma raised her eyebrows in a questioning manner as if asking whether we should give up. I pondered the same thing, but couldn't.

"Just one more lap around the hangar, and then I'll give up. Okay?" I coaxed.

"Well, okay," she said, looking toward the hangar door. The noise on the airfield was suddenly quite loud, and the audience applauded wildly as a new act was introduced. "I think the announcer just introduced a guy who's going to jump from the back of a convertible onto a plane. We're missing out. Could you please hurry?" she urged.

"Okay, okay," I reassured her. I felt a little silly being so persistent, but if I could find any evidence of smuggling, no matter how small, I'd save face with my cousins and Uncle Evert, which was important to me. I was in too deep to give up now.

I carefully retraced the steps around the interior of the hangar I'd just taken. Someone had gone to a lot of effort to empty the hangar completely and sweep the floor perfectly clean. There was no scrap of paper, cigarette butt, or loose screw. Not a ladder, tool chest, or airplane part, except for those stacked airplane tires. Nothing. Definitely no trace of Bobo, or a bird, lizard, or any other animal that may have been transported through there. Still a voice deep down inside me insisted there had to be a clue somewhere if I just looked harder. But where was it? All I needed was one little piece of *something*.

After I thoroughly checked inside the hangar again and still found nothing, I walked outside and searched the pavement and grass. Emma had already strolled outside and was watching the show. Everything was perfectly clean and orderly, just like inside. I was getting discouraged, until I walked behind the hangar and noticed a small shed standing only a few feet from the back wall. It was the kind of small building people sometimes put in their backyards to store mowers and yard tools. I'd never noticed it before and was surprised to see it. I walked up to the small door at the front and pulled on the latch. To my amazement, it opened.

After looking around and seeing no one, I slowly opened the door all the way and peered inside. It was dark, but I could see three large wire cages stacked on top of each other. A loud, screeching or trilling noise startled me. It sounded like something you'd hear in a *Tarzan* movie. I squinted and searched the darkness for the source. Then I saw it. A large, bright blue parrot-like bird perched on a swing in one of the cages, staring back at me. It had to be longer than three feet from the top of its head to the end of its tail, and it had a large, fierce-looking curved beak that looked as though it could snap a human finger in two with one bite. Its big black eyes were encircled by bright yellow feathers which made its stare even more menacing. As I stood in the door studying it, it let out a second loud trilling screech. At last! Here was my evidence.

"Well, hello boy," I said gently. "You're very handsome. What are you doing in there?"

"What's that?" Emma asked, looking over my shoulder. She'd followed me behind the hangar. I was wound a little tight from the excitement of my find, and she startled me.

"I don't know. It's definitely an exotic bird, just like Randy said he saw the other night," I answered. "I think this guy's proof there's something going on here. Why is he stashed back here like this if he's legit?"

"I don't know, but at last I have something to take a picture of," Emma said, tinkering with her camera. "Step aside and let me get a photo. I sure hope I can get it without a flash. It's such a bright day, I didn't think to bring it."

She paused as she focused, and then clicked the camera shutter and took the shot. "Got it. Now let's go," she said, wrapping the camera cord tightly around her wrist.

Suddenly, two men talking to each other emerged around the corner of the hangar. They appeared surprised to see us, and stopped abruptly. One of them carried a large box.

"Hey! You kids. What are you doing there?" one of them shouted. He looked like the guy who was with Pete in the airport restaurant when Emma, Daniel, and I had lunch there. I think his name was Ralph, but I couldn't be certain.

"Nothing, sir," I answered, slamming the shed door shut. "Let's get out of here!" I shouted to Emma.

Emma and I took off running around the opposite side of the hangar, as Ralph, or whoever he was, followed. "Hey. Bring that camera back here. Stop!" he shouted.

My heart pounded hard as we ran through the crowd, darting in and out of guests as they stood with their eyes fixed skyward at the planes flying overhead. We made a wide turn and ran through a line of people waiting to purchase ice cream cones. Then we ran past a group of people milling around three old World War II fighter planes. The stage was straight ahead, and we ran directly toward it. The rock band, The Fifth Wheel, was on stage performing "The House of the Rising Sun." Their speakers were small and it was difficult to hear them. Still the four local rock stars gave it their all, playing their instruments with gusto in their striped bell bottoms and shoulder-length hair.

It occurred to me we might blend in with all of the girls watching the band if we joined them, and shake Ralph that way. After all, to him, one teenage girl probably looked like the next. So we scooted into the middle of the crowd of girls and swayed along with them to the rhythm of the music. I looked eagerly for Margret and Wendy, but was disappointed not to see either of them. We could have used their help.

"Did we lose him?" Emma asked in a low voice, looking worried.

I looked over my shoulder as inconspicuously as I could and searched for Ralph. He wasn't very distinctive looking, only average height, but stocky and muscular. He had brownish-gray hair, a receding hairline, and wore the beige zip-up jacket with the red "S" on the pocket I'd seen before. I hoped we'd gotten lucky and lost him. I scanned the crowd and didn't see him. Things were looking good. But suddenly I spotted him standing at the back of the crowd, looking carefully at each girl. He'd identify us for sure if he saw Emma's brown box camera. A few other girls also had cameras of one kind or another, but not a Brownie.

"Can you stash that camera somewhere?" I suggested, looking down at it in Emma's hand. "It's a dead giveaway. How about hiding it under the stage?"

168

"What if someone takes it?" she asked. "Margret would kill me if I lost it. It's hers, you know."

"Well, do *something* with it," I urged.

She made a funny face and then abruptly stuck it under her shirt. It made a conspicuous bulge that under other circumstances would be funny. Maybe Ralph would move on if we just stood there for a few more minutes and acted cool. I was anxious and kept glancing at him out of the corner of my eye. After a few minutes, he began walking through the crowd looking at each person as he passed by. He wasn't giving up.

"He's standing a few feet behind us and getting closer," I whispered. "I hope he doesn't recognize us."

"I bet he will," Emma said. She sounded stressed. "He'll surely notice that long red hair of yours. Now what do we do?"

"Stay calm," I replied. "Maybe we should find your dad and ask for help?"

"And, have to explain why that guy is chasing us? No way," Emma said. "Dad would be mad for sure that we were snooping around the hangar again. Besides, I don't have a clue where he is in this crowd." She gazed nervously in Ralph's direction.

"Maybe we should go to the airport office," I suggested. "Surely someone there will help us if we ask them."

"If that guy finds us there he could complain that we were snooping in the shed, and get us in big trouble," Emma reasoned. "Nope. I think we should just find a place to hide from that guy so he never knows who we are and can't identify us to anyone."

I stopped talking for a moment so as not to draw attention to us. Other people were chatting, but those nearest to us were too absorbed in the band and the music for conversation. Our anxious chatter might make us stand out.

"Luke said to go to the tree house if we have a problem. If we can work our way through the crowd without that guy noticing us, we could hide up there. We'd be safe," I whispered, finally.

"Okay. Let's try it," Emma agreed. "We have no other choice."

Ralph was quickly making his way toward us as we began snaking our way through the throng of air show enthusiasts. We kept our backs positioned at him as much as possible as we wove through the crowd. I hoped he hadn't gotten a good enough look at us to be able to remember precisely which two girls we were. That was probably just wishful thinking on my part, though.

The airport office and restaurant weren't too far from the stage. We hurriedly walked there and slipped inside through a side door. I could see through the large windows that he was coming in our direction. I quickly searched through the office and restaurant looking for Luke and Jim, or even Buzz and Lars, but none of them was there. There were lots of people, but no one I knew, and no one I felt comfortable asking for help. So we moved on. We exited through a side door, crossed the refueling circle, and reached the large grassy area that extends to the access road where the tree house was. Groups of people were clustered here and there as we made our escape. I hoped moving among those groups helped conceal us.

The chain link fence along the access road was our last obstacle. When we got there, we crouched behind several parked airplanes, and pondered the best way to get over.

"There's no way to go over that fence without being seen pretty plainly," Emma observed. "Don't you agree?"

Before I could answer, the announcer suddenly boomed, "Ladies and Gentlemen! Please welcome Harold Krier and wing walker, Ray Krasgne, as they perform death defying stunts known the world over!"

Harold Krier's Great Lakes biplane with fancy red and white paint roared over the crowd. A man in a white jumpsuit and flight helmet stood on top of the two-winged plane attached to it by wires, and waved to the crowd as he flew by. The audience burst into thunderous applause and cheers.

"Let's jump over the fence while the wing walker is distracting everyone," I suggested. "Hurry!"

Emma and I ran to the fence and clambered over as quickly as possible. I had learned how to scale the fence more skillfully since the night of the UFO incident. Now we were only a few feet from the base of the tree house. Emma scaled up first and I followed. I was relieved when I finally made it through the opening and stood on the deck. At last, I was safe! I exhaled and caught my breath. Once I had collected myself, I walked to the other side of the deck and took in the view. It was a colorful scene to behold as I looked down at the sea of people, planes, and cars occupying almost every square inch of the airport grounds. I looked for our pursuer, but didn't see him.

"Boy, that was exciting, wasn't it?" I said, smiling with relief. "I didn't think we were going to be able to shake that guy."

"I know. I just hope my photo turns out," she said, looking down at the camera still attached to her wrist. "I'm kinda new at working this thing."

"I hope so, too," I agreed. "All of our evidence is in that little brown box."

"Harold Krier will now do his death-defying loops!" the announcer proclaimed. We could hear his announcements loudly and clearly.

Harold Krier flew large loops with smoke streaming out the back of his plane, and dove so low it seemed he'd crash for sure. Then, he flew low upside-down over the runway with that guy in the white suit still standing on top of the plane.

"Oh, I can't watch!" I said, covering my eyes. "I sure hope that pilot knows what he's doing."

"It's okay. He's the big star of the show. I heard he had his biplane custom made so he could do tricks like that," Emma reassured.

"Hey! You kids up there!" someone shouted from below.

I looked down, and saw Ralph staring back. I was stunned. I'd foolishly believed we'd lost him. He looked out of breath and enraged.

"Hey, I see you!" he bellowed. "Give me that camera. I'll come up and take it from you if you don't give it to me. You hear me? I want that camera."

"Oh, crap. Now what do we do?" I exclaimed as I pulled my head back out of his view.

"Hey! Do you hear me?" Ralph barked. "Bring that camera down here right now!"

"Get lost!" Emma shouted, looking down. She seemed more angry than scared. "I'm not giving you my sister's camera. Not now, not ever!"

"Disrespectful kid, huh?" Ralph muttered as he started climbing the ladder nailed into the tree. "Well, I'll teach you girls a lesson you won't forget." He would reach the deck in only a matter of seconds.

"Quick. Slide down the rope," Emma directed. "We can zip down before he gets up here and get away. Just like Luke said we should do." She started to crawl out on the limb.

"I. . .I don't know how to slide down the rope," I said sheepishly. "Please don't hate me, but . . . I don't think I can do it. I've never done it, you know."

"Oh, for goodness sakes, City Slicker. *Really?*" she chastised, pausing and making a face. "I can't believe this."

"You go ahead, and take the camera with you," I urged. "I'll figure out some other way to get away."

"No way," she said. "I'm not leaving you up here alone."

We didn't have time for further conversation. The top of Ralph's head came into view as he approached the opening in the deck and started to crawl up.

"Hurry. Go inside and lock the door!" Emma shouted, pushing me toward the door.

"Lock the door?" I asked as I stumbled inside and almost fell down. I didn't know how that was done with this door.

Fortunately, it didn't matter. She jumped inside behind me and slammed the heavy carved door shut. Then, she looped the small padlock hanging on its old brass door knob through a steel loop in the door frame, and pushed it down. With a "click" the door was locked, just in the nick of time. A second later Ralph banged on the door and pushed against it, trying to force it open. I stood back and stared as he strained against the lock. I wondered if the door would hold. The tree house was fairly well constructed as far as tree houses go, but it wasn't built to be a fortress.

"Can he push the door open?" I asked, shaking with apprehension. My eyes were fixed on the door frame where the lock hung.

"Don't know," Emma confessed. "I've never used the lock before."

Ralph continued beating on the door and shoving against it. Each time he did, the door moved in ever so slightly in the doorframe as though it might finally burst open.

Emma ran over to the window facing the airport, cupped her hands around her mouth, and let out a shrill "heyeric, heyeric, heyeric!" I recognized it as Luke's peacock call. She stopped, took a deep breath, and let out a second loud peacock call. Harold Krier and his wing walker were still performing, and the deep roar of his biplane's engine, coupled with the applause and cries of amazement from the crowd, drowned out her calls.

"I don't think they're able to hear you over all that noise," I concluded reluctantly. "What are we going to do?"

"They *have* to hear me. They just have to," she insisted, taking another deep breath and letting out a third ear-piercing peacock call.

It was suddenly quiet at the door. The banging and shoving against it ceased completely. The deck boards beneath Ralph's feet creaked, so I knew he was still there. What was he up to? Emma stepped back from the window and joined me in the middle of the small room where we huddled together, waiting for him to reveal his next move.

"Girls, come out," he cajoled in a quiet, but husky voice. "I won't hurt you. I just want to talk. You don't want to spend all day in there and miss the show, do you? Now, be good girls and come out. I want to be your friend."

"Balderdash," I whispered to Emma. Turning toward the door, I yelled "Go away! People are coming to help us, so you'd better get away from here!"

"Oh, is that so?" he replied gruffly, giving the door an exasperated kick. "Didn't your parents teach you lying is a sin? Just like tampering with other people's things."

"Go away!" I repeated. "The police are coming." I figured lying in a moment like this was allowed in the fine print of the rule against it.

"All I want is that camera. You give it to me, and I'll go away," he demanded.

"No. I'll never give you my sister's camera," Emma shouted. "Never! Go away!"

He was silent again, and then I heard something brush against the door. Moments later, there was a noise on the roof. It sounded as though he'd climbed atop the structure. But why? Then I realized why — there was no glass in the two large windows. Could he be planning to crawl across the roof and climb in through one of them? I was horrified as I heard him begin to make his way across the tin surface toward one of the walls with an opening. Yes, that had to be his plan.

"Oh, no! They *have* to have heard me. What will we do if they didn't?" Emma anguished, looking up at the ceiling with panic in her eyes.

My eyes were locked upward as the telltale thumps moved closer to a wall with a window. I was out of ideas, and trembling.

CHAPTER TWENTY-THREE

Trapped in the Tree House

*A*s Ralph made his way inch-by-inch across the roof, I considered our options for escape. Should we unlock the door, climb to the ground, and run away? After all, it'd take him a few seconds to get down from the roof to chase us. Maybe that'd give us enough lead time. Or, would it? Emma was almost like a circus performer when it came to her agility sliding down the rope, but I'd be much slower and vulnerable using the ladder. She'd probably be able to get away, but chances were he'd grab me. I felt safer remaining in the tree house, at least for now. Emma seemed willing to go along with that plan. On the optimistic side of things, there was always the possibility Ralph wouldn't be able to manage the gymnastics it took to climb down through a window.

I looked around the little room for something to use as a weapon, just in case. The furniture that was broken up when the tree house was vandalized had been removed, but one broken leg of the table conveniently remained and was propped up in a corner. I picked it up and considered its usefulness, and decided it would make a nice billy club. I stood poised, holding my makeshift weapon as Ralph began lowering himself from the roof to the window. When his boots were visible in the opening, I ran over and started beating on them with my make-shift cudgel.

"Get away! Get away!" I yelled as I landed each blow. "Leave us alone. Get away from here!"

"You girls stop that!" he yelled, kicking his feet. "Wait 'til I get in there. I'll teach you."

His boots were heavy, and my blows didn't appear to have much impact, except to annoy him. Even though I continued striking him, he continued lowering himself.

"I don't think he's going to stop," Emma concluded, looking frantic.

"Let's get out of here and climb down," I relented. "He won't be able to get off the roof so fast now that he's hanging from the side. That'll give me enough time to climb down. You take the rope and we'll both get away."

I turned toward the door and waited for Emma to unlock it and free us from captivity, but she didn't move.

"What's wrong?" I asked, puzzled. "Unlock the door. Hurry!"

"I. . .I don't remember what the combination is," she said apologetically. "I've never known what it is."

"What?" I exclaimed with disbelief. "Then why did you lock it?"

"There was no other way to get away from him. It made sense at that moment," she explained. "I figured we'd find a way out after he went away and everything was okay."

Suddenly, what had been our refuge was transformed into a trap. What could we do? In only a matter of only seconds he'd leap through the window, and we'd have no way to escape. My sorry little table leg wouldn't amount to anything face-to-face against a grown man.

"Try a few combinations and maybe we'll get lucky," I urged. "You've got to try. Hurry!"

Emma ran over to the lock and quickly tried several combinations, but each time the padlock remained locked tight. While she did that, I stuck my head out the second window and looked around for a way out. But there was no deck below the window — only a sheer drop all the way to the ground. We were locked in just like that exotic blue bird I'd just seen.

As I anxiously watched Ralph continue maneuvering in the window, he suddenly let out a loud whelp.

"What the heck? What was that?" Ralph yelled angrily as he dangled from the roof. "What just hit me?"

"That's what you get for being a big fat bully," a voice called from below. "Now, get out of there or I'll give you another big fat headache."

I ran to the window and looked down. Luke was below holding a sling shot already loaded, pulled back, and ready to fire. Daniel and Randy were with him.

"Oh, yeah?" Ralph sneered. "Well, kid, that was just a lucky shot. You couldn't hit the side of a barn with that thing."

"Oh, yeah?" Luke countered. A second rock flew up and hit Ralph hard in the middle of his back.

"Ouch! That hurt like the bejeezus! Cut that out, kid! You could kill someone with that thing," Ralph scolded.

"I'll hold my fire if you get down immediately," Luke said. "I brought several rocks with me, so I can keep this up all day if that's what you want. You decide."

"You're a lot of talk, aren't you, pee wee," Ralph jeered.

Ralph resumed situating himself in the window to jump in, ignoring Luke's commands. Luke fired two more quick shots. One hit Ralph on his arm, and the other missed him and hit the wall next to his head with a loud "thunk!"

"Cut it out, kid!" Ralph yelled.

"Get down. *Now!*" Luke shouted. "I can keep this up all day until you follow instructions."

"*Please give up*," I mumbled softly so Ralph couldn't hear. What would we do if he didn't? If he got inside we wouldn't be able to open the door to allow the boys in to help us. He said he just wanted the camera, but there was no telling what he might do to us. The situation could be very bad.

"Okay, kid. You win," Ralph shouted down to Luke. "That camera isn't worth the trouble, and neither are you. Just let me go into the tree house so I can get down. I don't want to climb back over the roof. I could fall, you know?"

"I don't think so, Lurch," Luke quipped. "You got there by climbing over the roof, so you have to go back over the roof the way you came. You read me?"

"What if I refuse?" Ralph dared in a mocking tone.

"Oh, you have that option. Mr. Slingshot will go to work again, that's all," Luke replied. "He'll aim for your head from here on out. You choose."

"You juvenile delinquent. I'll get even with you. You'll see," Ralph growled. "I knew I should have burned down this tree house when I had the chance, instead of just trashing it. Next time, I will. You can bet on it."

I knew it! It was Pete Scaggs who sent his henchman to vandalize the tree house. It wasn't the work of some wayward kids after all. Ralph maneuvered so he could pull himself up onto the roof. Then, he crawled over it to the deck and leaped down. It became quiet, and I assumed he'd climbed down the ladder and left. Since there weren't any windows on the deck side of the house, I had to rely on what I could hear. Emma and I stood inches from the door and listened. After a few more minutes, there was a loud knock at the door.

"Hello in there," Luke shouted. "Anybody home? This is Little Red Riding Hood bringing Grandma some goodies. Open up."

"I can't!" Emma shouted, leaning against the door. "I don't know the combination for the padlock."

"Well, then, I guess you'll just have to stay in there, just like King Tut in his tomb," Luke teased. "See ya' later. I'm going back to the air show now."

"Luke!" Emma cried. "Don't you dare leave! Give me the combination."

"I don't know it. Honest I don't," he replied.

"Sure you do. What is it? Stop playing games with me," Emma shouted impatiently.

"Honest Abe. I don't know it," Luke insisted. "You're stuck, kid."

Emma looked at me with an apologetic wince. "I guess I could climb out of one of the windows," she suggested. I knew she had acrobatic skills, but even for her that would be too risky.

"That's not safe," I insisted, shaking my head. "There has to be a better way."

Luke called down to Daniel and asked if he knew the lock's sequence, and he did. Apparently, when Buzz put the padlock there, he used his own birthday for the combination — 7-22-47. Emma quickly spun the numbers on the padlock and pulled it apart. When the door finally swung open, Luke, Daniel, and Randy stood on the deck grinning at us.

"Is that man gone?" I asked, looking around cautiously before stepping out.

"Yes, Princess. The boogie man is gone," Luke reassured. "You can come out now."

"How on earth did you hear my peacock call over all the noise at the show?" Emma inquired.

"I didn't," Luke replied. "I looked over here by chance and saw that guy climbing on the outside of the tree house, so I knew something was up. I brought these guys with me to check it out."

"Lucky for us. I could just hug you for coming to our rescue." I took a step toward Luke to hug him, but he quickly stepped backward.

"Get ahold of yourself, cuz," he said, waving his hands in front of him. "No mush, *please.*"

"So, he went away? Just like that?" Emma asked, looking around the deck and down below the tree. She seemed worried he might suddenly reappear. I wasn't too sure he wouldn't.

"Yeah. Luke had his slingshot cocked and ready to fly until that guy got down to Allisonville Road," Randy recounted. "He cursed at us as he walked by, but he went just the same."

"He was a big guy, too," Daniel said. "I'm sure he could have taken down at least two of us if he'd wanted to."

"That's why I always travel with two sidekicks," Luke said, smiling cockily. "Three is always a safer number than one."

"Where's Jim?" I asked as nonchalantly as possible. I couldn't wait any longer to ask. I knew I shouldn't be thinking about him, but I was.

"He saw a friend and said he'd catch up with us later," Luke answered.

A *friend*? Could that friend be Monica? I wanted to ask, but didn't. I had to start exercising some self-control where he was concerned, as difficult as that was.

"Why was that guy chasing you, anyway?" Luke asked.

"We found a small shed behind the hangar with a large, bright blue bird in it," Emma said. "I took a photo of it with the Brownie camera, and he wanted the photo." She held up the camera dangling from her wrist.

"No doubt to destroy the evidence," I added.

"A large, bright blue bird?" Daniel asked. "How large?"

"I'd say about three feet long," I reported. "Really bright blue, with yellow feathers around his eyes and a huge, scary beak."

"That sounds like a hyacinth macaw," Daniel concluded. "Those are on the endangered list because they're losing their native habitat in the rain forests. And poachers trap them to sell in the pet trade because they bring a lot of money. But for every bird that makes it to market, at least five die being caught or transported."

"It's a despicable thing to trade in exotic animals," Emma said solemnly. "Someone has got to stop them."

"When that photo's developed, we'll have undeniable evidence that Pete Scaggs is transporting exotic animals through Gatewood Airport," I said. "The authorities will have to listen to us and take steps to stop it. Did you hear that guy admit that he trashed the tree house? They know we're on to them."

"Hey, look over there," Randy said, pointing down to the hangar Pete Scaggs used. We all dashed to the edge of the deck and looked down. "Isn't that Pete Scaggs' plane over there? It looks as though they're loading stuff in it."

There was no mistaking Pete's DC-3 with the unique red circle "S" on the tail. Two men were loading boxes into the plane. The white panel truck I'd seen a few times before was parked near it.

"It looks as though we're not going to have much time if we want to stop him from flying that macaw out of here," Luke declared. "There could be other animals on that plane, too."

"Yeah, like Bobo. Don't forget I heard them talking about flying special cargo out of here during the intermission," Daniel said. "That macaw must be part of the special cargo, and maybe Bobo, too."

"We need a plan," Luke suggested.

"I'm going back to the air show to find Dad and tell him what's going on," Emma declared abruptly. "He'll know what to do. I'll bring him to the shed and show him the macaw."

"You might want to re-think that idea, little sister," Luke cautioned. "That guy we just chased away could be at the show and give you trouble. Especially if you're carrying that camera."

"Okay, then I'll give the camera to Vanessa," she replied, handing it to me. "Now I'll blend in with all of the other girls down there. I'll find Dad and have him help us. He'll listen to me."

"Okay, if you insist, but if you run into that guy and he gives you any trouble, scream your head off and get someone — *anyone* — to help you," Luke instructed. "When you find Dad, tell him to come to Scaggs' DC-3 right away. The rest of us will snoop around the plane and see what we can do to delay it from taking off. Bring Uncle Forrest and Buzz too, if you run into them."

I gave her a smile of encouragement, and then she crawled out to the rope, slid down to the ground, and was on her way back to the airport.

"I'm supposed to meet my dad at the office in five minutes to get my orders about hauling trash around the fair, so I gotta go. I'll tell him about the macaw," Daniel said. "He'll be interested about that, and want to go

179

to Pete's hangar to see what's going on. He won't like his airport being used for something as despicable as this. I know he won't, even if Scaggs tries to argue what he's doing is legal, which I just know can't be."

"Okay. We'll see you and your dad at Scaggs' plane. Bring him as fast as you can," Luke confirmed.

"Will do. Good luck you guys," Daniel said. Then, pausing, he looked at us and added, "If you can, please find Bobo and help me bring him home. You'd be the best friends a guy ever had if you could do that."

Luke gave him a thumbs-up, and then Daniel climbed down the ladder. He was over the fence running toward the airport office in only a matter of seconds.

"Let's go!" Luke rallied. His face had the determined expression of a Viking about to storm an enemy fortress.

Ralph and Luke popped down through the opening in the deck and I followed. *"Here goes nothing!"* I said under my breath.

CHAPTER TWENTY-FOUR

One Step Too Many

One-by-one, Luke, Randy, and I climbed over the fence and made our way over to Pete's plane. Just before we stepped off the grass onto the cement tarmac, Luke stopped and crouched behind a small parked plane, staring at the imposing DC-3 standing tall in front of the hangar.

"How are we going to go over there and look around without being noticed?" Randy asked.

"The guy from the tree house will surely recognize us," I pointed out. "I don't think this is such a good idea."

I was concerned Ralph might jump out of nowhere at any moment and exact his revenge on us, just as he promised he'd do. Luke had made a fool of him, and he'd surely be glad to get even and see us suffer for that.

"That's just a risk we'll have to take," Luke said without hesitating. "It looks pretty quiet over there right now. If we're careful, maybe they won't see us until Dad and Uncle Forrest get here."

"Why don't we just hang out here until we see your dad or uncle?" Randy suggested. "There's not a whole lot we can do by ourselves anyway, is there?"

"Look!" I said, pointing at the plane. One of the two engines had just started up. "Do you think they're getting ready to take off?"

"Well, dang it!" Luke said, grimacing. "They sure are. There's not enough time to wait for Dad and Uncle Forrest. We've got to take action *now*, with or without them."

"What are you suggesting?" Randy asked.

Without saying a word, Luke rose up and strolled slowly toward the DC-3. I guess he just assumed we'd follow him, which Randy and I did after exchanging confused glances. I didn't know what Luke had in mind, but I'd gone through far too much today to let that plane get away. I remained concerned about Ralph's whereabouts. But what harm could come to us with all these people around?

I wasn't really looking, but out of the corner of my eye I caught a glimpse of Jim and Monica walking together near the office holding hands. It was easy to spot her because she always wore red, and I seemed to have special radar where Jim was concerned, even if it meant seeing scenes like this one that I'd rather not see. I diverted my eyes and felt suddenly queasy.

The constant loud noise of plane engines suddenly died down, and it was quiet over the field. It was too soon for the air show to be over, so I figured this must be the intermission Pete's men had mentioned. Daniel said he heard them say they were going to fly out during the intermission, so if this was it, we had to hurry.

Luke led us around several parked cars located along the taxiway until we reached the area in front of the hangar where the towering aircraft stood. Just as we walked up near the tail, the propellers of the second engine suddenly began turning. I didn't know if it might taxi out for take-off at any moment, but I noticed that the back door of the plane was open and the stairs leading up to it still in place. Luke motioned for us to retreat back to a nearby parked car where we crouched together to strategize.

"Okay, you guys. This is the moment of reckoning," Luke began.

"What on earth do you people think you're doing?" Jim asked, walking up behind us.

"You goofball," Luke berated him, turning around "I could almost slug you for startling me like that."

"Ha. You're wound a little tight today, aren't you pal?" Jim observed, laughing. "Mellow out, man."

"Cut the hippie mumbo-jumbo," Luke barked. "Nessie has us playing detective, and we don't have time to horse around. We've got to stop Pete Scaggs from taking off in that plane with the bird in there."

"What bird?" Jim asked.

"After you left I found an unusual macaw in a shed behind the hangar, and we think it might be on that DC-3 right now, not to mention other animals," I told him.

"Well, then let's go see," Jim suggested without hesitation. "The back door's open, isn't it? We can walk over and look in. What are you waiting for?"

"Are you nuts?" Luke admonished. "We could get into a boatload of trouble. Don't you see those propellers turning? Someone's in the plane. Do you have a death wish?"

"Are you a man or a mouse?" Jim teased. "The door's still open. Come on. Let's get a closer look. They can't object to curious air show spectators trying to get a better look at their big, beautiful plane, can they? Let's do it while the plane's still on the ground. Time's a-wasting."

"All right, dude," Luke replied. "I'm in if you are, you crazy daredevil."

I couldn't believe they were really going to go to the open back door and look in, but sure enough, they walked across the pavement right up to the plane. I knew Scaggs' men had to be around, but at that moment the area appeared deserted. I hoped this wasn't a situation in which one-upmanship between Luke and Jim had overtaken their better judgment.

"I wish Uncle Evert and Uncle Forrest would hurry," I whispered to Randy. "They should be here any minute."

I turned and looked anxiously for the familiar faces of Emma and my uncles among the hundreds of strangers milling around in the distance, but sadly, didn't see them.

"I've always thought Luke and Jim were the greatest. I wish I was more like them. They're fearless. I guess I'll always be Robin, never Batman," Randy lamented as he crouched next to me.

I looked over at Randy as he watched Luke and Jim's every move with deep admiration in his eyes. I felt a little sad for him. I guess he wasn't such a bad person, really. Even with his messy hair and shirt hanging half out of his belt. He was just one of those guys who was always trying to fit in and couldn't, no matter how hard he tried.

I gasped when I saw Luke walk up one step, and then another, and finally stand in the doorway of the plane. Jim remained at the base of the stairs, probably as lookout. After a few moments, they both sprinted back to Randy and me.

"What did you see?" I asked eagerly. "Did you see the macaw?"

"No, but I think I heard it," Luke reported. "I heard a really loud trilling sound and a screech. Is that what it sounds like?"

"That's it," I confirmed.

"I saw the face of a monkey with black fur that I think could be Bobo," Luke continued. "It peeked out at me through the folds of a blanket hanging over its cage."

"Bobo?" Randy repeated. "Wow. We've got to rescue it and get it off that plane. For Daniel's sake."

"That would mean going on the plane," Jim said.

"That's too risky," Luke declared. "It's one thing to look inside from the steps; it's another to actually go inside and take something. I don't care if it's an endangered monkey or not, I don't want to be charged with trespassing and stealing. Besides, Dad should be here any minute, and he'll be able to take charge."

"Emma must be having trouble finding him," I said impatiently, looking again toward the crowd. "It's taking them a long time to get here." Painfully long, it seemed.

"Look!" Randy exclaimed softly.

Ralph came walking around from the other side of the plane carrying a small bundle. He walked up the steps and into the plane. After a few moments, he re-emerged and walked back around the plane to the white van parked on the other side.

"I've got an idea," Luke said. "Jim and I will go on the plane and stand in the door holding up the cages with the bird and Bobo, and Nessie can take pictures of them from outside. The photos will be our evidence, and we won't have to take anything. You've got the camera, don't you Nessie?"

"But that doesn't stop Pete from taking off with Bobo and the macaw," I pointed out. "How does that solve the problem?"

"It doesn't, but it's all we can do, unless you have a better idea," Luke returned.

"I'm nervous about going up to the plane," I admitted. "Can't I just give you the camera and let one of you take the photos?"

"Oh, for goodness sake, City Slicker," Luke replied in a disgusted tone. "Those cages are probably heavy, and we have to do all of this real fast before that guy at the van comes back. You're the one with the bleeding heart for these animals. Do you want everyone else to do the work for you?"

"No. I'm just being prudent," I said quietly, looking down to avoid making eye contact.

I didn't want to appear fearful in front of the boys, but my mind was spinning. I was terrified of getting caught. Sure, I wanted to get Bobo off the plane and stop Pete Scaggs from preying on helpless animals, but I didn't want to get in trouble doing it.

"Leave her alone," Jim chimed in. "Can't you see that she doesn't want to do it?"

"I'll do it," Randy volunteered. "Give the camera to me and I'll do it." He was beaming with resolve. "I'm not afraid."

"I'm not either," I said softly under my breath, although no one appeared to hear.

"Whatever we decide to do, we'd better do it in a hurry," Jim said. "Those propeller blades are turning and that guy could come back any minute."

"Okay," Luke agreed, taking a deep breath to brace himself. "Let's do this."

Randy put out his hand to take the camera from me. I paused for a split second and reconsidered what I was going to do. I couldn't live with myself if Jim or Luke thought I was a coward. What they thought of me mattered, whether or not it should.

"No. I'll do it," I said reluctantly. I felt a bit wobbly, but I had to do this.

"That's more like it, Agent 99," Luke said, beaming. "Here we go."

Luke and Jim walked ahead and swiftly tippy-toed up the steps and disappeared into the back of the plane. I took aim and clicked a photo of the whole plane for good measure and to practice my picture-taking skills. Then, I walked up the steps and stood on the top step and took another. Time crept slowly as I waited for them to bring a cage with one of the animals to the door. I felt apprehensive and checked behind me — first to one side and then the other —but didn't see anyone. So far, so good. Randy waved at me from where he still crouched behind the parked car. I turned back to the open door with the camera poised for a photo and nervously waited for the boys to appear in the doorway.

"Well, I declare. It's the troublemaker," I heard a man's voice say from behind me. "What do you think you're doing up there?"

I turned, and there stood Ralph! My heart jumped and my legs became numb.

"Nothing. . .nothing, sir. Just admiring your beautiful plane," I replied. Did the boys hear what was going on? They had to! Why didn't they rush out to help me?

"Well, get down from there, hand me that camera, and let me have the pretty pictures you just took," he demanded sternly. "Thanks for bringing it to me. You and your friends had some fun at the tree house today at my expense, didn't you?"

I turned and reluctantly descended the steps. As soon as I did, Ralph grabbed my arm and jerked the camera out of my hand.

"Ouch! You're hurting me. Give me back my camera," I insisted, reaching for the Brownie.

"I'm going to teach you a lesson you're never gonna forget," he growled, shoving me around while still holding my arm tightly. His breath had a foul odor, and his blood shot eyes had a mean look in them. I thought I would faint.

"Let go of me, you creep!" I shouted. "My family's here, and they know what you're doing. You're in big trouble."

"Oh, yeah?" he shot back. "I'll tell them I caught you trespassing and had no choice but to discipline you, you delinquent."

"I am *not* a delinquent!" I shouted. "Let me go!"

I tried to pull away from him, but it was no use. He was too strong and tightened his grip on me even more. Then, without warning, he slapped my face. I was stunned, and heard ringing in my ears.

"Settle down or there'll be more where that came from," he snarled.

"Let her go, you douche bag!" Randy yelled, running at Ralph with his head down ready to head-butt him.

Ralph let go of me and punched Randy hard in the face. With a stunned look of surprise, Randy stumbled and fell backward. The wind was completely knocked out of him, and he fell to the ground and lay unconscious on the pavement. He'd been brave and tried to rescue me. If only he'd succeeded.

"Get up them steps. Hurry up!" Ralph ordered. I turned and was startled to see him holding a gun pointed directly at me. "I said to get up them steps. Now!" he barked.

"Please let me go," I pleaded. "You can keep the camera. I won't tell. Why do you want me to go up the steps?"

"I told you kids I'd get even," he said with a self-satisfied sneer. "Well, now I am. Get up them steps!"

I quickly scanned the area, and no one but some people in the hangar were nearby. They didn't seem to notice what was happening at the plane. There was no one there to see what this man was doing to me, and no one to help. If I screamed, he might shoot me. I had no choice but to go up the stairs. But what would happen to me if I did? I couldn't believe this was happening. While the rest of the world enjoyed the festival atmosphere of the show, I was being kidnapped.

I slowly moved up the stairs and stepped into the plane. Several boxes draped in blankets and tarps were stacked in the back by the door. I glanced around for Luke and Jim, and was relieved not to see them, because that meant they'd found a good hiding place. I'd never been in a DC-3 before, but it looked as though most of the seats had been removed, perhaps to make room for cargo, except for a single row of seats lined up against the windows on the side opposite the door. Ralph, still holding the gun, pulled up the steps and locked the door behind us.

"Pete, we're fully loaded and ready to go," he shouted. I looked forward and saw Pete Scaggs sitting in the pilot's seat. He gestured okay without turning around.

"Sit down," Ralph directed, pointing with his gun to a seat just beyond some boxes.

I dutifully walked to the seat and sat down. The plane began slowly rolling down the ramp toward the runway. I looked out the small window next to my seat and saw Emma and Uncle Evert running up to the edge of the concrete just outside. They looked up and down the ramp, probably for me. If only they'd arrived a minute or two sooner! They had no idea I was on the plane, I was certain. How could they? I wanted to bang on the window and scream, but didn't dare. Ralph was next to me still brandishing the pistol. My heart sank as the plane finally arrived at the end of the runway, turned, and prepared for takeoff. This was unreal. I was petrified to fly. On top of that, I was the prisoner of a crazy man with and a grudge and a gun pointed directly at me.

CHAPTER TWENTY-FIVE

Air Mutiny

$\mathcal{A}$s the plane rolled faster and faster down the runway, I looked out at the unsuspecting crowd milling along the runway, and wished with all my being that I were out there with them enjoying a light-hearted day of fair food and breathtaking air acrobatics. My stubborn obsession with decoding the mystery surrounding Pete Scaggs had gotten me in more trouble than I could handle. What would these men do to me? Where were we going? Would anyone figure out I was on this plane? Even if they did, what could they do to help me? The more I thought about these things, the more despondent I became.

The plane slowly became airborne, and then quickly climbed higher and higher. The deep, droning sound of the two large engines filled the cabin. During the actual climb, Ralph sat in the seat directly behind me. No doubt he kept his gun pointed at me the whole time, even though it was unnecessary. Where could I go now that we were above the clouds? What options did I have? I was his captive, with or without the gun.

"Where are we going?" I asked. I was so nervous I could barely muster enough breath to make my voice audible in the noisy cabin.

"Be quiet. You'll find out soon enough," he replied in a gruff voice. "Stay in your seat and don't ask questions."

He walked forward to the cockpit and sat down in the co-pilot's seat next to Pete. Moments later, I heard them arguing.

"What? You brought a *girl* on board?" Pete growled. "Are you crazy? The last thing I need is to be charged with kidnapping on top of everything else."

Pete turned around to get a look at me. When he spotted me sitting among the boxes, I gave him the best angry glare I could muster.

"Oh, it's *that* girl," Pete replied to Ralph. "I remember her — always snooping around. But so what? You didn't have to snatch her. We could have dealt with her some other way. You always go off half-cocked. Like your idea to scare her off with that car stunt along the access road. Use your head, idiot."

"She saw too much," Ralph explained. "She took pictures of the bird. I had no choice, Pete. I had to act quickly. Really I did."

"Heck, Ralph. Do you ever think things through?" Pete chided. "What am I supposed to do with her now?"

"I don't know. We could throw her out over a lake or the ocean," Ralph suggested. "No one would ever find her if we did that. Even if they did, the authorities wouldn't know we had anything to do with it."

I couldn't believe my ears. *Throw me out of the plane?* Tears welled up in my eyes. I was beside myself with fear. If only Emma and Uncle Evert had come to the plane two minutes sooner! I wouldn't be in this trouble now. I gazed around the cabin looking for something to use as a weapon, and noticed a bottle opener lying on the floor near my seat. I slowly reached down, picked it up, and hid it in my hand. It was a long, thin aluminum bottle opener with one end designed to pop bottle caps open and the other pointed to pierce the tops of soda cans. Pete and Ralph were still absorbed in conversation and didn't notice me pluck it up. I didn't know what I was going to do with it, but I felt better holding it.

"Did anyone see you bring her on board?" Pete asked.

"No," Ralph replied.

"Are you *sure*?" Pete demanded. "Don't lie to me, Ralph."

"Of course I'm sure. Do you think I'm a fool?" Ralph answered indignantly.

"You tell me. Only a fool would steal the Kingwood kid's monkey, and only a fool would kidnap this girl. You've got two big strikes against you right there, and I'm just about fed up with you," Pete grumbled.

"I saw that monkey and thought you could make some money on it like the other animals," Ralph replied. "Isn't that the whole idea of this new enterprise of yours?"

"Yeah, but we get the animals through established channels," Pete said. "Not by stealing pets from neighborhood kids."

Ralph looked as though he was at a loss for words, and just stared back at Pete.

"All right. What's done is done. Let's hope for both our sakes no one saw you take her," Pete continued. "Go back and tie her up so she doesn't cause us any trouble. I don't want to baby sit anyone on this flight."

"Okay, okay," Ralph replied dutifully.

As they spoke, I heard stirring sounds behind me where several small boxes were stacked. I assumed the sounds were Luke and Jim moving about. I was curious what they were doing and wanted to turn around to see, but didn't want to inadvertently tip off Pete and Ralph that they were there. So, I stayed facing forward.

"Psst! Nessie monster," Luke whispered. He spoke so softly I could barely hear him.

I looked down and saw him on all fours in the aisle next to me. He winked and gestured to be silent. I was so glad to see him! Knowing I wasn't alone made part of my overwhelming fear melt away. He crawled over and squeezed behind a tall box just opposite my seat. The box, or crate, appeared to be made of wood and was about as tall as I was. It was the perfect place for him to hide. He had just gotten into place and out of sight when Ralph stood up and began walking back toward me.

I assumed he was coming to tie me up as Pete had directed, and I began hyper-ventilating. I grasped the bottle opener in my hand even more tightly, and braced myself to use it. He paused to dig around in a paper bag and pulled out a long cord, then jerked it to test its strength. Apparently satisfied, he smiled in a sinister way that made me shiver. He walked to my seat and stood over me with a deranged smile holding the cord, with the gun tucked into the waistband of his pants.

"You and your friends made a monkey out of me back at your little club house in the tree," he said, looking down at me. "Now it's my turn to give you a taste of your own medicine. Hold your hands out in front of you."

I looked up at him and knew this was my do or die moment. He was a big man and could easily fend off my attack. Still, I could at least inflict a wound that would make us even. What should I do? I sat motionless with indecision.

"Did you hear me?" he asked impatiently, snapping the cord between his hands.

"Even *I* heard you, Lurch!" Luke said, jumping out from behind the tall crate.

Before Ralph could respond, Luke jumped on Ralph's back and choked him with all his might. The gun flew out of Ralph's waistband and slid down the aisle toward the cockpit. They twirled around and around, and finally fell to the floor. Ralph's weight advantage helped him quickly get the upper hand over Luke, and he pinned Luke down and punched him over and over.

"Stop! Stop!" I yelled.

I dashed over to them and jabbed the pointed end of the bottle opener straight into Ralph's shoulder. He screamed in pain and reached back and grabbed my wrist so tightly I thought it would snap. After giving me an angry scowl, he let go of my wrist and resumed beating Luke.

Just then, Jim came running down the aisle and got a choke-hold around Ralph's neck from behind. Ralph was like an angry bear and stood up and whirled around while Jim held on for dear life. Jim quickly lost his hold and stumbled backward and almost fell down. Meanwhile, Luke managed to get to his feet, and walloped Ralph hard in the stomach. This didn't seem to have much, if any, impact, except to anger Ralph.

"I'll teach you!" Ralph shouted over and over again as he fought.

Time and time again Luke attempted to reach the gun lying in the aisle, but each time Ralph intercepted him and made him pay with a slug or a punch. On one attempt it looked as though Ralph would break Luke's arm after pinning it roughly behind his back, but Luke managed to wiggle free. Jim did everything he could to contribute to the cause, but Ralph seemed to know his way around a street fight and wasn't giving up easily, even against two young, healthy teenagers.

"What's going on back there?" Pete called out. "Who are those boys? Ralph! I can't leave the controls. There's no auto pilot of this plane. Answer me, Ralph!"

Ralph was too busy fending off Luke and Jim to answer. I looked at the gun lying on the floor only a few steps away and desperately wanted to pick it up, but the fighting blocked me. Each time I tried to reach for it, I had to draw back.

Suddenly, we flew into choppy air, and the plane dropped a few feet and vibrated. I managed to stay on my feet, but the tall crate next to my seat rocked as though it would fall over.

"Watch out!" Jim cried out.

The crate began to wobble more violently as the plane tilted from side to side as Pete struggled to get the plane through the turbulence. I was frozen and couldn't move. Jim suddenly stepped toward me and pushed me out of the way just as the box finally fell with an abrupt crash, trapping him underneath. He lay motionless, with his legs and feet extending out from under the box's heavy mass. I screamed in horror.

"Jim! Jim!" I shouted. "Are you okay? Please be all right. Oh, God. Please. . ." I knelt down and took Jim's limp hand.

Jim didn't reply, and I knew that couldn't be good. We had to get the box off him right away. Ralph stopped fighting for a split second and stared at the fallen crate. It was just enough of a distraction to give Luke the opportunity to get the gun. He ran down the aisle and picked it up.

"Okay, Lurch," Luke said, pointing the gun at Ralph. "Lift that crate off my friend, right now!"

"Ralph, take the gun from the kid, you blockhead," Pete yelled from the cockpit. "What are you waiting for?"

Ralph, disheveled and breathing heavily, looked at Luke, and then down at Jim. "Give me the gun and I'll lift the crate off your friend," he replied. "Otherwise, no dice and your friend can die under there for all I care."

"Do as he asks and give the gun to him, kid," Pete urged from up front. "Be smart and help your friend. You can't do anything with it, anyway. Think about it. You're in a plane ten thousand feet above the ground. If you shoot Ralph or me, you've got no one to fly this plane."

Luke paused and studied his options. Jim moaned and rustled under the box, and looked as though he was trying to push it off.

"Okay. You win. I know when I'm licked," Luke said. "Here you go."

He leaned toward Ralph holding the gun lying flat in the palm of his hand. Just as Ralph reached for it, Luke snatched the gun as fast as a bolt of lightning, and smacked Ralph across the side of his face with a powerful blow. Ralph staggered, obviously not expecting Luke to do what he'd done. Luke struck him again on the back of his head with the butt of the gun, and Ralph fell face down on the floor, out cold. It happened so fast I couldn't believe my eyes.

"Sucker," Luke smirked, tucking the gun into his belt.

Luke rushed over to the box and knelt down. Jim was pinned across his right arm and upper chest. "Jim. Jim, are you alive under there?" Luke asked.

"Get this off me," Jim moaned. "I can't breathe."

"Don't worry, buddy," Luke reassured. "We'll get you out of there in a snap."

Luke and I knelt down on opposite sides of the box and tried to lift it. It was so heavy that I assumed it must contain construction equipment or something. Straining with all we had, we were only able to lift it a few inches.

"Crawl out if you can," Luke urged, his face turning red from the exertion. "Can you do that?"

"I. . .I don't know," Jim said faintly. "I'll try."

Jim slowly moved his legs, wincing in pain. My muscles were straining and began to burn. I was overcome with worry that I'd lose my grip and drop the box at any moment. Jim slowly made progress, but not fast enough.

"Hurry, Jim," I pressed. "My arms are starting to give out."

"I. . .I can't go any faster. I think my arm's broken. Maybe some ribs, too," Jim said, suddenly stopping all movement. "Sorry guys. I can't do any more. I'm exhausted."

Luke and I gently lowered the box and let our arms rest.

"You're doing great, buddy," Luke cajoled. "Vanessa, you pull him out while I lift the box by myself. Do it fast as you can. I can hold this thing for only a few seconds."

"Can't we get Pete to come back here and help? You've got the gun and could force him to, couldn't you?" I asked. I wasn't certain I had enough strength to be able to pull Jim out. We needed more muscle power.

"He said there's no auto pilot on this plane, so he's got to stay at the controls. He'd have been back here by now if that weren't the case, you can bet on it," Luke reasoned. "So, it's up to you and me. Now, when I count to three, you pull him out. Ready?"

I nodded and looked down at Jim's face. He looked up at me and smiled weakly, even though he was in so much pain. He looked so pitiful lying there all rumpled and broken. It was up to me now to get him out, and I just hoped I was strong enough.

"Okay. One. . .two. . .three. Go!" Luke shouted.

With a big grunt, Luke lifted the crate a few inches. I knelt down and pulled on Jim's good arm with all my strength. He cried out in pain, but I continued tugging his arm and upper torso the best I could, and finally managed to just barely drag him out.

"I'm going to let go now," Luke said moments later. "Roll him over on his left side. Quick!"

I rolled Jim onto his left side just as the Luke let the box slam to the floor, barely missing Jim. We'd done it, and Jim was clear.

"Good thing I eat my Wheaties," Luke boasted, sweeping his disheveled blonde hair out of his eyes. "They've made me the he-man I am today."

Luke and I exchanged relieved glances. We carefully sat Jim up, leaned him against the box, and took inventory of his injuries. His right arm was definitely broken. Luke made a sling out of a burlap bag he found at the back of the plane and slid that over his arm. Jim also seemed to be very tender in his ribs. Some of them were probably broken. He might have other injuries we couldn't see. Not knowing where Pete was going or what would happen next, I wondered how long Jim would have to wait to get medical attention. His face was flushed and his breathing was shallow from the pain.

"Thanks, gorgeous," he said, his eyes half closed. "You're still the best, you know. And strong, too!" He tried to chuckle, but ended up coughing instead.

I touched his cheek softly and pondered what to do. I wanted to make him feel better, but didn't know what to do. It could have been me trapped under that box, not him. He'd selflessly put himself in harm's way to protect me, and I was grateful for that. I sat down next to him and took his left hand and squeezed it gently. He rested his head on my shoulder and nestled against me. All of the anger and jealousy I'd felt before evaporated.

Luke checked on Ralph, who was still unconscious. He tied him up with the cord Ralph was going to use on me. Then, Luke took the gun out of his belt and walked forward to the cockpit and pointed it at Pete.

"Turn this plane around and fly back to Gatewood Airport. Right away," Luke demanded. "Do as I say. I know how to use this, and I will if I have to."

Pete looked sideways at Luke and the gun, and chortled contemptuously.

"So, you're going to shoot me if I don't turn around, is that it, kid?" he sneered. "Well, I'm not about to turn around. So, go ahead and shoot me. I dare you. Like I said before, you need me to fly this plane. So, either use that thing, or shut up and sit down."

Luke looked confused by Pete's response. "I mean it Pete," he said in the most authoritative tone I'm sure he could muster. "Turn this plane around. My friend needs medical attention. The authorities will go easy on you if you take us back and get help."

"I'm not going back. So, like I said, either shoot me and fly this thing yourself, or sit down and be quiet," Pete snarled, turning his back on Luke. "Now get out of my face."

Luke paused for a moment, and then silently walked back to Jim and me and sat down next to us.

"I don't know what to do," Luke said, looking uncharacteristically defeated. "Pete's got a point. I can't shoot him and he knows it. I don't see any way to make him take us back to Gatewood. We're screwed."

"You mean — -we're back where we started? We're Pete's prisoners?" I asked, gulping. "After all that just happened?" I wanted to cry again.

"Yep," Luke said. "Looks that way."

"Luke — I'm in terrible pain. You've got to think of something," Jim pleaded, gasping and looking deeply distressed. "I hate to complain, but I need medical attention. I think I just coughed up a little blood."

Luke looked Jim up and down, and furrowed his brow. "Okay. I've got an idea. It's a long shot, but it's all we've got," he said.

"What?" Jim and I asked, almost in unison.

"Okay, listen up," Luke replied, lowering his voice and leaning in toward us. "You'll think I'm crazy."

"I don't care what it is. Crazy or not. What is it?" Jim asked, grimacing in pain.

"Maybe it's too crazy," Luke warned.

I studied Luke's face. If *he* thought it was a crazy idea, it had to be a doozie.

CHAPTER TWENTY-SIX

Amelia Flies Again

*J*im coughed and occasionally moaned a little. He looked miserable sitting on the floor, leaning against me clutching his injured arm. We had to do something quickly. He was in a lot of pain and needed medical attention.

"Okay. Here's the plan," Luke whispered. "If the plane's on fire, Pete'll have to turn around and return to Gatewood Airport. Right?"

"What're you suggesting?" I asked. "Are you going to set the plane on *fire*?" Talk about making the situation worse!

"That *is* crazy," Jim said, his eyes closed. "Even for a mad man like you. Next idea, please."

"No, no. I'm not really going to set the plane on fire," Luke clarified, smiling slyly. "I'm just going to make Pete *think* the plane's on fire."

"How do you plan to accomplish that?" I asked.

"There's a metal waste can in the back near the galley," Luke began. "I'll start a small fire with some paper in that. Pete'll smell smoke, and bing-o, bang-o. He'll do a three-sixty and turn around and head back to the airport. No questions asked, no shots fired."

"Wouldn't that be a one-eighty?" Jim asked, opening his eyes. "A three-sixty is a complete circle. Are we going to fly in circles?"

"All right. A one-eighty, then. I never said I was a math genius," Luke answered impatiently. "Well? What do you think?"

"What if the fire gets out of control?" I asked. "I don't want to die in a fiery crash."

"There's a fire extinguisher back there if anything goes wrong," Luke reassured. "But nothing will, you'll see."

"My vote is no. Let me tell you what's going to happen if you do this hair-brained thing," Jim began. "Pete'll smell smoke, come back here and get pissed when he finds the fire in the waste can, and throw us all out of the plane. Bing-o, bang-o."

"That can't happen. Pete's got to stay in the cockpit because this bucket doesn't have auto pilot. He told us that. He won't be able to tell from up there if it's a big fire or not. All he'll know is that he smells smoke, so there must be a fire, and he'll look for the nearest airport to get us on ground. Gatewood's the only airport for miles around that has a runway long enough for a DC-3, so he'll have to go back there. What d'ya say? Aren't I a genius?"

While we were discussing Luke's crazy plan, the plane flew through a cloud. The change in thermal temperatures made the plane jolt. Jim winced and clutched his arm even more tightly. It was clear he urgently needed medical attention, and we were out of other ideas.

"Okay. I'm in," I said reluctantly. "But I'll be really ticked off if you get me killed."

Luke grinned with a slightly demented look. I hoped he knew what he was doing. Fire was dangerous, especially on a plane.

"Be sure to make it a small fire, though. There are animals on board, you know," I reminded him. "Their respiration systems are delicate. Don't make too much smoke. Just enough so Pete can smell it."

"Are you certain that's the only plan you can come up with? Or, is it that you're just itching to set a fire? You've always been a bit of a pyro, you know," Jim teased.

"Well, if I've gotta go, I want to go in a blaze of glory," Luke replied, smiling. "Okay. Here I go. Good thing I've got some matches on me. You never know when you'll need them," he said, patting his breast pocket. The whimsy of his bowling shirt seemed oddly out of place now that we were in such dire circumstances.

Luke got up and walked to the back of the plane. I heard him moving things around. Moments later, the faint smell of smoke wafted through the cabin.

"Fire! Fire! There's a fire back here!" Luke yelled. "We're on fire! Help!"

"What?!" Pete shouted, turning around abruptly in his seat. "Damn you kids! What have you done?"

"Fire! Fire! The plane's on fire! Quick. Turn around and get us on the ground!" Luke continued, running up the aisle holding the fire extinguisher. "Fire! We've got to land! Hurry!"

The macaw squawked and rustled in its cage. It knew by instinct that the smell of smoke meant danger. Bobo let out a high pitched yelp from his cage as well. Even a small part of me instinctively felt agitated when I smelled the smoke. That must be proof that almost all living creatures are wired to be cautious of fire. I sure hoped Luke had made it a small fire.

"Damn it!" Pete bellowed again.

He turned back and forth in his seat, craning his head trying to see the fire. Apparently deciding he had no choice, he did exactly what Jim predicted. He left the controls and walked down the aisle to the back to investigate. By now the little fire was totally out, and just a hint of smoke remained in the cabin. Upon seeing the scorched waste basket, he realized what Luke had done, and angrily marched back with his gun drawn.

"What kind of a gag are you trying to pull, kid?" he chastised Luke sharply, pointing the gun at him. "I ought to shoot all of you right here and now. I could throw your bodies out over Lake Michigan and no one would be the wiser."

Luke didn't waste a minute. He flew at him swinging the red fire extinguisher he was holding as if it were a sword. Pete easily blocked the blow, causing Luke to drop the canister. It rolled down the aisle and stopped at my feet. The pilotless plane moved erratically, throwing Luke's footing off, and he stumbled and fell. Pete stood over him holding the pistol barrel only inches from his face.

"Satisfied? Now get up and drop that gun you've got in your waistband," Pete ordered, breathing hard.

Luke stood and pulled Ralph's gun out of his waistband and dropped it, then raised his hands in surrender. Pete quickly picked up the pistol and placed it in his pants pocket. We were back to square one, except now we didn't have Ralph's gun.

"Uh, don't you think you should get back to the cockpit?" Luke suggested, looking over his shoulder toward the front of the plane. "You can always shoot us later — if you feel like it, that is."

"Cute, ain't ya? You bet I'll take care of you later. Now sit down and don't make any more trouble," Pete growled. "I have both guns now, and make no mistake. It'll be my pleasure to shoot you with both of them if there's any more trouble. Capeesh?"

Pete pushed Luke down into a seat and then turned to rush back to the front of the plane. Just as he did, a flash of bright blue feathers flew by. Somehow, the hyacinth macaw had gotten out of its cage, probably agitated and disoriented by the smoke. It flew down the aisle, squawking and flapping its wings angrily. It landed on Pete's arm, and bit him over and over with its powerful beak which had the searing force of a chain saw. Pete screamed in pain as blood spurted out of his arm and hand. He was so stunned he fell backward, the gun discharging as he fell. He lay motionless on his side with the screeching macaw poised on his massive chest flapping its enormous wings.

"What was that?" Jim asked, straightening up to see. "Is everyone okay? Did he shoot the bird? What just happened?"

"I'm not sure. Pete? Pete?" Luke called, rushing over to Pete's motionless body.

The macaw had settled down now, and stood on Pete's corpulent body with a peaceful, almost casual attitude. Keeping a watchful eye on the bird, I knelt down next to Luke and studied Pete's wounds. Pete was very still, and his eyes were closed. I couldn't tell if he was dead or alive.

"Pete? Pete?" I said, jostling his shoulder. "Mr. Scaggs, are you all right? Mr. Scaggs, you have to get up and fly the plane. Pete?"

He didn't respond. I wondered how the bird knew Pete was his captor, and why he'd chosen him instead of one of us to attack. It had chosen just the right time to make its move. The animal kingdom certainly has its mysteries, and I figured it knew by some magic animal instinct that Pete was the bad guy, not us, and that we needed help. The macaw quickly lost interest in Pete and flew to an empty seat, and seemed content to remain there for now.

I looked down at Pete's sweaty, paunchy body, and saw bright red blood seeping through his shirt from a wound under his ribs. In addition to the gashes on his arms and hands inflicted by the macaw, it appeared he accidentally shot himself when he fell. Luke leaned down and checked for a pulse.

"Is he dead?" Jim asked.

"No. Not yet, anyway," Luke answered.

"Who's going to the fly the plane *now*?" I cried. A sudden panic descended over me. I was on a pilotless plane and would surely die. How could this be happening?

"Someone better do something real quick," Jim said. "Feels as though we've been steadily losing speed and climbing for several minutes now."

"I've flown in the Piper Cub with Buzz before, but this is totally different," Luke hedged anxiously. "What are we going to do?" I was surprised to see Luke waffling about taking charge of the plane.

"Help me up and I'll try," Jim volunteered, struggling to stand.

"Do you know how to fly?" Luke asked, taking Jim's good arm to help him up.

"No, but someone's got to try," Jim answered, working to get to his feet. He let out a small gasp of pain, and then fell back to the floor again.

"Forget it. I'll do it. You aren't in shape to do anything," Luke relented, running to the cockpit. "This flying thing can't be that difficult, can it?"

He jumped into the pilot's seat and pushed the yoke forward slightly. I felt the plane level off. Then, he put the headphones on and picked up a hand-held microphone stuck in a small pocket next to his seat.

"Mayday! Mayday!" he shouted into the microphone. "Anyone out there hear me? Mayday! Mayday! We have an air emergency! Over."

"This is Gatewood Airport. What's your emergency? Over," a voice came back after a few seconds. Luke must have pushed a speaker button, and I could hear the person on the other end.

"This is Luke Larsson. I'm in a DC-3. I don't know how to fly and there's no one else here to fly this thing. Over," Luke returned.

"Luke? Is that you?" the voice asked.

"Yeah, it is. Who's this? Over," Luke answered.

"This is Buzz. I was just walking through the office when I heard your call."

"Buzz! Thank God it's you. You've got to help us," Luke pleaded. "We're really screwed here."

"Did you say you're in a DC-3? How'd you get in a DC-3? What's going on?" Buzz asked, obviously confused.

"I'm with Vanessa and Jim Sparks. We were kidnapped by Pete Scaggs in his plane," Luke began. "You've got to help us. Pete's been shot, and there's no one here who can fly. We're desperate."

"Maybe I should get someone who flies a DC-3," Buzz suggested. "Stay put, and I'll be right back."

"No! Don't leave. No matter what you do, don't leave the radio," Luke implored. Taking a deep breath, he continued. "You know how to fly. You can do it. Just tell me what to do to get this crate on the ground without killing all of us."

"Okay, okay, but I'd I don't know that much about DC-3's. I'd rather get someone. . . ," Buzz said, his voice trailing off.

The radio suddenly went silent.

"Buzz. Are you there? Buzz? Buzz?" Luke anxiously clicked the radio button.

After a pause, Buzz came back. "Okay. I'll do my best. What's your location? Look out the window and tell me what you see."

Luke straightened up so he could see over the instrument panel. "I see fields, a few roads, and some grain elevators in the distance," he reported. "But I don't recognize anything. We could be anywhere. I have no idea where we are."

"You should see a compass located between the two front windows. What does it show?" Buzz asked.

Luke looked around and finally found it. "It shows a few degrees past north. What does that mean?" Luke answered.

"That's good. That means you're going almost due north. Look around again. Are you sure you don't see anything familiar?"

Luke straightened up and looked out again. "Wait a second. I see a big lake or reservoir on the left and a town almost directly below us. Wonder where we are?"

"The water could be Morse Reservoir, and you could be over Cicero," Buzz suggested. "You're going to have to turn around and follow Highway 19 back down to Noblesville. You can navigate visually using the roads."

"What do you mean turn around? How do I do *that*?" Luke asked, sounding stressed.

"You can do it," Buzz coached. "Remember when I let you turn the Piper Cub that time we were up together? It's almost like that, only you have to make a wider turn. Take it slow and easy. Let the wings bank, but not too much. And, watch your airspeed. If you speed up, pull back on the yoke just a little, and if you slow down, push it forward. Take a few minutes to get

comfortable with the plane before you do it. Move the yoke around a little to get the feel of it until you're ready."

I wasn't paying much attention to Pete, but Jim noticed he was bleeding badly. Jim suggested that someone help Pete before he bled to death. I
really didn't want to, but I agreed to do what I could, mostly because Jim
said it was the right thing to do. I found an old rag in the galley, placed it
over Pete's wound, and, closing my eyes, pressed it firmly against him. It
felt squishy beneath my hands. The sticky feeling of blood seeping through
the fabric made me pull away at first, but I resumed pushing hard anyway.
This was a day of firsts for me, and this was one of them.

Luke followed Buzz's instructions and moved the yoke to the left and
to the right, and slightly forward and back to get used to how the plane felt
and reacted. Each time he moved the yoke, the plane moved left, right, up,
or down. When he tried to execute a small turn which was a little too
abrupt, Jim and I almost took a tumble.

"Whoa! Take it easy, will you?" I shouted.

"Hey, I never said I was Sky King," Luke yelled back. After a few
more test moves, he told us he was ready to make the big turn. "Well, here
goes nothing," he said flatly.

With that, Luke moved the yoke to the left, the left wing dipped and
we began to turn. The wing banked steeply, and Pete and I slid a foot or so
to the opposite side of the aisle as the plane tilted. Jim grabbed one of the
seat supports with his good arm just in time to steady himself. Three or
four boxes near us teetered and looked as though they might fall, but none
did, to my relief. The macaw squawked in protest from its roost on one of
the seats, and Bobo let out a high-pitched cry from his cage. I was relieved
when the turn was completed and the wings were level again. Finally, we
were turned around, and the plane was still in one piece. Luke had accom-
plished the first step to get us home.

"Okay. I'm turned around," Luke confirmed in the radio. "What
next?"

"Good job! Now, what's your altitude? Look for the altimeter. It
looks like a clock with numbers from 0 to 9, with the 0 at the top. When
you find it, tell me what it shows," Buzz instructed.

Luke looked around the instrument panel for the altimeter until he
found it. He and Buzz discussed how to read it to determine our altitude,
and how we had to get our altitude just right in order to be able to land

without crashing. Buzz instructed him to move the throttles around slowly to see how the plane slowed down or sped up with each adjustment. I gathered that the throttles were a bunch of knobs on levers on a console between the pilot's and co-pilot's seats. Buzz told Luke not to allow the plane's airspeed to go below 120 miles per hour. They talked about a bunch of other stuff, too, that was too technical for me to understand. I was sure glad I didn't have to make sense of any of it. That was for Luke to do. All I had to do was keep pushing against Pete's wound to stop the bleeding. That, and pray that we'd get through this okay.

"You're going to need help navigating, getting the landing gear down, and doing lots of other stuff while you're landing. Did you say Jim Sparks is up there with you? Is he in the co-pilot's seat next to you?" Buzz inquired.

"What? Yes, I can help. For sure," Jim replied, struggling to get up when he heard his name.

"What are you talking about?" Luke countered. "You can't help with that bum shoulder of yours. Forget it. Vanessa can do it. Nessie, get up here."

I was stunned. I couldn't believe my ears. Me? Help fly this big plane? No way.

"Nessie Monster? Did you hear me? Get your keister up here in the co-pilot's seat. Pronto!" Luke commanded.

"I. . . . I don't think I'd be very good at that. Maybe. . .maybe Jim could. . .well he. . .," I sputtered.

Even as I spoke, I knew Jim was too injured to be able to help. He couldn't even get to his feet. I went numb as I faced the reality that it was up to me to help. But how could I do anything so complicated? This was never going to work. How could kids like us with no training land a large plane like this? It was crazy to think we could. Maybe Pete would wake up and be able to land. Now that he was injured, he wouldn't resist returning to Gatewood Airport. I looked down at him and jostled his shoulder again, but he was still out like a light. I nudged him again, but he remained unconscious. I had to face the fact he wasn't the solution.

Then I looked over at Ralph lying on his side all tied up. Luke must have hit him pretty hard, because he was still unconscious. Maybe we could rouse him and he could fly this thing. But he was still out, and I didn't even know if he knew how to fly. I realized I was out of options.

"Nessie!" Luke shouted. "Get up here. I need you. Move it!"

"You can do it," Jim said softly. He was on the floor just behind where I was kneeling next to Pete. "I know you can. You're a very brave girl, Vanessa. Go show yourself you've got what it takes."

I gazed at his weary face, and shook my head. "No. I can't do it," I blurted. "I'm too afraid. I just can't do it!"

All I wanted to do at that moment was to run to the back and hide under one of the tarps covering the animal cages.

"Of course you're afraid," Jim reassured gently. "But you're brave enough to do it anyway. That's what courage is. Doing what you have to do even when you're afraid. You've got that courage. I know you do."

"No, I don't. You're wrong about me," I said, shaking my head. "I'm too afraid. I can't do it. I want to be brave, but I'm not." I felt like crying, partly because I was worn out and afraid, and partly because I was disappointed in myself.

"You're wrong about yourself," Jim insisted. "You're much braver than you think. Go on. I'll take over with Pete."

He smiled and gave me a knowing look that steadied me. I lowered my head and closed my eyes. Taking a deep breath, I pulled myself together. If he thought I could do it, then maybe I could. I got up and marched to the cockpit, lowered myself into the co-pilot's seat, and took stock of what was around me. It seemed strange and scary to be up there. I felt out of place, like a tiny child sitting in her father's oversized chair. I gazed at all the dials and levers surrounding me. It was mind-numbing to think I'd have to figure them out. I looked out the front windshield at the fields and roads far below, and at the propellers spinning just outside my side window. The glass in the window vibrated from the roar of the engines. There was no way I could understand any of this. The situation was overwhelming.

"There you go, Nessie. Now you can see it all unfold before your very eyes," Luke said, giving me a quick wink.

Yes, but exactly what was going to unfold? I let out a heavy sigh and stared at the curve of the horizon far in the distance. If I ever flew again, I'd have to remember not to let the pilot accidentally shoot himself.

CHAPTER TWENTY-SEVEN

The General Would Be Proud

"Okay. So you've got Jim up there to help you. Right?" Buzz asked over the radio.

"Nope. Jim's been benched with a bad shoulder, so I drafted Vanessa for flight duty," Luke radioed back.

"Vanessa?" Buzz repeated in a surprised tone that I could detect even over the speaker. "Okay, okay. Why not? Sure. Tell Vanessa to put the headphones on."

I glanced around and found a pair of headphones hanging on a lever near the co-pilot's side window, and put them on.

"Can Vanessa hear me?" Buzz asked.

I nodded yes. "Yep. Loud and clear," Luke replied for me. Although I could hear Buzz perfectly well over my headphones, I had no idea what to do to allow him to hear me. Was there a button to push or a microphone to speak into? I didn't know, and Buzz didn't tell me.

"Vanessa, look under your seat. You should find maps to help you navigate," Buzz directed.

I reached under my seat and, sure enough, there was a map. That must be where pilots always stash their maps. I pulled it out and placed it on my lap. From the handwritten markings on it, it looked as though Pete was headed to Chicago.

"She's got it," Luke confirmed.

"Good," Buzz replied. "We'll use that later. Now, I want Vanessa to locate the landing gear lever and the wing flap controls. I'm not certain where they are in that plane. They should be somewhere on the forward instrument panel or around the center control pedestal where the throttles are located."

I looked around. If he didn't know where they were, how was I going to be able to find them? Everything looked the same to me. Lots of dials showing pressure readings of all kinds — hydraulic, oil, cylinder head, carburetor, manifold, oil, fuel, and on and on. There was a radio magnetic indicator, a glide slope indicator, and a pressure altitude gauge, whatever those were. I could find those, but not the landing gear lever. I carefully scanned all of the white labels under the dials, gauges, and levers looking for "landing gear" and "wing flap," but with no success.

"I can't find them," I shouted anxiously. "I can't find them! What are we going to do?"

"Calm down," Luke replied, studying my side of the instrument panel. "We'll find them."

"Did you find them yet?" Buzz asked.

"No. Not yet," Luke answered. "We're looking."

"Be careful not to allow your airspeed to drop. Keep it at least at 120 miles per hour. And hold your altitude at about 2,800 feet for now. You can accidentally let the plane slow down and lose altitude if you don't watch what you're doing," Buzz cautioned.

"There they are," Luke said, pointing to a lever that said "landing gear," and to another that said "flaps." "I knew we'd find them."

"Okay, you should be flying above Allisonville Road by now. Do you see it below?" Buzz asked.

I looked down and had no idea where we were. I could see a river on my right and a small town directly below.

"I think we might be over Noblesville," Luke replied. "I see White River off to my right, and some grain elevators, like the ones near downtown Noblesville."

"Okay," Buzz said. "Find Allisonville Road and follow it south. Watch where you're going, and when you're about to approach Fishers, turn southeast and head toward Geist Reservoir. Vanessa can look at the map and help you figure out when to turn. It's going to be very important that you know where you are at all times."

"Why are you sending us off to Geist?" Luke asked. "Are we going to ditch in the water?"

"No. Once you're out there you're going to circle back to Fishers and land at Gatewood. I want you to have a wide pattern in which to make your approach back here to give you more time and space to get things right and make corrections, if needed."

Buzz wisely knew we'd need lots of time and space to get things right. Luke and I sat in silence as the two loud engines droned on. I assumed we were flying above Allisonville Road, but all of the roads down below looked the same to me. I checked the map and then looked out the windows, comparing what I saw to confirm our location, but I couldn't be certain of anything. I kept changing my mind about where we were, and each time I did, I became more agitated that I wasn't doing my job. Luke was surprisingly calm. His eyes were fixed forward, except when he gazed down to check the altimeter or the air speed indicator. After a few minutes, he moved the yoke and the plane turned slightly.

"Is it time to turn toward Geist?" I asked.

"I think so," he replied. "That's Fishers High School down there. Boy, wouldn't the guys on the football team be impressed to know that it's me up here flying this DC-3? Too bad there's no practice today so I can buzz them."

"Hopefully, they won't learn about this from a story in the *Daily Ledger* about a DC-3 crash," I offered sarcastically.

We flew for a while until we were over the vast blue waters of Geist Reservoir. Luke asked Buzz if it was time to turn back west yet, and Buzz said he could do so whenever he felt like it. So, Luke got to practice his turning skills once again. Down went the right wing as he banked steeply and turned us back toward Gatewood Airport. I could hear boxes in the back slide as he made the turn.

"Hey. We're not in the air show, you know. Go easy on those turns, will you?" Jim called out weakly.

"Sorry buddy," Luke yelled back. "I guess I'm not ready to fly for American Airlines yet."

"After you make the turn over Geist, it'll be time for Vanessa to lower the landing gear," Buzz radioed. "Luke, you'll feel the plane slow down a little when the wheels come down, so be prepared for that and don't lose control."

I reached forward and moved the landing gear lever to the down position, and heard the wheels lower beneath us. A green light illuminated on the instrument panel under the words "landing gear down." It appeared that was all there was to it. Luke made some adjustments to our air speed, as Buzz had predicted he'd have to do, and all was well. Until the green light began flashing, that is.

"Is that light supposed to flash like that?" I asked. Something didn't feel right.

"Hey, Buzz," Luke asked. "The green landing gear light is flashing. What does that mean?"

"It means the landing gear isn't fully down and locked. Pull back on the throttles a little, and if the warning horn sounds, you'll know for sure the landing gear isn't down all the way," Buzz answered.

Luke pulled back on the throttles and, sure enough, a loud horn sounded.

"The horn sounded. What do we do now?" Luke asked.

"You'll have to manually lower the landing gear with the hand pump," Buzz said. "It should be on the floor near the central control panel between you. Vanessa should work that until the green light stays constant. Then, you'll know the gear is completely down and locked."

Luke and I looked around the floor until we found a red handle that looked like it could be the pump. Luke lifted it up and pushed it down. He nodded, indicating that was it.

"Your turn, Nessie. Time to build up those sissy biceps of yours," he said.

I lifted the handle up and pushed it down, over and over. It was diffi-cult and took all of my strength, even using the two-handed method. I couldn't tell if anything was happening, but as long as the green light flashed, I had to continue.

"When you pass over White River, turn ninety degrees to the left and watch for 116th Street, and then make another left turn," Buzz said.

"How will I know when I've made a ninety degree turn?" Luke asked.

"There's a compass in the middle of the instrument panel, but come to think of it, that might trip you up if you watch that. You should proba-bly just go by feel," Buzz instructed.

By feel? That didn't sound very scientific. At this rate I'd never make it to see my fifteenth birthday. Luke turned the plane, just as Buzz instructed. Everything and everyone slid a little to the left, just as with

Luke's other turns. When the turn was completed, Luke struggled to get the wings level again. We were caught in a pocket of strong wind. My stomach became queasy as the plane moved erratically. I took a deep breath and closed my eyes, trying to calm my stomach. I did *not* want to get sick, on top of everything else. My heart was racing, and I felt a wave of panic flow over me.

"Once you're through the turn, lower your altitude to about 1,100 feet," Buzz said "You'll know you're in the right place when you can see the airport straight ahead about one or two miles out. Can you see it yet?"

"Not yet," Luke said. "Nessie, are we where we're supposed to be? Look at the map and tell me."

I pulled the map back onto my lap and quickly examined it, but was so confused I could have been looking at a map of China instead of Indiana. "I. . .I don't know," I replied apologetically. "Where are we supposed to be again?"

"Oh, brother," Luke answered, pursing his lips together tightly. "Never mind."

I searched the horizon for the airport, but all I saw were fields and a few roads. The plane continued making its way as we went forward to meet our destiny. Luke looked out his side window and then forward, and then out his side window again as he searched for our location. I wasn't much help navigating, so I returned to my hand pumping duties.

"Um, I think I see it!" Luke radioed, finally.

I eagerly looked out the windshield and saw the silver-gray pavement of the runway glistening far in the distance. But my reaction was mixed. I was glad we'd found the runway, but now that I saw it, the reality of what we had to do hit me hard. How on earth were we going to be able to land this large and powerful plane on that little ribbon of pavement without killing ourselves? I had to hope for a miracle.

"Okay. Good job. Now, pull the throttles back to lower your airspeed to about 110 miles per hour, but no slower. Tell Vanessa to lower the wing flaps about half-way," Buzz said.

Lower the wing flaps? I paused from my pumping duties and reached up to the wing flap lever and moved it down one notch. Then quickly returned to pumping.

"Are the landing gear locked yet?" Buzz asked. "Is the light still flashing?"

"It's still flashing," Luke answered. "What should we do?"

"To tell you the truth, I don't know. You may have to just go for it and hope for the best," Buzz said.

I don't think I took another breath after that for a very long time. I was too racked with fear. The silver stretch of runway where my fate would be determined got closer and closer by the second. Even though I wanted to get out of this situation as quickly as possible, the closer we got to landing, the more on edge I became. I felt almost light-headed with dread. What would happen if the landing gear collapsed? Could we survive that? In the best of situations, the landing would be difficult. The uncertainty of the landing gear was one more strike against us.

"What about all the people at the airshow?" Jim asked from the back. "Are we going to land in the middle of the show?"

He made a very good point. What about the safety of all those people? What if we crashed and killed some of them? I suddenly realized that this was bigger than just the people in this plane.

"Buzz. What are we going to do about landing in the middle of the show?" Luke asked.

"Luther McKenstry just came into the office, and I told him to run out and tell the announcer to make an announcement for all spectators to take cover as far from the runway as possible," Buzz radioed. "One of the acts in the show was just about to take off, and I've told him and the others to stay on the ground for now. I've cleared the air and I'm doing my best to give you an empty field."

"We're going to be the next act in the show, huh?" Luke said, trying to add levity.

"Yeah, you could say that," Buzz answered. "Make it a good act, will you? Nothing with flames and broken bodies."

"Roger that," Luke answered.

The tree tops and fields came closer as we bounced along. The plane tipped from side to side with each gust of wind. At one moment, Luke had the plane lined up pretty well with the runway, and then the plane would jolt suddenly to the left or the right of it. The wings moved up and down as Luke struggled to keep them level. How was Luke going to be able to get us safely down on such a tiny strip of pavement? It looked impossibly narrow from up here. Luke stared intently forward with his lips pursed tightly together and a funny expression on his face. Rows of cars were parked in the grass not too far from both edges of the runway, so we didn't have much room for error.

"I can see you now. Keep your nose down," Buzz directed. "Your nose is too high."

Luke pulled the yoke forward slightly in response.

"Still too high," Buzz said again, a bit impatiently. "Bring it down. Bring it down."

Luke moved the yoke forward a little more.

"Okay. That's better. When you're directly over Allisonville Road, Vanessa should lower the wing flaps all the way," Buzz said. "Remember, Luke, when you make contact with the ground, pull the yoke all the way back, but don't brake too hard or you'll nose in. Let the tail fly itself down as the plane gradually slows. You'll steer with the rudder pedals and brake with the upper part of them. Just don't jam on the brakes. Go easy with them. Got it?"

"Got it," Luke answered.

"Do you think you can do it? Land this plane, I mean?" I asked, gazing at Luke. He was a hyper and brash kid, and now I was relying on him to save my life. I don't know why I asked. Maybe if he replied in the affirmative, I'd be less frightened.

"Sure. It can't be much different from landing a radio-controlled model plane, can it?" he joked, flashing me a big smile.

"I don't want to interrupt what you're doing up there," Jim said. He'd managed to crawl up near the cockpit and was leaning against the door looking very rumpled. "But I'd like to say something to the two of you before it's too late. It's at moments like this that you realize what's important in life, and I just want to say something in case I don't make it."

"Don't talk like that," Luke interrupted. "We're all going to get out of this in one piece with all body parts. So, go back where you were and brace yourself against something and find a flotation device."

"Why do I need a flotation device over a corn field?" Jim asked, looking puzzled. "Stop trying to confuse me. Look — I want to tell both of you how much your friendship has meant to me."

"Oh, great. Here comes the mush," Luke murmured. "I'd rather die in a fiery crash than hear this."

"Cut it out, Luke," I said, turning in my seat to look at Jim as he spoke.

Our eyes met, and I was touched by the sad look in his handsome eyes. I saw genuine caring, a tinge of regret, and something else that made a chill go through me. Was it possible he didn't believe we were going to make it? He must have sized up the situation and concluded it was doubtful. He smiled sadly, and somehow I knew what he was trying to say.

"Promise me you'll always remember how important you are to me," he said softly. "No matter what. Even if I'm not around to remind you."

I reached out and we managed to entwine our fingers momentarily.

"Uh, someone is supposed to lower the flaps about now," Luke said, struggling to keep the plane level. "Could you two do your Hallmark moment after we land, please?"

I turned back in my seat and moved the flaps down another notch. The plane was really getting low to the ground now. I could see crowds of people in the distance as they ran to get out of our way. The runway was less than a mile away now.

"When you get over the end of the runway, pull back on the throttles all the way and the plane will set itself down. Remember not to brake too hard. Good luck, you guys," Buzz said. "I know you can do it."

"Here goes nothing," Luke said. He jut out his jaw and held onto the yoke firmly with both hands. I heard him say something under his breath about General Savage on *Twelve O'Clock High* landing shot up planes all the time.

"Luke, I'm scared. So scared!" I blurted as I saw the runway directly ahead. "I think I'm going to throw up."

Luke didn't answer. Maybe he was too scared himself to speak. Time seemed to stand still in the final moments of our descent. A million thoughts streaked through my mind as the runway came closer and closer and the plane rocked from side to side. Would the landing gear hold? After all, the green light was still flashing. Would Luke be able to set the plane down on the runway without clipping a wing or landing too hard? What if we ran into cars parked along the runway? What if we ran into the office or a hangar — or another plane? What if we nosed in like a lawn dart? What if we burst into flames?

I saw Allisonville Road below us and lowered the flaps the final notch. Then, I closed my eyes, put my arms over my face, and waited for impact.

Seconds later, the plane touched down with a hard jolt about halfway down the runway, and bounced back up into the air. Luke held the yoke tightly and the plane went back down on the pavement again with a heavy thud, and then bounced up in the air again. It was like being on a roller coaster. When we finally touched back down to the pavement, this time we stayed there, and rolled fast down what was left of the runway. The landing gear was holding, even with the rough touch down, so my pumping efforts must have done some good. Luke followed Buzz's instructions and steered the plane with the rudder pedals and didn't brake too hard. Suddenly, however, something went wrong, and we veered off the pavement into the grass. The grass slowed the plane a little, but we were still going really fast. I opened my eyes and saw, to my horror, that we were headed directly toward a group of spectators standing near some parked cars.

"Oh, my god!" I shouted. "Watch out! We're going to mow down those people!"

Luke jammed on the brakes, which was exactly what Buzz told him not to do. The nose went down and the tail almost straight up as we skidded along the grass. The impact threw me against the instrument panel and I hit my head against the windshield. The propellers of the two large engines made contact with the ground, and spewed pieces from the impact for several yards all around. Then, the landing gear collapsed and Luke lost all control. I screamed and closed my eyes even more tightly and held on. We skidded for some distance as pieces of the plane were torn off or smashed, making hideous metal twisting sounds. The macaw let out a terrified screech. We continued skidding for what seemed like minutes, with loud thuds, bumps, and breaking noises deafening my ears as the plane plowed through the grass and disintegrated underneath us.

"Holy crap!" Luke shouted, still holding the yoke. "How do you stop this thing?"

We crashed through a spectator barricade and mowed down an empty lemonade tent. We plowed over a section of unoccupied spectator folding chairs. The right wing clipped a large Hoosier Air Sales advertising banner and its ripped material became entangled in what remained of a propeller. I didn't know how close we were to hitting a car or a hangar, but I assumed impact with one was coming, and braced myself even more securely. The plane continued to skid and bump along the uneven ground at an alarming speed, but then it began to slow down as it plowed through the grass.

Mercifully, after a few more seconds, we finally came to a rest, with the nose resting on the soft ground and the engines belching smoke. I was grateful all of the loud and terrifying noises of the crash finally stopped. I'd been thrown out of my seat and slammed against the instrument panel, but I was alive. I opened my eyes and looked around, and was relieved to see that we'd stopped just short of hitting the group of spectators by several yards. People were still running in all directions to get out of our path, and pieces of the plane were still falling to the ground. The plane was banged up pretty badly and so were we, but we were on the ground, and no spectators were injured as far as I could tell.

"Luke. Are you okay?" I called after I came to my senses, rubbing my head where I'd hit it against the windshield. A little blood trickled down my forehead, and I wiped it with my sleeve. Luke looked unhurt, but he still clutched the yoke with an iron grasp, as if welded to it.

"Luke? You can let go of the yoke now," I said, touching his shoulder lightly. "We're on the ground, and we're okay. You did it. Do you hear me? *You did it!*"

"Wow," he said robotically, looking stunned and still gripping the yoke. "That was some wild ride, wasn't it?"

"Jim! Jim!" I shouted to the back of the plane. "Jim, can you hear me? Are you okay?"

Several moments went by and my heart sank when he didn't answer. Was he alive? Why didn't he answer? It bothered me he'd talked the way he did just before we landed. Sometimes a person can have a premonition about his future. Why did he say good-bye?

"Jim? Are you alive? Please answer me," I called. I wanted to crawl back and look for him, but the large box that fell on him earlier and some other cargo was thrown to the front of the plane and blocked the door of the cockpit.

People ran to the plane from all directions. A fire truck from the Fishers Fire Department, an ambulance, and other vehicles streaked across the grass toward us. I'd gotten my miracle, and survived. I couldn't believe it. Tears welled up in my eyes. I took a deep breath and exhaled slowly. We'd beaten the odds and landed this sophisticated machine without any real flying experience. Sure, the plane was in pretty bad shape and may never be air-worthy again, but we were on the ground and alive. It was difficult to take it all in. Especially when I didn't know how Jim was, and why he didn't answer.

CHAPTER TWENTY-EIGHT

Picking Up the Broken Pieces

It occurred to me the plane might explode into a fireball at any minute, so I wanted out. *Now*! A couple of men climbed up and broke out the windows in the cockpit and helped Luke and me crawl out. We scooted down over the large crumpled nose, and then they helped us jump down several feet to the grass. It was wonderful to be on the ground again. I almost bent down and kissed it. My forehead hurt, and I was a bit stiff from the impact of the landing, but all-in-all, I was in pretty good shape. Luke was okay, too, at least physically. He walked in circles gazing up, shaking his head, and muttering to himself. I wondered if this was how he expressed his post-traumatic stress.

Buzz was one of the first to get to us. "You guys scared the daylights out of me, you know that?" he said, hugging first me, then Luke, then me again. "I was so worried. I wasn't sure you could do it, and if you hadn't, I would have never forgiven myself."

"Thanks, cuz," Luke said, slapping Buzz on the back. "I guess that means you didn't have much faith in your own flight instructions, did you?"

"Well, not entirely, to tell you the truth," Buzz replied, shrugging. "I told you I didn't have that much experience with DC-3s." Then, looking up at the plane, he joked, "Looks as though you have some explaining to do, now that you've wrecked Mr. Scaggs's beautiful plane."

The plane was indeed a mess. Nothing but broken propellers and windows and crushed aluminum, with landing gear and other parts strewn everywhere. Pete wouldn't be happy about this when he recovered from his injuries.

"I don't think so," Luke protested. "I believe ol' Mr. Scaggs has a whole lot of explaining to do to *me*."

A nurse from an Indianapolis hospital staffing the medical tent examined my head and bandaged my wound. She said she didn't think I'd need stiches, which was good news. She wanted to take me in an ambulance to the hospital to have my head checked out for a concussion, but I told her I felt okay. She made me promise to go later if I felt worse.

Meanwhile, two men pried open the back door of the plane and went inside. I ran to the back to watch as they brought Jim out. Monica pushed through the crowd and looked semi-hysterical when she saw him lying unconscious on the stretcher as they checked his vital signs and inserted an IV into his arm. I expected to see them load him into an ambulance right away, but they didn't. Instead, the medics continued working on him for what seemed to me like an unusually long time. He remained unconscious, and there was an air of concern on the medics' faces that worried me.

"Is. . . .is Jim going to be okay?" I asked Buzz who was standing near me.

"Sure, sure," Buzz reassured, looking solemn as he watched.

The paramedics gave Jim a shot of something in his arm, listened to his chest, and checked his pupils. The more they worked, the more anxious I became. I wouldn't be able to cope if I lost him. Not after all we'd just been through together.

Monica darted to the stretcher and gently pushed a strand of Jim's hair off his face and kissed him on the forehead. Maybe she really did care about him, or maybe she wanted to look as though she did. Who can explain the heart of a girl like her? I wanted to give her the benefit of the doubt, but on the other hand, I didn't really care. I knew how I felt about him, and that's all I was sure of.

Finally, the medics picked up the stretcher and appeared to be taking Jim to the ambulance. I quickly walked over and squeezed his limp hand as they carried him past me. I needed to touch him just once before they took him away. I was delighted, and surprised, when he opened his eyes a little when I did. He smiled weakly at me just as they lifted him into the ambulance.

"Nessie. . . I knew you could do it," he managed to utter ever so softly just before they closed the ambulance doors.

Monica looked at me with indignation as though I had just blown out her birthday candles. I smiled and slowly strolled away. If Jim survived, I didn't know where my relationship with him was going, but I knew we weren't finished yet. Monica would just have to get over it.

Emma and Uncle Evert ran over to Luke and me as I watched the medics take Pete and Ralph off the plane next on stretchers and load them into ambulances. Emma hugged me so hard and for so long that I didn't think she'd ever let me go.

"I was so worried!" she exclaimed. "I tried so hard to get Dad back to the plane in time, but Pete was already taxiing out when we got there. We didn't even know you were on the plane at first. Are you mad at me? I feel as though I let you down."

"Don't be silly. You didn't let me down," I said, giving her another hug for good measure.

"Are they going to live? Pete and Ralph, I mean," Luke asked as he watched the ambulances drive away.

"I think so. I overheard the medics say they didn't think they were too seriously wounded," Uncle Evert said. "I imagine you have quite a story to tell about what happened, mister. I can't wait to hear how they got you on that plane. I'm sure it's not because you were where you shouldn't have been."

"Oh, yeah," Luke said, smiling slyly. "It's *quite* a story."

I knew Uncle Evert was very happy that Luke survived the landing, but he seemed very curious about how Luke got on the plane in the first place. I'd been kidnapped, of course, but Luke would have to explain to his dad how he trespassed on it and got trapped. I would give him my complete support if he needed it. I knew fully well that if Luke hadn't been on the plane, Pete and Ralph would have followed through on their plan to throw me out over Lake Michigan or get rid of me in some other horrible way. There was no way I'd be standing here right now without him.

"Why do we always find you in the middle of big messes, little brother?" Lars asked, rushing up with Margret and Wendy. Looking up at the plane, he added, "I must say you've topped yourself this time."

"Glad to see you, too, big bro'," Luke replied.

"Well, I hope you're happy. You shut down our very first air show, and we were only half-way through," Uncle Forrest said, walking up in his usual quick gait. "That was some big finish, I must say. I just hope you get

a little more pilot training before you try landing anything in the future."
He laughed and put his arm around Luke's shoulders. "Seriously, though.
I want to hear all about what happened with Pete Scaggs. He's always been
such a stand-up guy. When you feel better, I'd like to hear what you know
about the shady activities Daniel and Emma tell me he was conducting at
this airport."

"Just my luck that I had to work the show," Daniel said, poking his
head through the small crowd that had gathered around us. "I missed out
on all the fun."

"Right. Some fun," Luke said, rubbing his stiff neck.

"We think we saw Bobo on the plane," I told Daniel. "We may have
wrecked the plane, but at least we were able to rescue him. I think they're
working on getting him and the other animals off the plane right now."

"Bobo?" Daniel said, his eyes searching the area. "Where is he? I
can't wait to hold him in my arms again."

Now that all of the people on the plane were out, the rescue workers
turned their attention to removing the animals. The animal cages were carried out one at a time and carefully placed on the grass. There were four
larger ones, each covered with a tarp or blanket. As the men pulled back
the tarps and blankets, I walked over to investigate, excited about finally
meeting Bobo.

The hyacinth macaw was really squawking and kicking up a fuss in
one of the cages. The rescuers had managed to get him back in his cage. I
was glad to know it was still alive. Another cage held the Komodo dragon,
which *did* look like a small dinosaur when I finally saw it. But where was
the black spider monkey that Luke saw? The animal in one of the cages let
out a ghostly shriek as I approached it. I looked through the holes in the
cage and saw two vivid yellow eyes staring back at me. It was clearly not
Bobo. The animal was covered in a patchwork of thick black and white fur
with a ruff of white fur framing its black face. I'd never seen anything like
it before. Daniel walked over and peered at it.

"That's a black-and-white ruffed lemur," Daniel declared. "He's on
the endangered list, too."

Of course he was. I'd never heard of that kind of lemur before, but it
didn't surprise me that it was on the endangered list. Pete didn't appear to
trade in any other kind of animals. What a shame he didn't have a con-
science when it came to animals, or people for that matter.

I approached a cage where two men were kneeling looking intently inside the open door.

"Is something wrong?" I asked, trying to get a look at the animal inside.

"We're afraid this one didn't make it," one of them said. "The stress of the crash landing must have been too much for his little system. He doesn't appear to have any outward injuries. Poor little guy."

"What kind of animal is it? Is it a monkey?" Daniel asked softly. I knew he was worried it might be Bobo. I was, too.

"It's a monkey with black fur," the man replied.

"What? Bobo? Oh no!" Daniel said, pushing in to see. A look of stunned grief replaced the hopeful expression he'd had on his face only moments before. "Oh, no. Bobo, my Bobo," he said, kneeling down to touch its lifeless little paw.

"Daniel, I'm so sorry," I said, touching Daniel sympathetically on the shoulder. "I can't believe it. Are you sure it's Bobo?"

Daniel silently nodded yes. A tear streaked down his cheek.

"Oh, Luke. I'm afraid we've killed Bobo," I said to Luke as he walked up. "All we wanted was to rescue him. How could this happen? I feel just horrible." I started crying. It was the last straw in a traumatic day, and I was overcome.

"Yeah, this blows," Luke replied, looking over at Bobo's cage. He walked over to Daniel and stood behind him. "I'm really sorry, buddy. Really I am."

"Don't feel too bad," Buzz said, walking up to us. "You did your best to try to save him. At least you saved the other animals on the plane. And, since Pete Scaggs is finished smuggling after this, you've saved all the animals he would've smuggled in the future. You should be proud you saw what was happening right under all our noses and put an end to it."

"I don't feel proud right now," I said, watching Daniel as he remained on his knees next to Bobo. Tears still welled up in my eyes.

"This is what happens when people trade in exotic animals," Daniel said through his tears. "Exotic animals often die in transit, even when there's no plane crash. Pete's the one who killed Bobo, not anyone else."

Just then, Randy walked out of the crowd gathered around us. He had a black eye, but otherwise seemed surprisingly healthy, especially considering the force of the punch he received from Ralph.

"Randy, you old scum bag," Luke said, slapping Randy on the back. "There you are. We were worried about you. How're you feeling?"

"Ralph hit me pretty hard, but fortunately all I got was this shiner," he answered, pointing to his black eye. "I'm kinda proud of it, to tell you the truth. I can't wait to show it to the guys at band camp and tell them how I got it."

"You look quite handsome with it," I said, wiping my tears and doing my best to pull myself together. "Heroic, even."

"Oh, well, I don't know," he replied, turning red. "Are you okay, Vanessa? I didn't know if I'd ever see you again. I felt pretty bad that I didn't stop that creep from hurting you. I tried. I couldn't stop thinking about you and worrying."

"He has a crush on you, you know," Luke whispered in my ear.

"Yeah, I know," I whispered back. "He has good taste, doesn't he?"

"Ugh!" Luke said, making a face. He walked back and stood beside Daniel.

"You don't have to worry about me any more. I'm fine," I said to Randy, and smiled. "It was sweet of you to care."

He looked at me with a look of admiration that used to bother me. "You know, you're okay for a girl," he continued. "You're not silly like a lot of them."

I laughed. *If he only knew!*

"Do you think? I mean. . . I was wondering," he mumbled, looking down shyly. "Would you. . . . Would you be okay going for a Coke or to see a movie with me sometime if I can get a ride down to Indianapolis?"

"Sure," I said without hesitating. "Just call me. We can talk about it."

"Cool," he replied, grinning broadly and looking me in the eye.

Randy was a good guy at heart. I realized that I should look beyond his outward appearance and his awkward way of interacting to the generous and caring person he really was. I didn't think we'd ever be more than just friends, but that in itself was something to cherish, I now knew.

CHAPTER TWENTY-NINE

Good-Bye and Hello

*A*lmost perishing in a fiery plane crash has a way of making a person take stock of one's life and think about who and what are important. After all, it was a miracle we survived, and that Luke and I came through it with hardly any injury. That must mean *something* in the scheme of the universe. Exactly what, I couldn't say, but I was going to do my best not to take life for granted ever again. At least, that's what I promised myself.

My little brother had the stomach flu, so my parents didn't make it to the air show. That meant they didn't see the crash, which was a very good thing. My mother would have had a heart attack if she'd seen it. Uncle Evert and Aunt Louise called my parents and filled them in on the details when we were safely back at their house. Aunt Louise told me my mother screamed and almost dropped the phone. Mom said she thought Emma and I were playing with Barbie dolls and doing crafts. Boy, was she mistaken!

The sheriff told us at the airport he wanted to come to the house later on and interview all of us before we forgot anything. So, everyone agreed it made sense for me to stay one more night to give him a chance to interview me, which made me very happy. I wasn't ready to say good-bye to everyone yet. I needed to talk through the experience with them, and let the dust settle in my mind. We'd been through a lot together, and it was going to be difficult to say good-bye.

The sheriff arrived just before dinner. He said he had just finished taking statements from Daniel, Buzz, and Uncle Forrest and was starting to piece together the puzzle involving Pete's exotic animal smuggling. I was a little intimidated to talk to the sheriff at first, but he was nice enough. He said we could sit around the dining room table and talk in an informal way, just as long as we gave him all of the important details. Before he started, he told us that the hospital reported Pete would probably pull through, and that Ralph would be okay, too.

"Yep. That Pete Scaggs sure is a lucky man," the sheriff began, "because that shot missed some important organs by only a centimeter or two. Yep, he would have been a dead man if that shot had been just a hair more to the left or right. Someone also did a good job of stopping the bleeding or he would have bled to death."

Hearing that made me feel pretty good about helping save a life, even if that life belonged to Pete Scaggs, the animal smuggler.

"Oh, that was Nessie here," Luke volunteered, pointing at me. "Did she tell you how icky she thought it was to touch Pete's wound? She's no Florence Nightingale, I can tell you."

"Oh, cut it out, Luke!" Emma scolded. I laughed and didn't say anything. It was just Luke's way of showing his affection for me, I knew.

I wanted to ask the sheriff if he knew how Jim was doing, but I managed to suppress the impulse. It was best not to mention Jim in front of everyone. I hoped the sheriff would bring Jim up on his own, but he didn't.

"Looks as though you were all very brave," the sheriff said after Luke, Emma, and I'd finished giving our statements. "It's amazing you caught on to what Mr. Scaggs was doing right under our noses, when the rest of us didn't see it."

"Oh, that was also Nessie's doing," Luke said. "She doesn't trust anyone. Comes from living in the big city, you know."

"It's just that I love animals and hate to see them harmed," I said. "It was just a lucky hunch."

"Well, then, I'd say you're a very smart girl," the sheriff said, giving me a nod. "Maybe you'll end up doing detective work when you grow up."

"Don't encourage her!" Luke interrupted. "She's already a pain in the ass about this stuff."

"Luke!" Uncle Evert reprimanded. "Be respectful, and don't use that word."

"Sorry, sir," Luke replied, pretending remorse. "Pain in the behind," he mumbled under his breath.

"Yep. I guess Mr. Scaggs found out that there was pretty good money to be made transporting those exotic animals from the Gulf Coast to the West Coast for resale to customers in Asia, so he used his plane for that dirty business," the sheriff explained. "Most of those animals were endangered, you know."

"What a creep," Luke declared scornfully. "Wasn't he making enough money in the construction business? Why'd he have to get into this exotic animal business?"

"Some people can never make enough money, no matter how much they make," Aunt Louise explained. "Pete must have been compensating for virility issues with money."

"Mom!" Luke protested, covering his ears. "Stop! You're grossing me out."

Aunt Louise laughed and waved her hand playfully at Luke.

"A couple of other details have also fallen into place," the sheriff continued. "That so-called ghost plane that landed at Gatewood a few weeks back, for instance."

"You mean that Cessna they found at the end of the runway in the middle of the night a couple of weeks ago with its propeller still turning and no one inside?" Luke asked excitedly. My ears perked up.

"Yep, that's the one," the sheriff replied. "Well, the authorities in California say the owner of the Cessna is in business with Mr. Scaggs to transport exotic animals to their area. Those unusual turtles they found in the plane were part of the flow of endangered animals they were smuggling. The pilot evaded radar the whole way here and ran off when he saw the security car making its rounds."

"See? I told you there was no such thing as a ghost plane," Luke said to Emma, bumping her leg playfully.

"You don't know everything," Emma grumbled. "Maybe that one wasn't a ghost plane, but I'm sure they exist."

"Sure they do. Just like Civil War ghosts in our graveyard out back!" Luke teased. Emma stuck out her tongue.

"You kids need to simmer down while the sheriff's here," Uncle Evert said flatly.

"Oh, it's okay if they want to blow off some steam. They've been through a lot today," the sheriff said as he closed his notebook. "But hey. Do you mind if I ask you a personal question, Mr. Larsson?"

"Sure. No problem," Uncle Evert answered. "What is it?"

"Looks as though you're moving, what with all those boxes over there," the sheriff observed. "Am I right?"

Several boxes that Aunt Louise had packed were stacked in the corner of the dining room, and a few more were stacked in the living room near the curtains to Emma and Margret's room.

"Yes," Uncle Evert replied. "You could say that. Seems we've gotten cross-wise with the company that has a mortgage on this farm, and they've graciously asked us to vacate the premises."

"That's interesting. You see, I did some research on Mr. Scaggs this afternoon before I came to see you. Would it surprise you to know that his construction company bought your mortgage from the bank a few months back?"

"What?" Uncle Evert asked, leaning forward intently. "So, *he's* behind those stern foreclosure letters. But why?"

"Probably so he could foreclose us out over nothing, and then have all this land to build houses on," Aunt Louise replied. "He's been interested in getting this land for a long time now. It's close to Fishers and would make a nice housing development."

"That's right," Uncle Evert agreed, nodding slowly as he gave it some thought. "Now that you mention it, Pete came by a few months back to ask if we'd sell, and I told him we weren't interested and never would be. He was extremely persistent. He must have figured buying our mortgage from the bank and foreclosing us out over a technicality was the only way to get it from us."

"I'm not the prosecutor, of course," the sheriff said, "but it sounds to me as though Mr. Scaggs will have three counts each of kidnapping and battery added to his list of charges, not to mention a federal offense for smuggling exotic animals. Let's just say when he feels better, he's going to be sent away for a long, long time. He won't have time to foreclose anyone or build any houses."

"Are you saying we can stay? That we won't have to move to New Jersey?" Emma asked excitedly.

"We'll get a lawyer to look into it," Uncle Evert said, reaching over and taking her hand. "Sounds promising we'll get to stay. Maybe I can even convince the bank to buy back our mortgage and give us some time to get it straightened out."

"Oh, thank heaven!" Aunt Louise gasped. She turned her back to everyone and looked down. I wondered if she was choking back a tear or two of joy.

The sheriff finished his business and thanked everyone, and then shook Uncle Evert's hand. "You've got some brave kids here, Mr. Larsson," he said. "I bet you're really proud of them."

Luke beamed. I felt pretty good, too. It felt great to hear the sheriff acknowledge my courage, even if I'd been forced by circumstances to be brave. Up until now, my life had been rather safe and ordinary. I'd never been in fear of being shot, or of dying in an airplane crash. Now, I knew what real fear felt like, and I knew what it felt like to act in the face of that fear. I'd never forget the terror I felt as we approached the runway, knowing we'd probably crash.

Uncle Evert thought we should celebrate, so he went out and bought a giant bag of White Castle hamburgers. The whole family sat around the table and gobbled them up, followed by giant chocolate sundaes made with Marsh brand vanilla ice cream doused with plentiful amounts of Hershey's syrup out of a can. Even Lars and Margret ate with us. No one made a cross remark or mocked anyone, except for Luke, of course. He was still dishing out his brand of good-natured insults. All in all, it was the most congenial I'd ever seen the Larsson family. I guess crisis really does bring people together, just like they say.

After dinner, Emma and I went outside and sat on the front stoop overlooking the yard. It was almost dark. The evening was beautiful, clear and still. Allisonville Road was busier than usual as air show stragglers were still leaving the airport.

"Were you scared?" Emma asked as she manipulated a foxtail leaf into a whistle. "In the plane, I mean?"

"Yes. I was in a panic," I confessed. "When I saw you and your dad run up to the hangar when we were taxiing out, I wanted to cry. The way those guys were talking, I thought for sure I was dead."

"Hey, Sky Queen," Luke said, suddenly appearing on the other side of the screen door. "Someone's on the phone for you."

"Who is it?" I asked, rising to my feet. "My mom?"

"I don't know. Do I look like your personal secretary?" he said, walking away.

I hurried inside and found the receiver lying on its side on the desk in the living room.

"Hello?" I said into the phone.

"Hello, beautiful," Jim said. "How are you?"

"Jim!" I exclaimed. His voice was faint, but it was unmistakably him. "How are you? Are you okay? Are you calling from the hospital?" I was delighted to hear from him and know he was well enough to make a phone call.

"I'm fine," he said. He didn't sound very strong, which wasn't surprising. "My parents brought me home from the hospital about an hour ago. The doctors wanted to keep me, but I was going crazy there, so they let me go home as long as I follow the rules. I have a broken clavicle, a couple of other broken bones, a small puncture in my lung, and a bad bump on my head. But I'll live."

"Are you in a cast?" I asked.

"Yeah, they've got me in all kinds of braces and stuff," he said. "I look like the Mummy when I walk. You should see me. You'd die laughing."

I giggled. It was so good to hear his voice.

"I'm going home in the morning, so I guess I won't be able to see you before I leave," I said.

"Yeah, that's the bad news," he said. "But I'll keep in touch. You can count on me. I won't let you down this time, I promise."

"Just get well," I said. "I always love receiving letters."

"Um, well, my writing arm is in a cast, so I'll have to call you," he replied.

"I love phone calls, too," I said.

"Well, I just want to say that it's been great hanging out with you. I hope you still consider me a good friend. A *really* good friend."

"Yes, of course," I replied. "I always will. You know that."

A moment of silence passed. I hugged the phone and felt his presence on the other end. It felt great just knowing he was there. He didn't have to say anything. I could feel through the line how he felt, and I knew he understood my feelings, too.

"Good. Well, take care of yourself. My mom says I have to get off the phone now," he said finally. "I — -well, you know. I care a lot about you, kiddo."

"You, too," I whispered.

"Um, one more thing," he added.

"Yes?" I said.

"Monica and I spoke this evening, and we've decided to take a time out," he began. "You probably don't want me to mention her name, but I feel I have to. I've got a lot of thinking to do, so we're going to take a breather."

"Okay," I said.

"I. . . I just want you to know that. She understands and says she agrees."

"You've been through a lot," I replied. "You need rest right now. I'll be here for you when you get better. I always will be."

We stayed on the phone a few more minutes, saying nothing. I guess neither of us wanted to be the first to hang up.

"I really have to go now," he laughed. "My mom's making faces at me. I mean it this time."

"Okay, okay," I said. "You go first."

"No, you go first, beautiful," he said.

"I don't think I can," I replied.

"Oh, darn it. I hate to do it, but here I go," he said. "Until the next time."

"Good night," I whispered.

"Good night, sweetness," he said softly.

I heard the click as he hung up. "I love you," I said, knowing he couldn't hear me. I held the receiver for a second or two, and then placed it back in the phone cradle. I'd never been in love before, but I knew this was how it felt. I knew it when I called his name in the plane and he didn't answer. It felt wonderful as well as scary, because now I could really get hurt, even more than I had been already.

I sat at the desk and gathered my thoughts. I was happy he'd called, but I didn't know where I stood with him any better than I did five days ago when I first arrived. Was I his girlfriend now, or just his good friend? If this was a romance, it wasn't how it appeared on TV and in the movies. There was always a super-romantic ending to those stories and everyone knew where they stood. It was great he'd called, but was Monica still in the picture? What did a time out mean? It didn't matter. I was back in the game and would fight for him. So whether or not Monica was in the picture, I wasn't letting go. I'd just have to wait and see what the next chapter was after Jim's body healed and we started again.

The next day my mother came out just before noon to collect me and take me home. I was extremely sore all over, and had a headache. Mom and Aunt Louise explained that people always get sore after accidents. I didn't understand why that was so, but I was proof they were correct. I felt pretty mashed up. Even all the aspirin I took didn't help much. My head was badly bruised where it had hit the windshield, and there was a big, ugly bump on my head that I hoped didn't leave a lasting mark. I was glad I was alive, but was miserably uncomfortable all over.

"Did you know you're famous?" Mom asked playfully.

"What are you talking about?" I asked.

"Look at this. *The Indianapolis Star* ran a story today about how you, Luke, and Jim landed a DC-3 in the middle of the air show yesterday," Mom said, handing me the newspaper. I opened it up and the headline read "Children Thwart Exotic Animal Smuggler in Fishers," and there was a photo of the crashed DC-3, with people walking around it.

"A reporter called Uncle Forrest yesterday right after the crash and interviewed him," Aunt Louise explained. "He said you gave the air show more publicity than he could have ever dreamed up—— or paid for."

"Really? I'm so glad he's not mad at us for shutting down the show," I said.

"No, he said next year, the show will be bigger than ever," Mom said. "Everyone will want to come see where the big crash happened."

I began reading the paper, which told the whole story, including how we used the tree house to spy on Pete. I had to admit it was pretty cool to see my name in the paper.

"Well, time to go, don't you think Vanessa?" Mom said as we finished some sandwiches Aunt Louise made. "Why don't you go get your things?"

I walked through the gold curtains into Emma's bedroom and lifted my suitcase onto the bed. Most of my clothes were already packed, so all I had to do was to stuff my pajamas into it. I was just zipping up the suitcase when Emma walked in and sat on the bed.

"I knew you'd figure out how to save the farm," she said, smiling knowingly. "And you did."

"Don't be silly," I said, sitting on the bed next to her. "I figured out what Pete Scaggs was doing, that's all."

"Yes, and that led to saving the farm," she said. "I'll always be grateful." She looked at me with her bright blue eyes. All of the worry that had lurked like shadows in her eyes was gone, and she looked like herself again.

"I'll always be grateful that your family moved here from New Jersey in the first place," I replied. "I'd miss you even if I never knew you and you weren't my best friend."

"You're too funny! I don't understand what you just said, but I know you're my best friend, too," she said, smiling. "I love you, cuz."

"I love you, too," I said, leaning against her affectionately.

Then, I lifted the suitcase and we walked into the living room together.

"'Bye, cousin," Lars said, standing in the dining room eating a bowl of soup. "It's been fun having you here. I hope the ridiculous antics of my siblings wasn't what drove you to attempt suicide in Pete Scaggs's plane. I'm worried they made you psychotic."

I laughed and gestured good-bye to him.

"Bye, Vanessa!" Margret called from the bathroom. I could see her working on her long, blond hair through the open door. "Thanks for keeping my little sister company."

I waved to her and smiled.

My mother, Aunt Louise, Uncle Evert, Emma, and I walked outside. I placed the suitcase in the back seat of the car. I wondered where Luke was. It would be just like him not to say good-bye. He didn't seem to like any show of emotion. I gazed around the yard looking for him as Aunt Louise and my mother talked. Finally, Aunt Louise looked over at me and smiled.

"'Bye, Aunt Louise," I said, hugging her. "I had a really good time. Thank you so much for everything."

"You were a delightful guest," she said as she rubbed my back affectionately. "You did us all a lot of good on this trip, young lady. You're welcome to come back any time."

"Do you have a hug for your dear ol' uncle?" Uncle Evert asked, smiling broadly with his arms outstretched.

"Oh, of course I do!" I said, hugging him.

"Nessie! Are you leaving us already?" Luke called from the barn. I looked up and saw him and Daniel running toward us holding BB guns. I was glad he came to see me off.

"After our crazy plane ride, how can you just up and leave me? I thought we meant more than that to each other," Luke asked, grinning mischievously. "Can't take the dangerous country life, eh? Running back to the city for safety?"

"Yes, I'm out of here," I agreed. "It's way too dangerous here. Take care, and stay out of planes."

I stepped toward him to hug him, but he backed away and gestured to keep my distance. But then he did the funniest thing. He stepped toward me and put one hand on my shoulder, and then stepped back again. I counted that as a hug in the dictionary of Luke's body language, and I was touched.

"As a matter of fact, I think I'm going study to get my pilot's license," Luke said. "I'm going to be one crazy-ass pilot, you can be sure!"

"You don't even drive well. How are you going to fly a plane? You're delusional," Daniel teased.

Daniel was wearing his favorite suede fringed jacket, even though it was a very hot day, which made me smile. I walked over to hug him good-bye, a little timidly at first because of my guilt over what happened to Bobo.

"Thanks for trying to rescue Bobo for me," he whispered as I hugged him. It was almost as though he'd read my mind.

"I'm so sorry," I began.

"Nah. Don't say another word," Daniel interrupted. "My dad says I can get another pet soon. This time it'll be an animal that's not endangered. Maybe a domestic ferret."

"How about a sloth?" Luke suggested. "Sloths are fine animals and are underrated in the pet world."

"I can't get a sloth, because it'd remind me of you," Daniel replied, starting to laugh.

"What? Why, I ought to give you a five minute treatment for speaking to me that way, you knucklehead!" Luke said, turning toward Daniel. Accustomed to the routine, Daniel immediately ran a few feet from him, and then stopped, turned, and laughed. Then, the two boys took off running and disappeared behind the house.

"Can you please take my brother home with you?" Emma asked, looking distressed.

"I've already got two brothers at home, and that's more than enough," I replied.

We laughed, and hugged again. Then, I climbed into the front passenger seat of my mother's car. She started it, and we slowly started to move down the driveway.

"'Bye, everyone!" I shouted, waving. "'Bye, Aunt Louise and Uncle Evert. Thanks for everything!"

We drove down the gravel driveway to Allisonville Road, and then turned to start the trip home. Just as we did, Emma, Luke and Daniel suddenly appeared on the bank of the yard overlooking Allisonville Road, jumping and waving.

"'Bye, Big Red!" Luke shouted. "I think that's what I'll call you from now on!" He appeared very pleased with himself.

Big Red? Maybe being called Nessie wasn't so bad, after all. I turned in my seat and waved out the open window as we drove along until I couldn't see them any more. After they were out of sight, I turned around and looked out the front window and thought how odd it felt to be leaving. I would definitely miss all of them.

As we passed Gatewood Airport, Pete Scaggs's crashed DC-3 was visible from the road, still sitting where it had come to a rest like a huge beached whale. Lying damaged on its side with mangled engines and broken windows made it a truly eerie sight. Peering at the plane as we drove by, I was even more amazed we'd survived.

"It gives me chills to look at that wrecked plane over there," Mom said. "I'm so lucky you're okay. So very lucky."

"I know. It seems surreal," I agreed.

"So, do you think you'll go ever up in a plane again? I mean, after what happened?" Mom asked.

"Yeah, I think so," I replied, nodding. "In fact, someday I might study to get my pilot's license. There are lots of women pilots, you know."

"Really? I thought you told me you were a nervous flier," Mom replied.

"Not anymore. I think I'm going to like flying from now on," I answered. "Mind if I listen to the radio?"

"Sure. Go ahead," Mom said.

I fiddled with the radio and came upon "Snoopy vs. The Red Baron" and stopped on that station. Settling back in my seat, I looked over at Mom and said, "That's a really good song, you know?"

Mom nodded and smiled.

CPSIA information can be obtained
at www.ICGtesting.com
Printed in the USA
LVOW07s2036051217
558761LV00001B/3/P